THE WAY OF A DOG

This, The

THE WAY OF A
DOG

By
Albert Payson Terhune
Author of LAD, A DOG

GROSSET & DUNLAP
Publishers   *New York*

THE
WAY OF A DOG

Copyright, 1932, by Albert Payson Terhune
Printed in the U. S. A.

J
T27w

THIS LATEST (AND PROBABLY LAST)
BOOK OF MY DOG STORIES IS
DEDICATED TO MY TWO FRIENDS
MARK AND SANDY SAXTON

CONTENTS

CONTENTS

THE WAY OF A DOG

I. GRAY DAWN, TROUBLE-HUNTER

To The Place came the little lame girl; a wisp of a child, big of eyes, pitifully frail, and tiny of body; leaning heavily on a diminutive crutch.

An invisible malady had swept the land, slaying children by the thousand. Its robe had brushed little Polly Weir but lightly in passing. But that light touch had changed her from a vibrantly healthy youngster to a half-helpless and wholly pathetic cripple.

She was the Master's niece. She had come to Sunnybank for the summer, on the chance that outdoor life and hill-country air might bring back a shadow of her former buoyant health.

On her first morning there, she limped out onto the vine-bowered veranda and stood looking over the fire-blue lake and at the green hills that circled it so lovingly. As she stood thus a dog came bounding up the slope of

I

the lawn, his black-stippled silver coat drenched from his recent swim.

Polly eyed him with keen interest as he caught sight of her and as he changed his direction and cantered toward her. The child had come to Sunnybank long after dark on the preceding night, and this was the first of the dogs she had seen.

At first sight the oncoming merle collie had a look of giant maturity. This because he was larger and more imposing of aspect than any of the other Sunnybank collies. A closer glance would have revealed to a dog man a loose-jointedness and clumsy gait that belong only to a puppy.

For gigantic Gray Dawn was barely seven months old. He had outgrown any semblance of gracefulness. He was a freak. In another year or less the awkward gallop would settle into a sweepingly powerful stride. The gawky young silver body would fill out and would assume lines of massive symmetry. The overgrown puppy would develop into one of the largest and most superb collies of his day.

But all of that was still in the future. Just now he was in the midst of the hobbledehoy age. In spirit, and temperament, too, he was infuriatingly bumptious; the very soul of destructive mischief.

Only the wise Mistress could look past his babyishly foolish expression and see the stanch loyalty that lay far back in his deepset dark eyes. For this promise of future greatness she loved him; and he repaid her love with utter adoration. To the Master and to the rest of the little Sunnybank world Gray Dawn was an unmitigated pest, with a startling genius for doing the wrong thing, not only at the wrong time, but at all times.

At sight of the tiny girl leaning on her crutch at the top of the veranda steps, this morning, Dawn came hurrying up to investigate the stranger. As he drew near, there was born in his heart a swift pity and protectiveness toward her. He liked such few children as he had seen. But there was something in this child's helplessness that stirred a deeper emotion in him.

Gaily he bounded up the veranda steps. Polly, wholly unafraid, chirped to him and held out one weak little hand to pet him. Dogs were a complete novelty to her. But this shambling giant puppy aroused no fear in her heart. Indeed, her own youth sought to respond to his.

Dawn came to a halt on the step below Polly. She stroked experimentally the silken silver-and-black-stippled head which was the only part of the dog that was dry after his swim. Dawn liked her caress. Pausing only to give himself a vigorous shake which sent a shower of spray over her from his lake-soaked gray coat, he ascended the final step and thrust his nose against her thin face, in friendly greeting.

The shoving impact threw Polly off her ever-precarious balance. With an involuntary exclamation of alarm she fell prone to the veranda rug on which she had been standing. The crutch flew from her weak grasp and clattered down the steps.

On the instant, the huge puppy was athrob with remorse at what he had done. Whimpering under his breath, he stooped and caught her bony shoulder between his mighty jaws, holding it as tenderly as if it had been

3

full of needle-points. He lifted her to her feet in this fashion, his brown eyes agonized with worry lest she had suffered harm.

Without her crutch Polly could not stand alone. To save herself from falling she threw both meager arms around the collie's furry throat and clung to him.

The clasp of the child's arms thrilled Dawn to the very soul. Moveless he stood there, except that he tried to twist his head so as to lick the pale cheek so close to him. Polly was as delighted by the pink tongue's moist caress as was he. She squeezed tightly the furry throat, and began to croon to Dawn as to one of her dolls.

It was thus the Mistress and the Master found them, as the sound of Polly's first involuntary exclamation and the soft thud of her fall had brought her hosts hurrying out onto the veranda.

"This is my dog," announced Polly as the Master ran down the steps to get her crutch and as the Mistress put a sustaining arm about the wisplike body. "He and I are going to be int'mit friends. He knocked me down when he kissed me. But that was only because he didn't know about my horrid crutch. I hadn't had time to tell him. He——"

"He ought to be thrashed, the big blunderer!" grumbled the Master. "You might have fallen all the way down the steps, baby, and been badly hurt. Are you sure he didn't hurt you, anyway?"

"I don't think," responded Polly, with due consideration—"I don't *think* such a nice dog would ever mean to hurt anybody. It's only that nobody had had a chance

4

to tell him I tumble down so easily. He won't do it again."

"You're right he won't," agreed the Master. "I'll see he is kept in one of the kennel yards, except at night, while you're here. He doesn't mean any harm. But he has a genius for *doing* all the harm there is to do. He ——"

"He is my dog," insisted Polly, slipping the crutch under one armpit, but keeping her other arm lovingly around Gray Dawn's neck. "So please don't shut him up. I'd like him to be with me all the time. Can't he?"

The Master frowned in perplexity. By experience he knew Dawn's bumblepuppy gifts for bumping against people and for getting into all manner of stupid mischief. And he resolved to interest the child in Lad or Bruce or some other of the older and more sedate dogs, instead of in this ungainly giant puppy. But the Mistress was wiser than he. With calm certainty she said:

"Certainly Gray Dawn is your dog, darling, for just as long as you'll stay here with us. And he won't knock you over again or hurt you in any way at all. Whatever he may do to the rest of us, he's had his lesson as far as you are concerned. I know Dawn well enough to be sure of that."

"Oh, thank you ever and ever so much!" cried Polly, squeezing the happy dog, ecstatically. "And now let's think up a nice name for him. I think I'll name him 'Mary.' I had a doll named Mary, once, and he ——"

The Master snorted, in an effort not to laugh. But the Mistress intervened:

" 'Mary' is a lovely name, dear. But you see we have named him already. His name is 'Gray Dawn.' I'm afraid

5

it would hurt his feelings if we changed it now. You wouldn't like it if people should change *your* name, you know. And he is so sensitive. He ——"

"Gray Dawn," repeated the child, under her breath, as if testing the name from every angle. "Gray Dawn. Yes. Maybe it's an even better name for him than Mary. I named my doll 'Mary' after her father. His name was Mary, too. He was a boy doll. He had blue trousers and yellow hair, and shoes that came off. But Gray Dawn is a nice name, too."

At each of Polly's hesitant repetitions of "Gray Dawn," the big gray collie pup wagged his tail and wriggled self-consciously. Polly released her hold on his ruff, and stood supported by her crutch. Dawn touched his nose again to her face. But now there was none of his former vehement bumptiousness in the salute. His black muzzle barely brushed the pallid cheek.

"What did I tell you?" demanded the Mistress of her wondering husband. "I said he had learned his lesson. He has all the queer collie gentleness toward anyone or anything that is weak. He'll never bump into her again. And he'd defend her with his life. I know it."

Thus it was that the rambunctious overgrown silver-gray puppy and the little invalid girl met and became at once dear friends. Thenceforth the two were inseparable. To everyone's astonishment, except the Mistress's, Gray Dawn put the soft pedal on his rowdy aggressiveness whenever he was near Polly Weir.

Turning his back on the temptation of a harum-scarum romp with the other collies of Sunnybank, he would pace slowly along close at Polly's side as the child limped with

6

painful slowness along the gravel paths or through the rose-garden or across the shaven green lawns.

He lay decorously alongside her chair in the dining-room, forbearing to snatch avidly at the morsels she offered him from her plate, although his eager snapping at such food offered by the Mistress and the Master had more than once led to bruised fingers and to a scolding.

At night he slept on the rug outside her door, forbearing to growl and yelp at the occasional fleas which pestered him. This noisy habit had led to his expulsion to the veranda during sleeping hours, before Polly's arrival.

In brief, the clamorously clumsy puppy toned down all his natural rough impulses when he was within sight or earshot of the sick little guest.

To Polly the dog was a never-ceasing delight. He was her best-loved playmate. Toward the other and older Sunnybank collies she was joyously friendly as were they to her. But for Dawn she reserved her chief affection.

The Fourth of July drew near. On The Place, firecrackers had always been barred. This year, at Polly's urgent request, several bunches of them had been bought by the Master; firecrackers of all kinds, from the cigarette-sized "sizzers" to a dozen enormous cannon-crackers.

Polly had memories of Independence Days in her own home, before infantile paralysis had stricken her. She had been filled with mingled delight and terror at the explosions of such pyrotechnics; and she begged for a supply of them now. As in everything, her wish was granted; though the Master demanded that the larger and more dangerous crackers be set off by himself for her

7

benefit, and that she handle only the semi-harmless "sizzers" and the torpedoes.

As soon as breakfast was over, on the morning of the Fourth, Polly limped out onto the lawn agog with joyous anticipation, while the Master carried the box of crackers and a stick of lighted punk, and the Mistress brought up the rear of the triumphal procession.

Already the muffled detonations from the mile-distant village across the lake had waked some of the Sunnybank collies to loudly excited barking and had sent others of them to crawling deep under their kennel houses. Collies do not like such explosions. Their dislike makes itself manifest in divers ways.

It was Gray Dawn's first Fourth of July. While the mile-off explosions annoyed and even frightened him, he forbore to take refuge anywhere and stayed close beside the little girl. Trembling, he remained by her side, his jaws flecked by spots of foam, his breath coming fast and heavily. He hated it all. Yet he seemed to feel Polly might need his protection from the distant peril.

Now, as the family went out onto the lawn, he remained close beside Polly, still panting and shaking, but resolved not to desert her.

The Master set down the box of firecrackers. Ever as inquisitive as a monkey, Dawn pressed forward and thrust his nose into the box, sniffing questioningly at the bunches of red cylinders. Then the Master picked out of the mixed lot a pack of smallest-sized firecrackers and handed them to Polly, along with the stick of smoldering punk. Trembling with eagerness, the child applied the tip of the punk to the knotted gray fuse at one end of the pack.

As it sputtered, she tossed it from her. Dawn made as though to retrieve the flung bunch of red. But the Mistress laid a restraining hand on him. Just then the mass of cigarette-shaped cylinders began to explode, in rapid succession; singly and by twos and threes, with a really creditable din.

Polly squealed with delight. She looked around for Dawn to share her joy in the machine-gun-like popping. But Dawn was not there. At the very first cracker's detonation he had torn frantically loose from the Mistress's light hold and had dashed under the veranda.

To the very farthest and cobwebbiest end of this shelter he crawled. There he lay, flattened against the foundation wall, shivering in stark fright. To the nervous puppy it was an unbearably hideous experience.

To some collies the report of a gun, or even of a target rifle, is mental anguish. A thunderstorm is a horror to them. Dawn was one of these not unusual types. Now the spittingly sharp series of single and multiple firecracker explosions drove him frantic. His mouth was slavering. His ungainly young body quivered as with ague. With all his strength he flattened himself against the foundation wall, peering in terror out on the group of noise-makers.

Worse was to come.

The Master picked up a monster firecracker, fat and nearly a foot long, and touched the punk to it. Then, as the gray double-fuse began to spit sparks, he flung it far away. A few seconds later the quiet morning air was shattered by the deafening report. Dawn all but went into a fit. Polly clapped her thin hands in rapture at the ungodly racket.

She lifted another giant cracker from the box and held it out to the Master to light. He did not see her action, as he was already arranging the fuse of still a third giant cracker and was blowing upon the smoldering punk. So Polly laid down the cracker she had taken from the box, and sat watching in laughing excitement the lighting of the cracker the Master held.

Dawn viewed the man with new horror. Always it had been the big dog's delight to retrieve any thrown object. Despite his dread, he had been about to dash out and pick up the first red cylinder the Master had flung, when the thing had exploded with that awful noise. Now he knew better than to try to retrieve the cracker the Master was making ready to throw.

He crouched flatter to the ground. His bloodshot eyes turned instinctively to the little girl he loved and guarded, as if wondering that she could take joy in such torture.

Thus he saw the cracker she had taken from the box and which was on the grass beside her, with her hand resting lightly on it. Dawn saw something more. Polly had laid the giant cracker near a still-smoking fragment from one of the tiny "sizzers" she had set off. The giant cracker's fuse was touching a spark from it.

As Dawn watched, the fuse ignited and began to throw off little sparks of its own. Engrossed in watching the Master fling the fizzing-fused cracker he held, Polly did not note what was happening so near to her. But Dawn saw, and understood.

Foolish pup as he was, he had intelligence enough to know, from what he had seen a bare minute earlier, the devastation that could be wrought by one of those swollen red cylinders when once its fuse began to burn. And now this one was burning—not far off on the lawn, but right against the hand and the side of the child who had roused all his protective zeal.

Ensued an instant's desperate battle between his shuddering dread of the queer-smelling explosive and his loyal collie heart. He would sooner have been thrashed to a pulp than go near one of the giant crackers. But the thing was menacing the helpless wisp of a child whom he adored.

Quaking, slavering, forcing himself to the hated effort, Dawn sped forth from his sub-veranda sanctuary, rushed at the sputtering cracker and seized it fiercely between his mighty jaws, starting off with it at a furious gallop. His impetuous dash had drawn the attention of all three of the humans away from their sport and to himself. They saw him snatch the cracker from under Polly's unheeding hand and carry it at top speed away from her.

Then, before his flying gray body had traveled twenty feet, the giant cracker exploded.

It exploded between his jaws, his pressure on it adding to the force of the detonation. Dawn pitched forward on his head, completely stunned. His gaping mouth was black with powder-burns and his pink tongue was bleeding and torn.

Polly screamed. She began to cry heartbrokenly as she crawled at the best of her feeble speed across the grass toward her senseless and wounded gray chum. But the

Mistress was already kneeling by the huge puppy, lifting his head. With a break in her sweet voice she was bidding the Master run for hot water and cloths and witch-hazel, and to have one of the maids telephone at once for a veterinary.

"He did it to save me from being terribly hurt!" sobbed Polly, hugging the inert silver-stippled head. "And it's killed him! Oh, he was so wonderful! Dawnie, dear! Dawnie! DON'T be dead! I love you, Dawnie. And you did it for *me*. Oh ——!"

"Hush, dear," the Mistress soothed her. "He isn't dead! See, he is opening his eyes and trying to get up. He's cruelly injured, but he isn't dead. And he isn't going to die. You mustn't cry like that, darling. It's bad for you. Dawn will be all right again in just a few days. And we are going to do everything we possibly can for him. He's a gallant, *gallant* puppy, and we must make up to him for the splendid thing he did. Now, suppose you hold his head in your lap—he'll like that—while I bathe his mouth and see how badly it is hurt. Don't cry any more, baby. It makes him so unhappy to have you cry! See, he is trying to lick your face with his poor mangled tongue, to comfort you."

Dawn, coming groggily to his senses, was aware, through his pain and dizziness, that Polly was weeping. Instantly, he forgot his own plight in a clumsily fervent effort to abate her grief. Waveringly he raised his head and, with his tormented tongue, licked at the tear-blotched baby face that bent above him. He even made a right valiant effort to wag his plumed tail. Polly gathered his head in her arms, straining it against her breast and sobbing incoherently:

"Oh, Dawnie, DAWNIE—of—of all the dogs that ever were—you're—you're that dog! And thank you a trillion times for not being dead, you beautiful Dawn! I'll give you all my dolls to play with if you'll just get well. And I didn't mind, a single bit, when you tore the—the sawdust insides all out of Charlotte Amy, yesterday. I—I only made believe I minded. You—you can tear every one of the dolls all to smidgins, if you want to, Dawnie beautiful!"

The Mistress was working with swift skill over the dog's blistered and lacerated mouth, with the hot water and the soft rags and the solution of witch-hazel. Gentle as was her dear touch, the process was infinitely painful. Yet not one whine did it wring from the patient. Dawn had been able, somehow, to make Polly stop crying. And that was far more important to him, just then, than his own agony and fright.

"Won't you please put the rest of these firecrackers away somewhere?" Polly asked the Master. "I don't believe any of us want to play with them again just now."

A human, injured as was Dawn, would have incurred lockjaw or other septic trouble, or at the very least would have had a useless and tormented mouth for many weeks, and perhaps a fractured jaw as well. Being a dog, and young and in supreme health and vigor, Dawn was almost as good as new within a week after his experience with the giant cracker. By that time he had ceased to hold his mouth ajar all the time and to flinch with pain whenever he tried to chew or to lap.

Throughout, Polly had been his tireless volunteer nurse

and playmate. She magnified to stark heroism his plucky deed in her behalf. She tied gay votive ribbons around his neck and brushed and petted him and saved him morsels of cake and other dainties from her own desserts.

One night, a month later, as the Mistress and the Master sat on the veranda, toward bedtime, they started up at hearing the hurried tap-tap-tap of Polly's crutch descending the stairs from the third-floor bedroom, whither she had retired to sleep two hours earlier.

As an accompaniment to the crutch's tapping, sounded the awkward slithering scurry of Gray Dawn's feet on the stairs. The dog slept always now on a rug across the doorway of Polly's bedroom. He and she were coming downstairs in much haste. The Mistress and the Master came quickly indoors at the sound, to meet the descending pair.

Polly looked very small and very fragile in her white nightgown. Also she was a shade paler than usual. Her voice was steady, but was controlled with evident effort. She said, in elaborate calmness:

"Please, I'm sorry to disturb you, but there's a ghost in the attic. I thought you would like to know."

"What!" exclaimed the Mistress, astonished by the matter-of-fact announcement.

"A ghost," repeated the child. "It makes awfully funny V-shaped noises just above the door of my room. Not the regular door. The door that leads to the attic—the door just beside my bed. It woke me up by making them, the ghost did. And it keeps right on nearly all the time. I thought Dawnie might scare it away, so I opened the attic door and I whispered to him to run up and drive it off. But just as he took the first step up the stairs he wheeled

around and came scampering back, with his tail between
his legs. I'm sorry he's so afraid of ghosts. They aren't
nearly as dangerous as cannon-crackers. But he ——"

The Mistress had gathered the frail little figure up into
her arms.

"That's nonsense, dearest," she soothed the forcedly
brave child. "There aren't any such things as ghosts.
There is nothing in Sunnybank House that would harm
you. Sometimes squirrels or rats get into the attic, and
they race around there or roll nuts to and fro. That is
what you heard. There aren't any ghosts. And ——"

"Of course," acceded Polly—"of course it *may* have
been a bear. It sounded just a little bit more like a bear
than like a ghost. But you told me there aren't any bears
at Sunnybank. So I s'posed it was maybe a ghost."

"But ——"

"And it didn't scamper around and roll nuts on the
floor," continued the child. "It went like this:"

Shutting her lips, she made a most dolorously ghastly
sound through her nose, by way of illustration, adding,
apologetically:

"It wasn't quite exactly like that. But it was pretty near
like it. That's the nearest I can make it sound. It wasn't
always either. Just off and on, and with times between
with no sound at all. Then it would begin again. And
Dawn ——"

"Dawn turned tail and ran, eh?" asked the Master.
"Your noble hero! With all his ten million crazy faults,
Gray Dawn has never shown cowardice, except once when
he was little and an angry hen chased him; and always
at thunderstorms or any other explosions. He's foolishly

fearless about everything else. I can't understand his turning tail when you tried to make him climb the attic stairs."

"Neither can I. But he did. Maybe dogs don't like ghosts. Or maybe ——"

"Dear, there aren't any such things as ghosts," declared the Master. "But we're not going to let you be nervous. I'll tell you what we'll do: You shall sleep in the room next to ours tonight, with the door open between. And before then I am going up to the attic and hunt all through it and find out what silly thing frightened you. And more than that, Gray Dawn is going with me. If he is silly enough to be scared at wind moaning in the chimney ——"

"There isn't any wind tonight," protested Polly. "I thought of that, right off. There isn't. There isn't even a breeze. The air is as still as anything."

The Master started upstairs, a flashlight in one hand. He whistled to Gray Dawn to follow him. Willingly the dog obeyed. But as the two reached Polly's room and the Master opened the door leading up to the attic, the collie hesitated.

"Up!" commanded the Master, crossly, yet sinking his voice lest Polly should hear him speak thus to the dog she loved.

Dawn took a hesitant step forward. Then, as he planted one forefoot on the lowest of the curved flight of open ladder-like stairs which led to the attic, he shrank back as in craven terror, flattening himself at the Master's feet and looking up at the provoked man with a world of pleading.

"You mangy coward!" grumbled the Master. "I ——"

The silence of the attic was broken by a long-drawn

guttural sound—a sound which was wafted down the black stair-shaft with eerie dissonance.

Dawn's terror seemed affected in no way by the unearthly groan, nor by another that followed it. Yet when the Master pointed once more to the stairway, he shrank back in panic.

The Master was puzzled. He shot the ray of his flashlight along the winding open steps. At the foot of the stair and in the space behind the lowest stair stood a wooden box. From the top of one corner of it protruded the fuse-tasseled end of a giant cracker. Here, carelessly, the Master had thrust the box of firecrackers after Dawn's mishap.

Gray Dawn had sniffed the pungent odor of the box's contents when Polly first had opened the door. In sharply reminiscent fear, he had refused to go nearer. The Master saw. The Master understood. He was glad the bungling young dog had not shown fear except for the things whose explosion had terrified him and one of which had caused him such shock and anguish.

Stooping, he pulled the box from under the stair and carried it across the room, depositing it temporarily on Polly's dressing-table as yet another gruesomely gasping groan resounded from the attic above.

Dawn had retreated scramblingly from the advance of the firecracker box as it was carried out into the room, even eyeing it apprehensively as it was set down on the far side, fifteen feet away from where he stood trembling.

Then, somewhat reassured by its distance from him, his puppy-mind reverted as ever to what it had been dwelling on before the diversion. The Master had bidden him go

17

up into the attic—the dark attic whence issued at intervals those highly entertaining sounds. Yes, and Polly, too, had bidden him go up there. Also, the attic was even farther away from the firecrackers than where now he stood.

Gaily, the big young dog frisked up the narrow semi-circular stair. The Master, stirred to curiosity by the same sounds, ran up the steps close behind him.

Lishe Biggs was a neighborhood character who made his devious way by the acquiring of other people's possessions. On the third of August he had finished a two-year term at Trenton State Prison for burglary, and had come back to his own village. There certain boon companions had celebrated his release by filling him with ardent moonshine whisky. The debauch had lasted a full twenty-four hours.

Then it had dawned upon Lishe that if he wanted to continue eating he must have money. The friends who so generously had provided him with booze were chary as to spot cash. Lishe fared forth into the countryside to see what portable and pawnable goods he might acquire without too much danger or labor.

At dusk his roving steps carried him to the roadway above The Place. Here, if he could keep to windward of the dogs and out of sight among the oaks and shrubbery of the grove through which the driveway ran down to the house, he might have the good luck to find something worth stealing. In safety he made his way to the house and in through a back door.

The house dogs were sprawling on the front veranda with the humans of the family. Lishe took a step toward the empty dining-room, in quest of silver. At the same moment he saw, through the twilight, that some one was coming into the house from the veranda. A child; a cripple at that. A big dog paced slowly beside her.

Lishe stepped back onto the stairs until she should pass by. But Polly made for the stairs. She was on her way to bed. Lishe crept catlike up to the landing. Below, he could hear the tap of the crutch as Polly and Dawn ascended the first flight. He moved fast and noiselessly up the second and shorter flight of stairs. But the child and the dog continued to follow.

Nerve-wrenched from his long debauch, Lishe slithered into a third-floor room. Still, as if on purpose, the child and dog followed. They were almost at the threshold when Lishe, glaring about for means of escape, saw another door at the far end of the room he had hidden in. To this he tiptoed. It was not locked. It led up to the attic. Thither Lishe fled, shutting the door with great caution behind him.

Well, here he was, safe from exposure, unless that strangely persistent child and her brute of a dog should follow him up here, too—which, to his relief, they didn't.

He must stay where he was until the little girl should be asleep and the dog should have been put out for the night. Then, with all the household slumbering, he could creep downstairs and rummage the dining-room at his will, for silver. He dared not risk exploring the bedrooms. On the way out he could ransack the kitchen for a tin of red pepper—a terrible weapon against any pursuing watch-dog.

In the meanwhile there was nothing to do but wait. And he stretched himself at ease on the floor boards.

The drinking bout of the day and night before had left Lishe approximately sober. His capacity was great. But it had left him worn out and sleepy. Without realizing it, he dozed. The doze became a booze-drugged slumber. The slumber was punctuated presently by an occasional deeply raucous snore.

Up the steps galloped Dawn. The dog smelled the alien presence there, even as he had smelled it all evening. But he was not yet eight months old. He still lacked the training needful to a watch-dog. More than once he had been scolded for barking in harrowing menace at newly arrived guests. For all he knew, this ill-smelling intruder might well be some such guest.

Scoldings were ever a keen humiliation to Dawn. He did not care to incur another one by giving the alarm as to this new visitor's presence. Moreover, the hated and feared reek of the firecrackers absorbed the bulk of his mental processes.

Up the stairs he ran, the Master, flashlight in hand, at his heels. Dawn halted in grave inquiry at sight of the man sprawled there dead asleep on the floor in front of him. Then, in pursuance of his inquiry, he bent down and pushed his coldly moist nose with inquiring vehemence against the sleeper's face.

Lishe Biggs lived by his wits, as I have said. Thus, while drink sleep had drugged him heavily, yet when the prodding shove of Dawn's nose awoke him, all those wits awoke with him. Sitting up, he saw the huge puppy confronting him, and alongside the puppy the Master.

With the speed of a cat Lishe gathered himself together and made a lightning-quick dive for the attic stairhead. The Master struck as Lishe whizzed past him. By that deceptive light, the blow all but went wild. It missed Lishe's jaw, but glanced heavily along the side of his head.

Lishe reeled, ducked a second and harder blow, and dived down the stair.

But while he had eluded cleverly the Master's attack, Dawn was less easy to escape from. At the Master's first ill-aimed blow the puppy decided instantly that this newcomer was invited thereby to a glad romp of some kind. The smashing blow seemed a rarely merry form of horseplay. Gaily, Dawn bounded into the game, eager for a share in such a promising frolic.

The gigantic puppy frisked waggishly toward the fleeing man. Youth and over-haste and natural awkwardness made him miss his mark, and miss his balance as well. He skidded fast toward the stairhead, along the smooth worn boards. This through no volition of his own.

He reached the top of the stairs, thus, at precisely the same instant as did Lishe Biggs. But the dog was moving even faster than the man.

Dawn's head and shoulders jammed themselves squarely between the sprinting legs of the fugitive. Together, in an inextricable tangle, Lishe and the collie rolled, crashing and bumping, down the whole flight.

At the bottom they lay still for a second or so. Then Dawn, bruised and breathless and indignant, wriggled free from his fellow-passenger and lumbered to his feet. The game was getting too rough, even for him.

Lishe Biggs lay where he had fallen. This because of a broken leg and concussion of the brain.

"It was through no virtue of Gray Dawn's that the man was caught," said the Master, an hour later, when the state troopers had carried the injured thief away in a car. "It was just one of his eternal blunders."

"Yes," assented the Mistress, stroking the collie's silken silver head, "But did you ever happen to notice that Dawn's 'eternal blunders' have a queer way of turning out all right? And the more egregious they are the better they turn out. He——"

"Dawnie," rebuked Polly, "don't you think if you tried very, *very* hard you could stop being so rough? The first day I came here you knocked me down. And just see what you did to that poor man, tonight, just because he happened to make noises like a ghost! Next time he goes to sleep, up there, be nice to him and give him your paw."

"Yes," said the Master, "and, after that, tell him where the silver is kept. It would be right in line with the rest of your work, Dawn."

II

"VALUED AT ONE THOUSAND DOLLARS"

* *

The car had been driven up to the house by the Mistress, who then had gone indoors for some letters she had forgotten, and to summon Polly Weir to drive over to the village with her.

Polly was a wisp of a child, old-fashioned, fragile, altogether lovable. Two years agone she had spent a summer at Sunnybank, while she was recovering from a dire illness. The air and the outdoor life of The Place had wrought wonders for her. Accordingly, she had spent the ensuing summers there.

This morning she had been happily busy in wrapping up with loving care a little silver cup she was to send as a christening gift to her baby sister in New York. The cup had been ordered from New York by the Master, at Polly's urgent request. Today it had been swathed by her in successive layers of white tissue-paper, each layer fastened with wide varicolored ribbon.

When Polly came to binding the cumbrous bundle in

23

stiff wrapping-paper and cording it for expressage, the package was fully thrice as large as it need have been.

With infinite care and neatness the little girl addressed the bumpy parcel. Then, after considering for a moment, she printed in large letters the words: "SOLID SILVER. Valued at ——"

Here she paused again, glancing down at the huge gray collie that sprawled lazily at her feet. Sunnybank Gray Dawn had been Polly's adored and adoring chum since the day, two years earlier, when she had come first to The Place, crippled and pitiably weak. From that hour the great young collie had constituted himself her guard and comrade. She talked to him, often, as to a fellow-human, declaring that Dawn understood every word.

"Dawnie," she said now, "when people mail things that cost ever so much, they write on the outside of the bundle just how valuable the things in it are. I've seen that, lot of times. Now how much do you suppose a wonderful solid silver cup like this would be worth? I'll have to say, on here. And I don't want to make it too small, for fear the post-office people won't take good enough care of it. I suppose it couldn't have cost a million dollars, Dawn, but it must have cost as much as a thousand dollars. Suppose we say a thousand dollars, Dawnie?"

The big dog thumped his plumed tail on the floor in drowsy contentment at every iteration of his name. Then he dozed again. Polly Weir picked up her pen and printed in very black and very distinct lettering, "One Thousand Dollars," directly after the words, "Valued at." Then she sat back and surveyed her artistic work with pride.

It was a bit of writing which was destined to have queer results.

The Mistress called up the stairs to ask if Polly were ready for the drive. The child hurried to the veranda, clutching the precious parcel to her breast. At sight of the car, Gray Dawn cleared the steps in one effortless bound and cuddled luxuriously into a nest of two rugs which had fallen from the rail to the bottom of the back seat. He was daft about motoring, as are at least nine collies in ten, and he had no intention of missing this particular drive through getting aboard too late.

Polly deposited her parcel on the front seat. Then she went indoors to speak to the Mistress, who had been delayed by answering a telephone call. At sound of the car's approach from the garage, the Master had left his outdoor hammock-desk, a hundred yards away, and started toward the house with a handful of letters to be posted in the village.

But, for the moment, Gray Dawn was left alone in the machine; lying expectantly in the bottom, half-hidden by the rugs into which he had burrowed.

It was at this psychic instant that Destiny sent Bat Sibley past the car on his way to the upper garden, from the shed whither he had gone for a hoe to replace one whose handle he had just broken.

Sibley was an unlovely local character who used to be hired from time to time as an extra man at The Place during the busy season. He was a fairly good workman when need for food drove him to working. For the most part, he preferred to live by his wits, such as they were.

Doubtful stories were current in the neighborhood as

25

to the courses these wits now and then had led him into.
Moreover, he hailed from the Ramapo Mountain settle-
ments, a few miles away, where dwelt the notorious
"Jackson Whites," a primitive and often unsavory breed
of mountaineers.

Today, hoe on shoulder, Sibley slouched past the waiting car, on his way back to the garden. On the front seat
lay Polly Weir's much-bewrapped bundle. Its printed ad-
dress was large enough and black enough and legible
enough for a purblind man to have read it from twice
that distance. Idly, with a mountaineer's born curiosity,
Bat Sibley loitered to con the black-lettered words. Then
his gaze and his furtive brain focused sharply on the inscription:

"Valued at One Thousand Dollars."
One thousand dollars! ! ! ! With that much money in
hand or even with some article which could be sold or
pawned for half as much, a work-hating mountaineer
might live in royal laziness for months and months.

Nobody was in sight. Nobody could prove anything on
him. He could grab the package, hide it away safely
somewhere among the lawn's shrub clumps; and sneak
back at his leisure to carry it off. It was a chance of a
lifetime.

Out shot Bat Sibley's right hand, flashing as swiftly
and as furtively as did his warped brain. Without so
much as halting in his slouching stride, he seized the
bundle. It would be the work of a second to thrust it into
his shirt and thence carry it to the nearest safe hiding-
place.

His fingers clenched themselves around the parcel. He

drew it to his breast, to shove into the front of his loose flannel shirt. But the package did not reach its destination.

This because something else reached forward—something even faster and more accurate than the swift swoop of Sibley's arm. Gray Dawn had gone into action.

From puppyhood, Dawn had been taught to guard The Place's cars, when he was left alone in them. It was a lesson taught to all Sunnybank's successive car-dogs.

Today, he had noted with no interest the slovenly approach of this laborer. He had roused himself instinctively as Sibley's stride had slowed down alongside the machine. Then he had seen the shooting out of the long arm and had seen its hand close around the bundle. It was Gray Dawn's job to protect not only the car, but everything in it. He had seen Polly toiling over this package. He had seen her put it on the seat, leaving it in his care.

Nobody except the Mistress or the Master or Polly or the superintendent could touch with impunity anything that had been left in a car with Gray Dawn on guard. There had been no time, just now, for a warning growl or a show of teeth. The theft had been too sudden. Action must be just as sudden, if the parcel were not to be stolen from under its defender's very nose.

There is perhaps nothing quicker in the animal kingdom than the motions of an aroused collie—unless it be the workings of a collie's strange brain.

Before Sibley's hand could reach Sibley's breast with its plunder, Dawn's slashing jaws had raked his wrist to the bone.

27

Sibley jerked his hand back convulsively from that snarling onslaught. His fingers still clutched a corner of the parcel. A fragment of the stiff, ill-made wrapping-paper was yanked away, unnoticed, in his convulsive grip —a fragment containing part of the painstakingly printed valuation.

The package itself fell unheeded to the ground. For Dawn had launched himself from the car and at the man. Sibley leaped back, out of reach, swinging his hoe aloft for a blow at the charging collie's head. In his right hand, pressed close around the hoe handle, Sibley held unknowingly the torn scrap of paper.

It was then that the Master came on the scene. Dropping the handful of letters he carried, he caught Gray Dawn by the ruff as the collie was renewing his attack upon Sibley and as the man poised the hoe for a smashing cut at his angry assailant.

Indeed, the blow had been launched. Despite Sibley's sudden effort to avert it, the sharp edge of the hoe scraped Dawn stingingly on the shoulder in the course of its checked flight through the air. Dawn snarled afresh at his foe, under this sting and the ignominy of the striking. The Master held fast the struggling collie.

"Well?" he demanded of Sibley.

"I was going past here, minding my own business," responded the flustered man, "when this cuss set onto me. I'll have the law on ——"

"You mean you were going peaceably along and he went for you?" broke in the Master. "That's nonsense. Even a bungler like Gray Dawn wouldn't do that. He has seen you around here for weeks and he knows you're not a trespasser. He's never bothered you before. There's something more to this. He ——"

"He bitten my wrist!" vociferated Sibley, strong now in his certainty that his story would pass muster. "He lept out at me—right out from that machine there—and ——"

"Out from the machine, eh? Were you trying to get aboard it? If you were, he may have thought it was up to him to ——"

"No, I wasn't! I was minding my own business. I didn't even see him. If there's a law in the land ——"

The Master had stooped and was picking up the torn parcel that lay at his feet. He noted its condition and looked about for the missing scrap of wrapping-paper. Dawn took advantage of the slackening of the grasp on his ruff to struggle once more to get at Sibley. The latter shrank back and swung the hoe aloft with a menacing flourish.

The shifting of his clasp on the smooth handle caused a shred of paper to slip from the palm of his right hand and flutter to the earth. The Master paused in the tightening of his own hold on Dawn's ruff, to watch the odd happening. To the ground fell the bit of paper. From its surface glared blackly the words: "—ued at One Thous —"

"Oh!" cried Polly, from the top of the veranda steps, as she and the Mistress came out of the house. "My beautiful bundle. I trusted you to watch it on the seat, there, Dawnie. And now you've gone and torn it, you *naughty* dog! I'll have to wrap it up, all over! If I didn't love you so much I wouldn't speak to you again all day! It ——"

The Master caught the eye of his wife, and said to her, in French:

"Take her indoors, please. Quick!"

As the Mistress led the child into the house again on some pretext, the Master stepped hastily after Sibley, who was moving from the scene with much more than his wonted speed.

"Wait!" he ordered, his hand falling detainingly on the man's squirming shoulder. "I wanted to let the little girl get out of hearing. We try to keep the rotten things of life away from her. I don't want her to know there's a dirty thief on The Place. She's not going to know, now or later. But——"

"If you're talking about *me*," blustered Sibley, "I'll have you to know I'm an honest man. I——"

"Good!" approved the Master. "I never yet heard of an honest man who called himself one. It's the patter of every caught thief. You tried to steal that bundle. You didn't see Dawn was there. He grabbed you just when you had grabbed the bundle. Part of the paper came away when you yanked your hand back. You saw that 'thousand dollars' sign—on a tiny cup that cost only fourteen dollars— And it seemed to you a good haul."

"I'll have the law of——"

"Go to it!" said the Master. "But first go to Robert Friend and get your money, and then get off my land. Ten minutes from now I'll come hunting for you, and I'll bring Dawn with me. You and your breed talk a lot about the law. Be grateful I don't turn you over to it. I'd hold you here, for the State Police, if I wasn't afraid

the little girl might be called as a witness or get otherwise to know about this. *Out!*"

Thus it was that Bat Sibley lost his job. Thus it was
that he slunk from The Place with a burning hate in his
heart, a hate less for the Master who had exposed and
discharged him than for the silver-gray giant collie that
had caused the exposure and had bitten him.

As often with the strange mountaineers of the Jackson
White type, hate oiled the workings of Sibley's brain, not
only for mere revenge, but for a revenge which would
profit him. He trudged to the cabin of his sister, high up
in the Ramapos, for food and shelter during his period
of joblessness—he knew the tale of the theft would travel
fast from one end of the Valley to the other and would
bar him from employment at any estate or farm there—
and to mature an idea which had sprung all but full-
grown into his fast-working mind.

At first he flinched at the thought which flashed into
his head. For the man was an arrant coward. But, as it
kept forcing itself upon him with new details and ramifi-
cations and possibilities, he toyed more and more with it,
testing it from every angle. And ever it seemed to promise
an increasingly golden reward.

Sibley had been at Sunnybank long enough to know
that Polly Weir was inexpressibly dear to the Mistress
and to the Master, that they would do anything in their
power for her welfare or happiness, that a supposed peril
to her would hurt them more than would anything else
he could devise.

He had seen that inscription, "Valued at One Thousand

31

Dollars" and he had discarded craftily the Master's asser-
tion that it referred to something worth only fourteen
dollars. People who could send out thousand-dollar parcels must be wealthy beyond belief; for all the simplicity
of their mode of life.

In brief, if he could kidnap Polly and hold her for ransom—the annals of the Jackson Whites are full of such
ancestral legends—he might not only revenge himself
upon the man who had berated and discharged him, but
he might make himself rich for life.

No more hateful work; no more tightening of the belt
in hard times; no more need for dangerous petty thefts;
no more fear of the police—for the rest of his career.
Wealth, ease, all the moonshine whisky he could swig;
three heaping meals a day; ten-cent cigars; a brand-new
store suit every single year or oftener; the slavish adoration of his fellow-mountaineers; and at a momentary risk
which the simplest caution would render negligible.

It was no part of his scheme that the slightest harm
or terror should befall Polly Weir. Too well did he know
that a tale of ill-treatment, on her return, would rouse the
whole county against him. No, he would find means to
steal her without her so much as guessing she was stolen.
He would take her to his sister's cabin. There she should
be housed and fed and amused, in a way which would
make her give a glowingly high account of her captors.
She should be sent back to Sunnybank, unhurt in body or
feelings, when a three-thousand-dollar reward should
have been paid.

He broached the subject to his sister—a widow whose
husband had spent much of his married life in jail. She

passed for a wise woman in her own circle of acquaintances. His sister asked many questions as to his plan. Then she did much thinking, with a brain that was even more furtive and shrewd than Sibley's own.

After which she took a day off from her overt trade as washerwoman, and went down into the Valley. There she made certain seemingly careless inquiries of servants and of tradesmen's boys. Then she came back to her cabin and reported favorably. Moreover, she polished Sibley's rough-hewn notions for the kidnapping and for the safe collection of the ransom.

She even told him where and how he could secure the forced loan of a high-quality motor-car for an evening. She made a second journey to the Valley, where, at the village of Hampton, she bought toothsome food and attractive toys. Presently all was set for the venture.

The Master and the Mistress went, one moonlit night, to a large and formal dinner given by some friends of theirs, several miles from Sunnybank. On the same evening Robert Friend, The Place's English superintendent, took his family to an amateur minstrel show in the village across the lake. This much, among other things, Bat Sibley's sister had foreknown from her inquiries through the Valley.

The maids were in the kitchen quarters of Sunnybank House. Polly Weir and Gray Dawn were sitting together on the vine-hung front veranda; the child reveling in the glory of the almost tropical moonlight, the dog snoozing at her feet. Down the oak-bordered driveway, from the highroad above, came a sedan. It stopped at the veranda.

33

Polly went forward to greet whomsoever might have called and to explain the absence of the Mistress and the Master.

Gray Dawn started forward with her. But before he reached the veranda edge his nostrils told him who was driving the car. He paused, his hackles bristling, his curved upper eyetooth gleaming in the moonlight. A growl of wrath surged up from his furry throat.

Well did Dawn recognize the scent of the man who had stolen Polly's bundle and who had smitten him so stingingly with the hoe. Ire burned hot in his friendly heart. At the time of the encounter the Master had held him back from punitive assault. But tonight the Master was not here to stand between him and the debt he longed to pay.

Polly, ashamed at her chum's dearth of hospitality, spoke sharply to him, catching him by the ruff and leading him indoors. Dawn went, reluctantly, yet obediently, deeming that she was coming into the house with him. But after she had piloted him through the doorway she shut the portal upon him and went back to the head of the porch steps.

"I'm sorry," she said, politely, addressing a man who stepped out of the car as soon as the front door was safely shut behind the collie, "but I'm the only one left at home. They have gone to ——"

"Yes, Miss Polly," interposed the man, "I know. They've gone to Colonel Ryerson's for dinner. That's why I'm here. They sent me for you."

"Why," exclaimed the child, "it's Sibley! I asked

34

Robert Friend what had become of you, and he said you had gone away to work somewhere else. How do you do?"

"First rate, miss, thank you," answered Sibley, with his best-rehearsed manner and speech, "and I'm Colonel Ryerson's chauffeur now. The dinner folks have all figgered out they'd like to go and see that new wild-animal movie up at Suffern, this evening. And they thought maybe you'd like to see it, too, because it's all about bears and such. So Colonel Ryerson sent me to bring you along."

"*Oh!*"

"Your folks said you needn't bother to go inside and get your hat and your coat, because they sent along a coat and a hat that belongs to little Miss Helen Ryerson. And they told me to ask you to please to hurry right along as fast as you can, because they've only got just barely enough time to get there before the second show. Could you hop in, Miss, quick?"

He had delivered the long-rehearsed speech beautifully. And as his sister had predicted, Polly was down the steps and halfway into the car before its laboriously conned lines were finished.

The child was wildly eager for the promised outing. The evening had begun to drag, for her, despite the glorious moonlight; and in spite of the company of Gray Dawn, who had insisted on going to sleep and snoring in the middle of a story she was telling him.

The prospect of seeing a wild-animal movie and of sitting up long after her usual bedtime and of a motor ride through the moon-drenched night—all these delights captivated her and set her heart to beating rapturously. She

35

scrambled into the back seat of the sedan without waiting
for Sibley's proffered help.

The car was in motion again and on its way up the
drive before the maids, chatting in the kitchen, had so
much as noted its arrival. Then, drawn by Gray Dawn's
thunderously imperative barking, one of them came slowly
into the front part of the house to investigate.

The great dog had raged at the trick whereby he had
been cooped up when the man he detested was standing
at the foot of the veranda steps. He had snarled and
growled venomously, and had clawed in futile eagerness
at the stout paneling. Then he had heard the car depart,
and Polly with it.

Something seemed to tell the raging dog that this child
he worshiped was in danger. The feeling was even
greater than his craving to avenge himself upon the man
who had struck and hurt him with the hoe edge. The man
was carrying her away, and Dawn was imprisoned where
he could not help her. His barks shook the house with
their wild vibrations and his nails tore at the unyielding
door. He was beside himself with apprehensive fury.

The maid supposed he smelled a stray cat outside. She
opened the door amusedly, prepared to watch a farcical
chase of the intruder.

In a trice Gray Dawn was outside in the flood of moonlight and was tearing up the driveway, toward the road,
at top speed. He ran, head low, seeking and isolating the
fresh trail of the car that was just turning out of the gate
into the highroad. By sight as well as by scent he followed
it, his rushing body ashine in the moon's rays as he sped

through patches of light between the black shadows of the trees.

Into the white-lit highway spun the pursuing dog, every sinew astrain, his silver-stippled gray body a long and gleaming flash as his spurning feet sped over the road. He was in the full glory of his youthful prime. He was one of the largest and strongest and fleetest collies of his day. Beneath his external boisterousness, he was endowed with the white courage of a crusader.

He flew at an incredible pace, the soft night air beating against his nostrils and bearing to him the hated and desired scent of his quarries. Far ahead, and going fast, he could see the tail-light of the car which was his goal. Strain as he would, he could cut down only a little at a time the distance between him and that light. For Bat Sibley was stepping on the gas and taking every advantage of the smooth stretch of roadbed.

Nor was Dawn's race unobstructed. This was a night, for warmth and for breath-taking beauty, to bring out innumerable cars on pleasure jaunts. More than once the dog swerved aside barely in time to avoid being struck by such whizzing vehicles. These detours impeded his progress, even if they saved his life.

"I thought the Ryersons lived over there, to the left," said Polly as the sedan whirled past a crossroad. "Are you sure we're going in the right direction?"

"I ought to know," laughed Sibley, reassuringly. "I've lived hereabouts since long before you was born, miss. We're going to take a short cut to their house, so as to be sure to get there in time. I'd hate to have you miss that wild-animal movie. We ——"

He ceased to speak as the breath was jounced out of him by a sharp turn he made, at full speed, out of the smooth concrete highroad into a rutted byway. There, perforce, he slowed down a little.

This byway was one of the two ingresses to the mountain track he planned to take to his sister's distant cabin. The second byroad was a mile beyond. He had turned into the nearer of the two.

"Here's the short cut I told you about, Miss Polly," he reassured the child, at the same time slackening speed still further as the sedan lurched and pitched. "Right ahead is the Ramapo River that runs into the lake past where you live. Pretty, in this moonlight, ain't it? See, we're coming to Doty's Bridge."

"But I'm almost sure the Ryersons don't live in this direction," expostulated the child. "They—*Ooh!*"

The squeal of delight that broke off her protest was caused by an enormous bass breaking water just below the bridge they were crossing. There was a grand splash and a rainbow of spray as the fish smote the stream again from his leap after some night-fly. Polly leaned far out of the sedan's open window to look down at the wondrous sight.

The resounding whack and the cataract of spray made Sibley start nervously. The man was under terrific tension. When a coward keys himself up to a decisive deed, his nerves take toll from him. Sibley had had much ado to keep his teeth from chattering. Even now, when success seemed assured and when everything had gone as well as his best hopes had forecast, he was jumpy and apprehensive.

Nor had the several drinks which he had taken to steady him had the desired result.

Liquor is tricky, in that way. Not always can it be relied on to fulfill the purpose for which it is drunk. Instead of calming Sibley, tonight's potations made him tenfold alive to the peril he was incurring and ripped his sorry nerves to ribbons.

More, they had loosed within him the flood of rank superstition which is the heritage of every Jackson White mountaineer. They had awakened olden memories of sprites which ride the moonlight and play mischievous havoc with such humans as are so unwise as to venture abroad without protective charms.

The splash of the huge fish might well be the rising of some water-devil from the fast-flowing river's depths. What was the charm against river-devils, by moonlight? The fingernail parings of an old woman and the hair of a black sow and the ——

With a slam Bat Sibley brought the sedan to a halt, just beyond the bridge.

Clearly defined in the narrow and rutted byroad, fifty yards in front of him, was a touring car—a car without lights. It was lying at a curious angle and it stretched across the narrow space, effectively blocking it.

With a start, Bat Sibley came back to normality. Some automobile had sought to traverse this road, and had paid for its temerity by a breakdown. Its occupants doubtless had deserted it and had fared to the nearest telephone along the highway to summon a wrecking-crew and another car to take them home. Meantime, the crippled machine was blocking the whole narrow passage.

Polly, too, saw by the sedan's headlights the wreck in front of them. It did not interest her. But as Sibley climbed down to the ground and clumped forward to investigate, she slipped out of her seat, on the other side, bent on running back to the bridge, directly behind them, for another view of the leaping bass. As she clambered out of the car she heard the fish leap again. Eager to see a repetition of that shower of pale rainbow light, she ran to the bridge.

Panting from his three-mile top-speed sprint, Gray Dawn flashed alongside the sedan on the left side, even as Polly climbed down from the right. Straight ahead of Dawn and moving toward a disabled machine in the middle of the road, Bat Sibley was running.

At sight and scent of him, Gray Dawn forgot everything but his hate for the man. Snarling rabidly, he sprang in pursuit.

Sibley heard the menacing sound. He spun around in terror to face it, even while Polly was trotting gaily in the opposite direction, toward the near-by bridge, with her back to the car and to him.

The man saw and recognized the dog bearing down upon him at express-train speed in the flood of moonlight. With Sibley's fear of a mangling from the murderous brute was a tinge of superstitious awe at this impossible thing which had occurred. Dawn had been left at home, safely prisoned behind a closed house door. Yet here he was now, on this rough byway, miles from Sunnybank. The thing was impossible.

Fright surged through Sibley, completing the upset of his jumpy nerves. Instinctively he had whipped out a pis-

40

tol from his hip pocket, at sight of the dog, and had leveled the weapon. At point-blank range, with palsied
finger, he pulled the trigger.

The sweet moonlit silence was shattered by the report.
Dawn was stricken down in mid-rush. He tumbled headlong to the ground, rolling over twice from his own momentum. Then he lay very still in the weed-choked ditch
at the side of the road.

His enemy's collapse, and the sound of the shot, served
to jerk Bat Sibley back to sanity. Shoving the pistol into
his pocket, he hastened to his sedan to try to sooth Polly,
in case she had witnessed the slaying of her beloved pal.
But she had not seen. So intent had she been in leaning
over the bridge to look for another spectacularly leaping
fish that she had noticed nothing until the shot startled
her.

She looked around in amaze. But the sedan was between her and the dog. Moreover, the high ditch weeds
hid Dawn from any casual view.

But she did see Bat Sibley running toward her as he
caught sight of her light dress on the bridge.

"I tried to haul that busted car to one side," he announced, his voice shaky. "But one of the tires blew out
when I pulled at it. Hear the racket it made? Say, we
can't get past there. No room. We gotta turn around and
try the next short cut. It's only about a mile ahead.
You stay there, if you like, while I make the turn."

He was fearful lest the child's eye might fall on Dawn's
inertly crumpled body in the ditch, during the process of
turning in that narrow space. Thus he was relieved at her

glad consent to watch the shining water for a moment longer.

Deftly he maneuvered the sedan, in spite of the quivering of his clammy hands on the wheel. It would be a matter of only a few minutes at most before he could reach the next byway which led into the mountains. He did not like to linger in this hoodoo spot where his way had been blocked and where the dog had charged him— the dog whose presence seemed an utter impossibility.

After much backing and twisting the sedan was turned, and Sibley headed it for the bridge where Polly still watched for another fish-splash. Coming to a halt, he called to her to hurry. Obediently, she turned from the delight of watching the moonlit swirl and eddying of the river below her, and she sought to twist the handle of the sedan's nearest rear door. But her fingers were not strong and the handle was stiff.

Feverishly impatient at her slowness, Sibley got down from his seat to open the sticking door for her and to lift her in. The delay was doing queer things again to his wrenched nerves. That shot might well bring some one to investigate. Or the people whose car was wrecked, might be coming back at any moment; they or a wrecking crew. There was no time to waste. Down to the bridge's planks Sibley stepped, on the side of the sedan farthest from Polly, and he started around the rear of the machine toward her.

But he took only one long stride in that direction. Then his legs refused their office. Eyes bulging, jaw agape, he stood staring in front of him in shuddering horror.

42

Coming to meet him, down the byroad from the direction of the deserted car, Gray Dawn was galloping!

The collie's big body loomed gigantic in the deceptive moonglow. It gleamed wraithlike. A shimmering halo of light encompassed it where the moon's rays touched the edges of the silver coat.

It was a ghost—a ghost, past all doubt! No real-life dog bulked so huge as that, nor shone with that unearthly light. Sibley had shot Dawn at point-blank distance, sending a heavy-caliber bullet crashing through his brain. He had seen the collie roll dead in the ditch.

Yet now, not one minute later, a devil had entered the slain body and was coming for the slayer's life and soul! Mountaineer folklore has been jammed with such tales since first the legend of the werewolf was coined. No bullet could prevail against a demon. What was the one way to escape such a hell-born pursuer? Oh yes! A 'ha'nt' cannot cross or enter running water! Every mountaineer knows that. There was one way of escape. Running water!

In the merest fraction of a second these thoughts raced through Bat Sibley's brain, even as Dawn bore down upon him.

With a screech of stark fright the man flung himself headlong over the low rail of the bridge, pitching down into the fast-flowing moonlit river. This although he could not swim a stroke. Better any fate than the horror he was fleeing from.

Moonlight is fatal to accurate marksmanship. Nor does a convulsive shivering of the marksman's whole body tend to make a shot go straight. Sibley's bullet had grazed the edge of Dawn's skull so lightly that the skin was

43

scarcely abraded. But its velocity at that close range had given it the power to knock the collie over and to stun him for perhaps fifteen seconds. It was a far lighter and less injurious knockout than is sustained by players in hundreds of football games. Moreover, the gray young dog's system was in far better condition than is that of the best-trained football player.

Dawn had come to his senses, with only a slight momentary grogginess to show for his experience. Even this daze began to pass away as he stood in the ditch, looking about him. The last of it vanished as he saw and scented Bat Sibley dismounting from the sedan on the middle of the bridge. Head down, Gray Dawn went for his enemy. Before he could reach him, he saw Bat vault the bridge rail and go crashing into the river.

Now this was a most highly entertaining performance. The screech and the dive and the splash thrilled Dawn's ever-present love for the dramatic. Eagerly he trotted to the bridge and peered downward, ears cocked, head on one side. His brain was clearing fast.

Polly was hopping up and down in gay excitement as she, too, peered down through the alternate moonglare and shadow at the spot where Sibley's body had smitten the water and had vanished beneath it.

The child had seen Bat make the spectacular leap. Again and again she had seen men dive for fun from bridges. Not for an instant did it occur to her that this was anything more serious than a prankish bit of horse-play. And the fact that Sibley went into the water with all his clothes on made it the more amusing. He was a funny man! Of course he had done this spectacular stunt for her amusement. Politely she clapped her hands.

Sibley's sleekly wet head came to the surface just under the bridge's edge. The current had caught him. He was floundering wildly. Polly clapped louder, and prepared to see him strike out for shore. But he only splashed and gasped and floundered in panic helplessness. He screeched raucously.

His mortal peril and his fright went unrecognized by the child. But Dawn's mystic collie sixth sense caught instantly the stark terror of that screech.

Over the side of the bridge the dog sprang. This was no time to nurse injuries. A human was drowning. Dawn struck the water resoundingly and went under. In another second his head was above the surface and he was striking out, downstream, with all his wiry strength, at a speed which carried his shoulders high out of water.

Downstream he swam, following the sputter and flopping of Sibley as the current swept the impotent man along. Bat's clothes kept him more or less afloat for a minute. Then he began to sink. Dawn flashed alongside and seized the nearest part of him, which chanced to be his sleeve.

At the contact the panic-crazed Sibley flung both arms spasmodically around the collie, cramping Dawn's every motion.

Underwater went the two, man and dog; far under. Sibley's arms loosed their grasp on Dawn as he began to strangle. As a result, both of them came to the surface again, the dog as lightly as a cork, the man more slowly and soggily. Dawn had had his lesson. Keeping clear of

45

the weakly moving arms, he struck for Sibley's coat collar as his late foe began anew to sink.

Straining every splendid muscle, the collie made slant-wise for the nearer bank, letting the current do the bulk of his work for him, while he strove to keep Sibley's face above water. The two had passed on into the dense shadows of the river-edge trees. Seek as she would, Polly Weir could not see them now; these two merrily-romping moonlight swimmers who were trying so finely to amuse her.

Then, at a sharp bend of the stream, the current flung the struggling pair against a sandbar which jutted far out under water. Sibley felt something solid beneath his feet. The sensation pierced his terror madness. With a final struggle he got his legs under him and stood up in waist-deep water.

There were several people on the bridge now. He could hear their voices through the clogging of his water-filled ears. The man splashed drunkenly through the shadows to the bank and toiled up it. Thence, taking advantage of every patch of black shadow, he made for the mountains at what pace his sodden clothes would permit. Nor did the Valley folk see him or hear word of him from that time on.

Polly, too, had heard voices and had turned to look. From the highroad two white-clad women and two men in flannels were advancing toward the bridge, on their way back from telephoning for garage men to come for their broken-down car and to carry them home. The shadowy beauty of the byroad had tempted the four from the smooth course of their evening drive, and their car had succumbed to the deep ruts before they had traversed a furlong of the alluring stretch. Now, coming back from telephoning, they saw a child move forward to greet them. The foremost of the women exclaimed:

"Why, if it isn't little Polly Weir! What on earth are you doing here all alone, this time of night, darling?"

"I'm not alone, Mrs. Maclay," denied Polly, recognizing the quartette as friends and close neighbors of the Sunnybank folk. "I'm with Sibley. We are going to the movies. But he just stopped a few minutes for a nice swim, and Gray Dawn went swimming with him. I don't know how Gray Dawn happened to be here. But then Dawnie is always doing things nobody knows the reason of. They'll be back in just a —— Why, here's Dawnie, now!" she broke off as the collie came scampering up the bank and over to where the child stood.

He frisked gleesomely into the center of the astounded group before he remembered he was still soaking wet. Hitherto his one idea had been to get back to Polly and to guard her from further peril. But now he saw she was safe and laughing, among old friends of hers and of his, he had time to notice the volume of river-water that filled his mighty coat.

With a tremendous shake he sent a Niagara of spray over the women's white dresses and the men's snowy flannels.

"Isn't it just like Dawn!" cried Mrs. Maclay, in annoyance, as she backed hurriedly from the shower. "I suppose that worthless clown of a dog never *will* get any sense!"

47

III. *GRAY DAWN, JINX-FANCIER*

There were times when Gray Dawn resembled painfully the misanthrope who said:

"I had a run of bad luck for seven years, and then all at once it began to get worse."

For months the big silver-and-snow collie would live on, serenely and happily, as did the other collies at The Place. Then his hoodoo would reappear. As the years went on, the Mistress and the Master grew to recognize the beginnings of these mishap periods and to worry mightily at their advent. For seldom did they run their odd course without involving one or more of the Sunnybank humans.

While Dawn was still in his early prime and still given to moments of idiotically puppy-like bumptiousness, one such jinx season set in. It had a simple enough beginning.

The itinerant newsdealer was wont to make the round of the neighborhood at daybreak, leaving at doorways

48

GRAY DAWN, JINX-FANCIER

the various morning papers. The rattling of his car down
the furlong of driveway from the highroad to Sunnybank
House was always a signal for the collies to smash the
dusky silences with a salvo of challenging barks. This
din had scant attraction, either for the folk of The Place
or for their nearest neighbors, a quarter-mile away.

Wherefore, the man was bidden to leave the papers
just inside the gateway at the entrance of the drive. The
superintendent or one of the workmen, later, brought
them down to the house.

One July morning the Master chanced to get up before
daylight, to go up into the forest for a two-hour tramp
with the dogs. For the promised heat of the day would
make later exercise a burden to him and a menace to his
collies. On the way back to the house, as the trampers
turned in at the gates, Gray Dawn spied The Place's
three morning papers lying in their wonted place, a rubber band around them.

For some reason best known to himself he swooped
down upon them and carried them gaily to the Master.
He held them lightly between his great jaws and showed
no sign of playing doll with them. So the Master patted
him on the head and let him carry them all the way
down to the house. There, laying the papers at the Mistress's feet, Dawn was patted again and praised—not that
the simple exploit called for any such reward, but because he was so joyously self-important about it.

Next morning, the superintendent reported that the
papers had not arrived. The Mistress replied that they
were lying on the breakfast table. A maid said they had
been on the front-door mat when she opened the house.

49

The mystery was cleared up, the following day, when the Master, rising early, saw from his dressing-room the huge gray collie pacing right pompously down the driveway with the bundle of papers in his mouth. Dawn had hit on a new accomplishment.

Memory of the praise that had been his, two days earlier, for acting as paper-carrier, evidently had led him to make a regular morning duty of it. The Master was at the front door as Dawn laid the rubber-banded parcel on the mat. He petted and praised the collie again for the cleverness of thinking out this simple form of service. And that was where the Master made a grievous mistake.

No temperamental opera-singer ever was half so susceptible to the plaudits of her public as was Dawn to the approval of the two humans he loved. The giant collie shuffled and danced with delight under the laudation and the careless head-pat of his master. Then he snatched the papers afresh and galloped upstairs with them, dashing into the Mistress's room and dropping the bundle lovingly, if thuddingly, upon her sleeping face.

Had it been the Master who was roused thus violently from slumber, Gray Dawn would have learned instantly and drastically that his paper-carrying trick was no longer popular; and he might thenceforth have foregone it. But the Mistress was different. The Mistress understood. Always she understood. She petted the clownish destroyer of her sleep, and thanked him for bringing her such a nice present.

Next morning, the usual daily papers were at the breakfast places of the Mistress and the Master. But also the waitress was holding out toward her employers a pile

of eighteen other morning papers. She was confused by
their numbers and variety. But she supposed they must
have been ordered; because all eighteen of them, as well
as the three regular papers, had been lying on the door
mat when she opened the house an hour or so earlier.

While the Mistress and the Master were eyeing amaz-
edly this journalistic avalanche, the telephone rang. The
village newsdealer's voice asked worriedly whether or not
The Place had received its papers that morning.

"Yes," answered the Master, "we did. And we——"

"I'm glad, sir," came the response, "because all my
other customers on your side of the lake have been calling
me up and asking why I forgot to deliver today. Some
smart Alec must have tried to be funny and followed me
around and pinched them all. You're the only people
who got yours. I wish I knew who——"

"I can help you out, perhaps," said the Master. "The
'smart Alec' rounded up the whole lot and dumped them
on my door mat. I'll save them for you. There are eighteen
of them, besides our three."

He went back to the veranda corner where he and the
Mistress were breakfasting. There he launched into
a contemptuous tirade against practical jokers in general
and the rustic sense of humor which could devise so silly
a prank. The Mistress heard him out. Then she said:

"Dawn and Wolf and Bobby were loose all night. How
far down the driveway do you suppose they would have
allowed any stranger to come, at early daybreak, with
that stack in his arms? And the kennel dogs would have
seen him, too, and given the alarm. Wolf sleeps on the
mat where Fifine found the papers. The man never would

have gotten off the veranda—or on it. Wolf would have seen to that."

"Yes," agreed the Master, dazedly, "Wolf would. I never thought of that. So would the others. But ——"

Wolf was curled up as usual at the Mistress's feet. At sound of his name, the fiery little gold-red-collie's tail smote the veranda floor. Dawn, ever jealous of word or look lavished on another dog than himself, got up from the shade of the vines, stretched himself fore and aft in true collie fashion; and came lounging over to the table. The Master eyed sourly the big young gray dog.

"Dawn," he said, "just as I was trying to figure out the answer, you hove in sight and supplied it. I think I have the rights of the matter now. In fact, I know I have. It's quite clear. You went to fetch the papers again, this morning. You got there in time to see them put inside the gateway; and either in time to see them left at one of the other houses, or else you followed the newsman to see what a car was doing on the road so early. Anyhow, you saw the different papers left at the different houses, and you went and annexed them. Because three papers belonged to us, you figured that every other paper must be ours, too. *You're* the 'smart Alec' who ——"

"More likely when he watched the newsman go on to the next house and stop there," suggested the Mistress, "Dawn went over to investigate. He found a paper there, and then he made a tour of all the houses on this side of the lake and brought us a collection."

"Anyhow," said the Master, "we seem agreed he is the 'smart Alec.' His exact process of paper-stealing doesn't matter. I'm not going to tell on him. But he can't be allowed to do it again. People are crankier over missing their morning papers at breakfast than if they missed their coffee. If he keeps it up, some early riser is bound to see him on his paper-grabbing circuit. Then Old Man Trouble will be due to visit us. The only thing to do will be to tie him up for a week or so at night or let him sleep in my study, till he forgets this newest crazy idea of his."

Accordingly, that night, Gray Dawn slept in the study. There, sometime during the hours of darkness, he pursued a mouse under a table and then beneath the desk, and thence under a low bookshelf. The Master awoke from a dream of watching the battle of the Marne; and found the house still reëchoing with noise. He discovered his study in a woeful snarl of upset chairs, smashed bookcase, cascaded books, and strewn papers.

At an angry glower and angrier rebuke from the man the supersensitive Dawn slunk from the devastated room and out through one of the open French windows of the library. At sunrise a peace-offering in the form of twenty-one newspapers adorned the front-door mat.

But this time the usual performance had been varied. Dawn apparently had gone for a swim before starting on his paper-route, and then he had rolled in the cool lakeside mud. Having placed the last mouthful of the carefully collected newspapers on the mat, he had lain down on the heap of journalistic endeavor, for a nap. The papers were in hideous condition.

"There's only one thing for me to do," said the Master as he surveyed the pile of muddy news sheets. "I'll go around and distribute these, myself, and I'll say truthfully that I found them in this crumpled and mud-smeared state, in front of my door. But Dawn ought to be tethered somewhere on an ox chain, with a ten-foot stockade around him, if we're to keep out of trouble. He has one of his jinx fits on him again. If the newsman calls up while I'm gone, will you tell him all the papers were here again today and that I'm saving him trouble by delivering them for him?"

That night, at bedtime, Gray Dawn was taken to the cow-stable and ignominiously locked in there.

"Good night, you mischief-making old ruffian," said the Master, motioning him back into the warm darkness of the stable, as Dawn sought to push past him and out into the freer air. "Stay there and behave yourself. There's a bed of fresh hay in that corner; and you'll have the cows for company. You needn't look so forlorn. You're not being punished. But you're going to be kept safely out of trouble, for once. Good night."

Gray Dawn scratched imperatively at the shut door, as he heard the Master's steps recede. He was indignant and his feelings were hurt. This was no place for a watch-dog to spend the night in. There must be a mistake somewhere. At last he curled himself moodily on the pile of sweet hay and went to sleep.

One of the laborers, arriving for work, took the papers from behind the gate and laid them on the door mat, then made his way to the stable for the morning's milking. As he opened the cow-shed door, Gray Dawn bolted out to freedom. The dash was mildly disastrous, since the collie ran between the somewhat bowed legs of his liberator, causing the man to sit down hard and suddenly on the stable threshold. Dawn cleared the prostrate and blasphemous worker in one glad bound and frisked forth to liberty.

The summer sun was up. But that did not deter Dawn from going about his new trick of newspaper-collecting. Up the driveway he ran, to the gates. The papers were gone. Well, that did not prove there might not be other newspapers still lying on the piazzas and front steps which he had learned to visit at daybreak each morning. He set off for the nearest neighbor's, a quarter mile to northward.

But there, too, he drew blank. The papers were not on the steps, as usual. At three succeeding houses they had been taken in before his late arrival. Dawn began to lose heart. His beautiful morning game, for some occult reason, had been spoiled for him.

Being only a real life dog and not a canine fiction hero, he had no way of knowing that daily papers usually are taken indoors as soon as a household is stirring and that he was nearly three hours behind his usual time schedule for collecting them.

It was not in Dawn's nature to give up any project until he had assured himself from every angle that his venture was hopeless. Accordingly, leaving the main road, he struck up into a steep byway that skirted several hillside bungalows commanding a grand view of mountains and lake. In this bungalow settlement, on other mornings, he had annexed several newspapers from verandas and from low mail-boxes.

His quest, this time, was not wholly in vain. True, the first four porches were bare of papers. But on the topmost step of the fifth reposed two neatly folded journals, awaiting the perennially late arising of the bungalow's occupants.

Dawn's tulip ears went up happily. The white-plumed tip of his silver tail wagged. His journeyings had not been in vain, after all. True, this would not be an occasion of going patiently back and forth half a dozen times between The Place and the neighboring houses with successive mouthfuls of crackly and crinkly news sheets. But here at least was one mouthful to bear home in triumph, for the admiring praise of his two deities. It was far better than nothing.

He pattered up the flight of high steps, to the veranda summit. With meticulous care he nosed the two papers against a porch post, where he could encompass both of them in a single wide stretch of his jaws. As he picked them up and turned to descend the steps he halted; irresolute, troubled.

He sniffed the still morning air, then dropped the papers from his mouth that he might sniff the better. His ears were up. A strange sound had come to them, at the same time that an unwelcome reek had assailed his sensitive nostrils.

The sound had a pleasant allure to it. The scent was one which, from puppyhood, Dawn had loathed. For a moment he stood thus, listening and sniffing. First of all by scent and next by sound, and last and least of all by sight, does a dog record his impressions and carry his memories. His uncanny senses of smell and of hearing can guide him to any spot far more accurately than can the evidence of his near-sighted eyes.

Thus, Gray Dawn had no trouble at all in locating

the sources of the sound and scent which had arrested him. Ever as inquisitive as a monkey, the big dog padded around the piazza corner. The papers had been on the side steps. Now the collie made his way toward the piazza's rear.

Rounding a chimney outjut, he came alongside a wire-screened sleeping-porch. It contained a bed and a crib. On the bed lay a large woman who slept with her mouth open and who breathed stertorously with static noises. In the crib was cuddled a chubby pink-and-white baby, perhaps a little more than a year old—a baby whose tousled gold fluff of hair curled moistly above two wondering dark-blue eyes.

The baby had awakened early. Her nurse had not awakened at all.

The nurse had lost three good situations in a year through a cureless craving for drink. She had taken this job in the country to be far from temptation. But on the preceding evening she had come upon a hidden bottle of Scotch whisky in the bungalow cellar. She had carried it to bed surreptitiously, and had swigged from it at intervals until the drugged sleep of drunkenness had overtaken her.

The baby had waked a half-hour earlier. She had waked to a world of sunrise and of bird song. In her crib she had lain, wide-eyed, content with the glory around her. Nestling happily there, she had enlivened her loneliness by crooning a chuckly little wordless song, very soft to herself.

It was this jolly subdued gurgle which b
Dawn's ear. Like most collies, he was do

to babies, although he had seen but few of them. There was an irresistible lure for him in this musical mumble he heard. Accordingly, he had trotted along the porch in quest of the child.

At his every padding step the sweet crooning became more audible. But also at every step that disquieting scent waxed sharper and more repellent.

Even as he came in sight of the child he saw the cause of the reek which had disturbed him.

On a stand between the bed and the crib stood a candle. The nurse, in one of her nocturnal gropings for the whisky-bottle, had failed to find the object of her search, which had rolled out of her reach. Accordingly, she had gotten up and had lighted the candle. By its aid she had seen the bottle and had borne it back to bed with her. Being fuddled from drink, she forgot to blow out the light again.

During the past few hours the candle had been burning down. At last its guttering flame had lapped against a canton-flannel doll that lay on the stand close beside it.

The breath of fire had run swiftly along the fuzzy length of the doll, presently touching the thrown-back folds of a mosquito-bar at the head of the crib.

The folds of the netting were close-pressed, so they did not break at once into flame. But they set up a preliminary smolder which filled the air with pungent smoke.

This was the odor Gray Dawn had recognized so uncomfortably. From puppyhood, fire and thunderstorms the big collie's only fears. Nor was he to overthat reasonless dread of flame and smoke stant day when his life-and-death struggle

58

through the burning forests above Rainbow Lake should
cure him forever of fright at any lesser conflagration.

(Those of you who have read my book, "GRAY
DAWN," will remember Dawn's gloriously mad race
through the hell of fire.)

Dawn stood with his nose against the rusted wire which
inclosed the sleeping-porch. At sight of him the baby's
crooning song swelled to a crow of delight. She stretched
out her chubby arms eagerly toward the grinning dog
that had come to lighten her loneliness.

The slight jarring of the crib, from her jerkily welcoming gesture, shook free the smoldering outer folds of
mosquito-netting, above and behind the aureole of golden
fluff that crowned her head.

The air reached the looser folds of the netting. It flamed
up. Two or three hornet-like sparks fluttered down on
the baby's cheek, stinging sharply. The bedclothes received a like baptism of sparks. The inflammable outer
blanket of floss, across her tiny plump body, began to
smoke, where it was spark-ignited in a dozen spots.

Even as the crooning had changed to crowing, so now
the jocund crowing broke off in a surprised whimper
of pain. The tender pink cheek was stung by the red
sparks. Also, the smoke was getting into the baby's nostrils.

But she was one of those rare children whose sweetness
of nature extended even to her crying-spells. She did not
bawl lustily as would the average hurt youngster. Rather
did she wail softly, and more in amazed heartbreak than
in pain-wrath. Her weeping could scarce have been heard

59

twenty feet away. It did not so much as disturb the snoring nurse.

But the note of hurt and unhappiness in her crying went straight through Gray Dawn's all-tender heart, like a breath of torment. He could not endure the sight of human suffering, at any time. And now, when it was something helpless and tiny that suffered, the surge of sympathy and of desire to be of help swept aside his dread of fire and smoke.

Dawn seldom wasted much time in lassitude when once an impulse seized him. Just now he wasted not a fraction of a second. The thin rusty wire alone shut him away from this baby who was so frightened and hurt. He had no way of knowing whether the wire might be as strong as an iron wall or as flimsy as cobweb. But that question did not interest him.

He drew back a step. Then, nose down, he charged. His dappled silver head smote the wire with all his strength and with his eighty pounds of weight behind it. Through the screen he went as though it had been meshes of cotton threads.

The impetus of his rush carried him to the crib before he could come to a standstill. His terrible jaws closed upon the nearer shoulder of the baby as lightly as they had closed on the bundle of newspapers, as tenderly as a bird-dog picks up a shot partridge.

Yet the gentleness in no way marred his mighty strength. With no effort at all he lifted the crying and gasping child from the crib and, wheeling, bore her toward the gap he had made in the wire.

Before he had traveled three feet the baby ceased to

cry. To her this was a decidedly new and not altogether comfortable form of locomotion. But the novelty of it interested and entertained her vastly. Moreover, she was entranced with this furry friend of hers. The pin-prick pain of the sparks was lessening on the baby's cheek. And here, away from the bed, the hot smoke no longer tormented her nose and throat.

Arrived at the breach that his onset had made in the wire, Dawn had the wit to realize he could not hope to carry his living burden out through so small an exit.

Gently he laid the baby on the floor, close to the wire, after one tentative effort to push her through the hole whose ragged edges had sagged close together after his crashing assault. Then, drawing back, again, he hurled himself, once more, furiously at the wire; near to the opening through which he had entered the sleeping porch. He ripped his way through it. Back he charged again, butting once more through the much-widened rent in the screen.

His nose and ear and one paw were scored cruelly by the saw-like rusty wire edges. But he had cloven a gap, now, through which a wardrobe trunk could have been shoved. He glanced back in fear toward the crib. The floss had begun to blaze. The rest of the bedding was afire. The mosquito-net was sending a sheet of thin flame to the tin-tiled ceiling of the sleeping-porch. The nurse snored on.

She had scarcely stirred when, at his second impetuous leap into the room, Dawn had upset a flower-stand with three potted plants on it; although the racket resounded like a ragged thunder-clap.

Picking up the baby, Dawn carried his unprotesting pink-and-gold-and-white burden swiftly through the wide gap and far out onto the safety of the open veranda. There, gently he laid her down; having no clear idea what next to do for her.

Unharmed, unruffled, she laughed up at her big and friendly new chum. Wagging his plumed tail and quite oblivious of his several scratches and cuts, Dawn bent down to lick her face.

As he did so the bungalow's back door was flung open. On the threshold appeared a pajama-clad man, blear-eyed with sleep, crossly seeking to locate the noise which had disturbed him.

Blinking, he saw his adored baby daughter lying on the floor in front of him, while a monstrous gray dog ravened above her with blood-stained jaws. With a yell the man rushed forward; snatching the child from her presumptive death-peril. In the same move he delivered a furious kick with his slippered foot at the part of the murderous dog's anatomy which chanced to be closest to him.

The kick, softened as it was by the woolen bed slipper, caught Gray Dawn sharply and bruisingly in the short ribs. The collie had been eyeing with mildly amused interest the advent of this excitable human. He had even begun to wag his tail again. But the ferocious kick changed his attitude toward the stranger; and changed it with ludicrous suddenness.

The dog gave a wild-beast roar and sprang ragingly at the man. But almost in mid air he swerved. For, unconsciously, his assailant was holding the baby in front of him with one arm. The dog's raging jaws clicked shut scarcely an inch from the child. The leaping gray body dropped back to the floor.

Before Dawn could gather himself for another and better-directed attack, the man had darted backward across the threshold, carrying the baby close to his chest, and had slammed the door against the snarling jaws that threatened him. Dawn stood growling in baffled indignation, his side smarting from the padded kick. Then the door flew wide and the man reappeared on the threshold. He had laid the baby down somewhere and had grabbed up a large service revolver of antique pattern.

By the time the door was open he had leveled the weapon at the fiercely advancing collie.

Gray Dawn had not the slightest idea what the metal thing might be which his enemy was pointing toward him. All he knew or cared was that he had been kicked, right maddeningly, and that the kicker once more was within his reach.

But even as the dog sprang and as the man's finger tightened on the trigger, a woman pushed frantically past the pajama-clad figure in the doorway jostling him and disturbing his aim.

She was in a kimono and her face was smeared with traces of last night's cold cream. Apparently she had just been roused from sleep and had no knowledge of the scene in progress between her husband and the collie. Indeed, so excited was she that she noted neither the leveled pistol nor the dog. As she pushed forward past the man, Gray Dawn halted with scrambling suddenness.

Between him and his recent assailant, this newcomer

had thrust herself. He could not get past her at the man. The collie, like most members of his breed, would not molest or even willingly frighten a woman. He paused, irresolute, listening with genuine entertainment to the shrill volley of language which accompanied the kimono-clad housewife's advent.

"Phil!" she declaimed, tremulously, beginning to speak while she forced her way past her husband. "Phil! The house is on fire somewhere! Something waked me, and smoke was drifting through my windows. It must be that chimney again. Quick! It——"

Then she saw the hesitant collie; grinning up into her convulsed face with queer elfin amusement. At the same instant she and the equally excited man were aware for the first time of smoke clouds rolling from between the rusty wire meshes of the near-by sleeping-porch.

They cried out shrilly, in unison, and sped toward the smoke-belching screen. As they ran their clamor was augmented by a Valkyr screech from somewhere amid the smoke. Out through the gap cloven by Dawn's gray body, rolled and scrambled and bumped an obese figure to whose entangling nightclothes a galaxy of sparks clung and smoldered. The nurse's sweet repose had been disturbed at last.

While Dawn had found it mildly amusing to hear one woman make funny hysterical noises and wave her arms distractedly, yet the ear-racking bedlam raised by two women and a man disgusted him. It began to get on his hair-trigger nerves. The baby's unhappy wail had stirred him to the heart. These wild squawkings merely annoyed him.

The women were scampering about and ripping open the sleeping-porch's locked door in an effort to get into the swirl of flame and smoke and rescue the baby. The man was bellowing to them that the baby was safe indoors. As he bellowed he was wrestling grotesquely with the veranda's unwieldy fire-extinguisher.

Dawn had had enough of the clangor and silly commotion. Uncouth antics on the part of humans had always one of two immediate effects on the collie. Either they stimulated him to a gale of merry excitement and set him to gamboling thunderously in the very center of the activities, or else they jarred upon his nerves and temper.

This multiple loss of self-control on the part of strangers waxed vaguely irritating to him. He was not accustomed to shrieking and uncontrolled women. Also the smoke reek gave him an innate fear. None of the trio had eyes or thoughts for him. He favored them with a loftily contemptuous look. Then he turned and trotted away.

At the foot of the steps he paused and came back. He had forgotten something. He searched the smoky veranda, and found the two newspapers. They had been trodden on and had been scuffed into a corner during the wild footwork of the three fire-fighters. Still, as trophies their value was unimpaired. They were what Dawn had come for, and it was not Dawn's way to let such minor obstacles as fire and rescue and human hysterics come between him and anything his queer brain had set itself to do.

Wherefore, he picked up the torn and trampled papers

solicitously and gently and set forth, still unnoticed, for home.

He arrived at The Place just as the Mistress and the Master were sitting down to breakfast. Bearing the disordered news sheets, like an enormous irregular rosette, between his jaws, he capered delightedly up to the breakfast table. And now, in addition to their earlier disarray, the papers were flecked with blood from his wire-scratched face and head.

The Mistress and the Master sat gazing dully at him. Long custom ought to have braced them for anything he might do. But somehow they never could armor themselves completely for the next shock.

"*Dawn!*" gasped the Mistress.

At sound of her loved voice Gray Dawn frisked over to her, dropping the papers at her feet and laying his blood-wet head adoringly in her white voile lap.

It was a fitting conclusion to his morning's adventures, but he improved on it. One of his forepaws had been cut somewhat deeply by the wire. In puppy-like desire for sympathy he held up the bleeding paw for inspection, then planted it on the Mistress's shoulder.

He was awaiting eagerly the Mistress's ever-ready compassion for his hurts, when a sizzling gush of language from the Master made him slink cringingly off the veranda and toward the lake. He was abnormally sensitive to the slightest rebuke from either of these two humans whom he worshiped. The Master's swelling volley of invective turned the dog's first slinking retreat to a gallop. Nor did he pause until he was shoulder deep in the healingly cool waters.

"What's the answer?" demanded the Master, looking from the fast-receding collie to the tangle of newspapers on the floor. "I suppose this time some one objected to being robbed of his morning papers and Dawn annexed them by conquest. Well, we're due to find out soon enough. That's the only compensation about bad news. You don't have to go looking for it. Stay quietly where you are and it's certain to come and find you."

A little later, part of his glum prediction was fulfilled. As he and the Mistress were finishing their apprehension-marred breakfast a car came down the drive. Out of it stepped a man, who turned to help a woman descend from the tonneau. In her arms the woman carried an adorably fluffy pink-and-white-and-gold baby. The baby was the only one of the three who did not look nightmare-ridden.

"My name is Soden," the man introduced himself, speaking in staccato breathlessness, as one whose frayed nerves are hard-held, "Philip Soden. This is my wife. This is our baby daughter. I have come here to tell you about that great gray collie of yours."

"If you have any just complaint—" began the Master, stiffly, while his eyes strayed in guilty uneasiness toward the bunch of stolen and mishandled newspapers in the veranda waste-basket—"if you have any just complaint against our dog, I am willing to ——"

He broke off short in his ungracious speech, for the woman all at once broke into convulsive weeping and clasped the baby tight to her.

"Good Lord!" inwardly pondered the troubled Master. "Dawn must have done more than just to steal their papers. He's killed some one! This is going to be worse than I thought. He ——"

With one arm thrown soothingly around the weeping woman's shoulder, Soden continued his jerky harangue, while his wife fought for self-control.

"Our baby's nurse got drunk," said he. "She set fire to Baby's crib. It was one mass of flame and embers when we got to it. Baby would have been lying in the middle of that blazing crib—all helpless and—and ——" His throat thickened. He cleared it impatiently, then added: "Your dog tore a hole through the wire wall of the sleeping-porch and dragged her out, just in time. That's—why we're here. There—there isn't anything we can say or do, to—to ——"

His voice bogged down and refused its office.

But if two members of the Soden family were mute, the third was not. The baby gave a squeal of utter delight and squirmed to get to the ground. Up from the lake a dog was galloping. The baby had seen and recognized her dear playfellow of an hour before.

Dawn's scratched head and paw had profited greatly by the plunge into the cool water and by a subsequent roll in the mud. So had his scratched feelings. Hearing the approach of a car, he had left off his dual swim and roll and had come houseward to investigate.

At sight of the baby and at sound of her welcoming squeal he broke into a tearing run and bounded dramatically into the center of the veranda group. There he halted long enough to shake a liberal shower of mud and water from his shaggy coat impartially upon everyone within range, and then tried to reach up to lick the baby's radiant little face.

Even as he had neared the group, his psychic collie perceptions told him he was no longer in disgrace, but in unexpectedly high favor. He was taking a characteristically Dawn-like advantage of this change in public sentiment toward him.

The Sodens had departed; after taking up a full hour of a morning which the Master had planned to spend at hard work in his study. The Mistress was sponging Dawn's superficial hurts with warm water and witch hazel. The Master looked dazedly down at the huge collie sprawling happily on the veranda floor.

"Dawn," he said, at length, "almost half of that wasted work hour was taken up by us in persuading those noisy people not to give you a gold collar set with diamonds. And I know they're both thinking I'm a heartless brute because I told them you'd much rather have a pound of chuck steak than all the jewelry that ever happened.

"If Charlie Chaplin should play 'Hamlet' one week and save a passenger train from wreck the next week," went on the Master, perplexed, "the whole world would be talking about it. But that's the kind of thing *you're* doing, every year of your clownish life, Dawn. Perhaps if we live together fifty years longer I may get to understanding you."

"And you won't shut him up at night any more?" pleaded the Mistress. "He hates it so!"

"No," answered the Master. "When this rescue story gets around the neighborhood, nobody will have the nerve to object to his stealing every paper in the county. I'm glad I didn't tell Soden about that fool stunt of his, though. The poor man would have taken out a life subscription to fifty newspapers a day in Dawn's name; or bought him a paper-mill."

IV. GRAY DAWN, DIRECTOR

On the pretty vine-draped steps of the Inasmuch Orphanage were grouped ninety jolly little boys and girls.
Their faces and bearing proved past doubt the truth
of the Orphanage's proud boast that this institution was
a Home in the truest and biggest sense of the word.

Behind them, on the top step, just below the carven
motto, *"Inasmuch as ye have done it unto the least of
these—"* was a line of the Home's directors and patrons.

On the lawn in front a camera man was focusing his
machine.

The children were eagerly alert as they held the graceful poses taught them for the occasion. They had been
told that if this picture should turn out well, it was to
be printed in the illustrated sections of many Sunday
newspapers, besides appearing on the front page of the

71

Home's new booklet. Also, an enlarged copy of it was to be framed and hung in the dining-hall—the sunny blue-and-white dining-hall whose wall friezes were wonderful scenes from *Mother Goose* and Hans Christian Andersen.

Small wonder that each and every one of the young-sters posed with breathless eagerness! This was an Occa-sion; the climax of the merry proceedings of Visitors' Day.

The camera man waved his hand—a prearranged sig-nal that everything was ready and that he was going to press the shutter bulb. As if in immediate response to the signal, a huge gray-and-silver-and-snow collie ap-peared from nowhere in particular, rounding the corner of the porch at a hand gallop.

As he reached the precise center of the proposed pic-ture, and just in front of the group of children, he seemed aware that something extraordinary was going on. For he halted and stood at gaze, statuesque, magnificent, if wholly out of place, while he peered inquisitively at the camera.

The photographer pressed the bulb, his eyes ranging the ranks of children to make certain they held their as-signed postures. Then he looked down as he noted that ninety pairs of bright eyes were all centered at one spot. He saw the big collie standing there, in a natural pose worthy of a sculptor's chisel.

"Plate spoiled!" commented the photographer, dis-gustedly. "The picture would have been a beauty, too. And the light's going."

"No, the picture is *not* spoiled, either!" indignantly

declared a shrill voice from among the ninety. "It will look ever and ever so much nicer with Dawnie in it."

"And with everyone of you kids staring goggle-eyed at him instead of in the directions I told you to!" scoffed the disgruntled camera man. "Nope. Plate's spoiled. It ——"

"Gray Dawn!" called the Master, crossly, from his place among the handful of invited guests.

At the call, the big collie wheeled and cantered up the steps, straight through the middle of the artistically grouped children, their careful formation crumbling as a score of them reached out to pat him during his unceremonious progress. The camera man groaned aloud. The collie danced up to the Master and stood looking in his face, waiting for further instructions.

"I'm so sorry!" the Mistress was saying to the president of the board of directors and to the Home's matron. "It's a shame he ruined such a fine picture. He ——"

"He can be counted on to wreck anything he comes within a mile of!" grumbled the Master. "He has a genius that way. He's five years old and he'll never stop being a fool puppy. I'm mighty sorry he made toad pie of the picture. I'll shut him in the reception room while the next one is taken. He ——"

But a multiple and vehement protest burst forth from the children on the steps below. Over and over again, in many high keys, they insisted that their beloved Dawnie must be in the next picture, and indeed must be in any and all future pictures.

The juvenile group had stampeded from its primly correct pose. It wanted Dawn. It wanted to be photographed with Dawn in its center or it did not want to be photographed at all. The mutiny was frolicsome, but there was a subnote of tearful pleading behind it.

The matron of the Orphanage smiled apologetically at the president of the board. Had this been an icily correct and standardized refuge for parentless children, the mutiny could and would have been annihilated at a word from her; if, indeed, the unlucky little inmates of such an institution should have dared to mutiny.

But it was the directors' boast that every child in the Inasmuch Orphanage had the same chance for individuality and for happiness as if it were the only offspring of wisely loving parents. It was for this reason that they had engaged their present matron.

The president of the board laughed back indulgently in response to the matron's appealing smile.

"It seems unanimous," said he. "For my own part, I'd rather be photographed with a gallant and clean-souled collie like Sunnybank Gray Dawn than with a number of humans I could mention. Go ahead with the picture, please, Mr. Camera Man. And use Dawn as the pivot for your grouping."

Amid a raggedly ecstatic chorus of squeals, the photographer set sourly to work on his new composition of the sitters. The Mistress turned to the board's president, whispering:

"No wonder the babies are all so happy here! It was beautiful of you to let them be photographed with Dawn. I am going to borrow the plate and have post-card-size reductions made from it. Ninety of them. I'm going to give each of the children one of them, with Gray Dawn's compliments. Do you mind our doing that?"

"It'll be fine!" approved the president. "They'll treasure those pictures more than you or I would treasure the Koh-i-noor. I'm glad you people bring the big dog over here with you on these Visitors' Days. He is so gentle and friendly with the children, no matter how much they haul him around or pet him or make him shake hands. A fine dog like that is a wholesome influence in any coterie of children, besides being a real delight to them. It is touching to see how they love him."

"Indeed they do," assented the matron. "If a popularity vote could be taken at the Inasmuch, I know Gray Dawn would win. If the children had the electing of the board—or if the rest of us here had—Dawn would be made a director, by acclamation."

"Gray Dawn, Director!" quoted the president, whimsically. "Well, I've served on boards whose membership's moral and pulchritude average would have been improved, one hundred per cent, by his presence on it. Besides," turning to the Mistress, "think of the money your big collie has earned for our Home! More than the average director bothers to raise. His cash prizes from those two dog-shows, and all the contributions he got during our last drive. Why, the manager of Blankberg's store told me more people stopped and turned back and dropped coins and bills into your basket, after they saw Gray Dawn lying there so majestically beside you, than had ever been contributed to any other drive the store helped out in. Yes, we could have a worse director than Dawn, if there weren't a foolish prejudice against admitting wise dogs to governing boards instead of foolish humans."

As the Mistress and the Master drove home to The Place, that afternoon, with Gray Dawn lying contentedly on the car's back seat, their talk was all of the Inasmuch Orphanage and its growingly pressing needs. The unusual homelikeness of the institution was beginning also to overwhelm it with applicants, who, perforce, were refused because of lack of funds and lack of space.

In spite of many donations and of frequent drives, the Inasmuch was having no easy time to maintain its high standard of comfort and of home surroundings. There was increasing need for a new building or for a new wing on the present building, if any of this swarm of applicants were to be admitted. But money for the purpose was coming in with maddening slowness.

As the car rounded a bend in the wooded road at the farthest boundary of The Place, it all but ran into another machine that lay half across the none-too-wide highway and half in the ditch.

The Master got out, in the gathering twilight, and examined the derelict machine. Its axle had snapped, letting down the rear wheels in splayed uselessness. The car sagged like a broken-backed animal.

Whoever had occupied it had not troubled to hide the cushions or rugs, in going to telephone for help. Nor could the mishap have occurred more than a little time before. Though there was not overmuch traffic on this road in the late afternoons, yet if the broken-down vehicle had been there for any length of time, some one surely would have notified the local State Police.

The radiator was still hot. The license plates were those of Illinois, some thousand miles distant from this North Jersey hinterland region. The machine was of expensive make and almost new.

The Master ceased from his inspection and got into his own car to continue the homeward trip.

"It's foolish to leave it unguarded, like that," he commented, "especially in these days of motor thieves and cheap crooks. When the man from Illinois gets back from telephoning, he'll be lucky if he doesn't find the cushions and the tires and the robes and the carburetor and the windshield-wiper gone. Some passing motorist is liable to stop there and clean out everything portable. I'd take some of the things home for safe-keeping, but I don't care to have him come back and accuse me of robbing him. By the way, I've been accused of larceny, once, today."

"What!"

"Little Myrtle Robertson, at the Inasmuch, told me she knew I must have stolen that rabbit-doll you gave her," laughed the Master. "She said she had left it on the bench where I was sitting, and it was gone. I was lucky enough to clear myself. For just then we both saw Gray Dawn burying the adored doll in a flower-bed. I don't know what's come over the crazy dog. He never buried anything, or dug up anything, except bones, in his life, till lately. But now he's taking to digging, like any fool puppy. The only thing anyone can be sure of about Dawn is that he'll do something no other grown dog on earth would think of doing."

"It's just a phase," said the Mistress, "like the habit he

picked up, once, of carrying all kinds of food to those puppies of Lass's; and his trick of climbing into cars, in the garage, every night, so as to be ready for next morning's drive; and the way he used to leave his white elephant everywhere. He'll get over it. He always does. Remember, he isn't like any other dog. He never was."

She spoke affectionately, and leaned back to pet the collie's classic head. Dawn's tail thumped loudly on the leathern seat and he strove to nuzzle the petting hand.

Just as the Master came downstairs for dinner, that evening, Gray Dawn returned from a ramble of the grounds. In his dirt-smeared mouth he carried an exceptionally dead hen, covered with earth. One of the men had buried the fowl, which had died a natural death. Dawn, in his wanderings, had come upon the new-shoveled spot and had investigated, then bringing his fascinating find to his owners.

"Take that thing out of here!" shouted the Master. "*Out!*"

Grievously offended, as ever he was by a single sharp word, the gray collie turned and stalked out of the house, his ears pinned back to his drooping head, his plumed tail down.

The Master glared after him, then went out on the veranda to make certain the hen had not been left close to the house. In the starlight, he could see Gray Dawn mournfully interring the fowl in the middle of the Mistress's cherished heliotrope border. With lavishly effortful forepaws the collie was hurling into air an indiscriminate mass of dirt-clods and of fragile heliotrope plants.

"I've got to break him of that idiocy," declared the Master as he and his wife sat down to dinner. "It's bad enough for the moles to have gotten into the lawn this week, without that great hulk of an eternal puppy tearing up what's left of The Place. He's a pest. I———"

The whir of motorcycles on the driveway set the kennel dogs to barking wildly. Presently the waitress returned to the dining-room, from the front door, with the announcement that Captain Trill and a sergeant from the village's State Police barracks would like to see the Master.

Puzzled, he went out to greet them. After a five-minute chat the sputter of the two cycles proclaimed the departure of the visitors. The Master came back into the dining-room.

"Well," he said as he sat down to his interrupted dinner, "the mystery of the smashed car is solved. Trill came here to see if we had happened to be anywhere around when it broke down, or if the men in it had happened to pass through our grounds on their get-away."

"Get-away?" echoed the Mistress. "What do———?"

"Here's the idea," explained the Master. "Another episode in the robbery wave. The biggest one yet. The Croyden post-office was looted this afternoon, Trill says. He says it was evidently the work of old hands and they must have had an inside tip that a swad of cash and a lot of other valuables were in the registered-letter sack just then. It's pay day at three of the Croyden factories, and it's a day some of the Croyden banks happen to be sending valuable stuff to New York.

"Two men got into the back rooms—it's a disgracefully ramshackle little old building for such a busy town's

post-office—and one of them held up the clerks with a
gun—he was masked—while the other went through
everything he could lay his hands on, including the safe.
They got clean away, too. They had stolen a tourist's car,
somewhere downtown, in Croyden—an Illinois car. Trill
thinks they were on the way to the mountains, back of
Rotten Pond, to hide the stuff or to divide it, when the
car broke down just outside our woods.

"They had a good start, and by the time the police
hit their trail they had stolen some other car or legged
it to the nearest railroad station. Anyhow, they're gone,
and a good many thousand dollars are gone with them.
. . . Yes, the Automobile has placed successful robbery
as well as immorality within the reach of all. We live in
a wonderful age."

Next morning, as the Mistress and the Master took
their after-breakfast stroll of the grounds, Gray Dawn
went with them, as usual. In the middle of a velvet green
oval of sward—still known as the "croquet lawn" in
memory of the purpose for which it had been laid out
seventy years earlier—the Master came to a stop, pointing
to a long and crooked and ugly weal which cut the care-
fully-tended oval of shaven turf.

"Look!" he exclaimed, in disgust. "The moles are still
at it. I'd rather have had them furrow any other part of
The Place than this croquet lawn. It's the sweetest bit of
lawn this side of England. There have been seventy years
of steady care spent on it. And now, in one night, a
mole ——"

"It can be rolled smooth," consoled the Mistress. "By

the way, did you get the mole-traps you were talking about?"

"No," sheepishly admitted the Master. "I forgot to. I was going to get them yesterday. We'll stop and buy them when we go over to the village."

With his foot he was pushing flat a part of the up-heaved turf. Dawn watched him with mild interest.

"Why don't *you* catch moles?" the Master asked him, jokingly. "Then you might be good for something besides burying dolls and exhuming buried hens. That would be a real outlet for your talents, Dawn. Get the mole."

The collie listened gravely, his head a little on one side. Naturally, he could not understand the meaning of one word in ten. But the Master very evidently was addressing him and was telling him to "get" something.

Also, to Dawn's preternaturally keen scent, the presence of the mole was wholly distinguishable. He gathered that the Master was trying to catch the mole; though the man was putting his feet down on the furrow-welt, several yards away from the spot at which Dawn's nostrils located the underground digger. Humans were so stupid, that way. Gray Dawn yearned to give skilled assistance to the Master's clumsy mole-hunting.

But just then the two humans moved away, and the Master whistled Dawn to follow. Still, the big gray dog had a queerly retentive memory. In that memory, as he trotted off obediently in the Master's wake, the collie jotted down a certain exciting deed to be performed at the first convenient chance.

He did not drive to the village that morning with the

Mistress and the Master. For they took the small car, wherein there was no room for an eighty-pound collie whose interest in brake and accelerator was sometimes more than academic.

The mole-traps were bought, and were stored between the Master's knees as the Mistress drove home. As soon as the car was put away the two fared toward the croquet lawn, to set the first trap where the most recent and most destructive underground tunneling had been done.

Just as they neared the corner of the house whence the croquet lawn would become visible, Gray Dawn came capering up to meet them. Vastly pleased with himself was the collie. His silver-and-snow coat was not at its cleanest. His white paws were brown; his nose was browner.

Daintily, between his massive jaws, he was carrying something. Running to the Mistress, Dawn dropped this trophy at her feet.

It was a newly-killed and unmangled mole; large, fat, heavy. Dawn laid it in front of the Mistress. Then he stepped back, in self-conscious pride, and waited for the praise that was his due. He got it.

"See!" cried the Mistress. "Isn't that clever of him? He kept staring up at you and then down at your feet while you were telling him he ought to kill the mole and while you were trying to stamp on it. Then he thought the whole thing out for himself, and he killed the mole and brought it to us. Oh, Dawn, you're splendid! *Good* old Dawnie!"

She patted him, extravagantly praising his cleverness. Dawn wriggled until he looked like an animated silver-

and-white interrogation point. He grinned vacuously, in sheer delight at the laudation.

Then, picking up the defunct mole again, he sought to lay it at the Master's feet, in hope of hearing more and louder praise of his exploit. But the Master was looking more interestedly at the egregious quantity of dirt on the dog's paws and muzzle than at the dead mole. He was drawing pessimistic inferences.

Ignoring the proffered trophy, he hurried forward around the house corner to where he could see the croquet ground. The Mistress, seized suddenly by the same suspicion, followed him. Then both of them stopped and gazed in wordless horror.

Along a ragged line of perhaps eighteen feet, down the very middle of the erstwhile exquisite bit of lawn, an irregular trench had been dug, from two to six inches in depth and at a width varying from three inches to a foot.

The shaven and tenderly-cared-for emerald carpet was blotched and marred thus, by a ghastly brown stain across its middle, ruining its beauty; a beauty which could not be restored in full, by the most expert gardeners, for another several years.

The mole had been crafty and elusive. He had burrowed erratically and fast while the eager dog above him had been clearing away the roof of his green tunnel in patches and rents. For an hour the digging chase had gone merrily on across the desecrated lawn. Not until the Mistress and the Master were coming up from the garage after their drive to the village, had Dawn at last overtaken and caught the inspired tunneler.

Fresh from the kill he had borne his grisly trophy to the Mistress.

For a long minute nobody spoke; as the man and woman stared aghast at the devastation wrought upon their beautiful lawn.

Here, almost seventy years agone, the Master's parents, as young people, had played the then fashionable game of croquet. Here the Master himself had been laid, as a baby, for his daily sun-bath. Hither, for a half-century, had come envying neighbors, to gaze on an oval of perfect lawn which their best efforts could not yet duplicate.

Just now, it looked as though a drunkard had driven a deep-shared plow through it. Perhaps nobody but a lawn fanatic can realize to the full what such desecration means and how long it takes for such a scar to vanish from the face of the verdant turf.

It was the Mistress who broke the spell of silence. Glancing apprehensively up at the Master and reading his chaotic thoughts, she said:

"You mustn't punish him for it, dear. You told him to get the mole. He did what he thought we wanted him to. You could see that by the triumphant way he brought it to us, just now. It's awful, I know—awful—to see the dear croquet lawn like that, and I feel as if it was my own face that had been slashed with a raggéd knife. But, honestly, Dawn isn't to blame. Can't you see he isn't?"

"I can see how beautiful he'd look at the bottom of the lake, with a stone around his worthless neck," fumed the Master. "But you're right, I suppose. I told him to get the mole. I didn't suppose he'd understand. The longer I study dogs, the less I know just what impossible thing they are going to understand and what absurdly simple thing they aren't going to. . . . Take him away, somewhere, won't you, dear? Somehow I feel he's apt to live longer if he and I aren't in each other's company for the next few hours. Gee! but I'm glad my father didn't live to see his croquet lawn, the way it looks now! He was prouder of it than ever he had reason to be of *me*."

The Master stamped away, to break the news of the devastation to Robert Friend, his English superintendent —an unpleasant task, by itself—while the Mistress called Dawn into the house with her.

The collie was almost psychically cognizant of human moods. The stark silence wherewith his two deities had surveyed the scene of his mole hunt affected him more keenly than would a storm of kicks and curses. Inch by inch he had shrunk to earth, close beside the Mistress, and had laid there trembling.

Now, at her gentle word of command, he followed her into the house as if into a torture-chamber. She petted him and told him it was all right. But Dawn knew that somehow it was not at all right. Miserably he crept under the piano, which for so many bygone years had been old Laddie's "cave."

There the disgraced and perplexedly unhappy dog lay until late afternoon. He had not the remotest idea why he had been praised loudly at one moment and at the next had been made aware that he was an object of detestation. It did not make sense to him. Naturally, he did not connect his disgrace with his destruction of the lawn. For had he not been petted and lauded for that?

The Master's first gust of temper cooled; and he came back to the house at lunchtime, to talk over the annoyance with his wife.

"Something's got to be done," he said, worriedly. "This can't go on. It's a sort of obsession that has overtaken Dawn in just the past few weeks. If we don't break him of it there'll be all sorts of trouble."

"But he ——"

"Robert told me, this morning, how he thinks it began. Salvatore had a walrus-skin vest that some one on an Italian whaleship brought him. The other men guyed him about it. It had a fish-oil smell that made them sick. One day Salvatore took off the vest while he was working. For a joke, Sam buried it in the melon-patch. Salvatore was mad as wrath; and he went all around, looking for it. At last Dawn happened by. As he was walking through the melon-patch he either saw the disturbed earth or else he smelled the walrus vest through the ground. Anyhow, he dug up the vest. Salvatore gave him all his dinner-pail's greasy contents as a reward; and then swaggered around, praising him to the skies. I suppose it went to Dawn's head and started him on his digging orgy."

From the piano-cave Dawn could hear the talk distinctly. He could catch his own name mentioned once or twice in a tone of indubitable disapprobation. He shrank the lower, head between paws, profoundly and bewilderedly heartsick.

"I've never struck him since he was a puppy," went on the Master, none too happily, "but he's got to be cured of this in some way. And a good licking seems to be the only cure. Naturally, I've got to catch him in the act or it won't do any good. But I'm going to keep my eye on him. Next time I catch him digging—whether he's burying something or digging it up—he's going to be whipped."

The Mistress was listening, a crease of pain between her brows. Her husband ignored the look.

"I don't see any better way out of it," he insisted. "Do you?"

"You've said again and again," she protested, "that no grown dog on The Place is ever whipped, and that none of them ever need to be."

"Then this will be a good punishment to me, for bragging," he rejoined, sulkily. "I'm going to watch Dawn as closely as I can. When I catch him digging, he's going to catch a thrashing. If you can cure him any other way, go to it. I'd rather be kicked than have to lick him. You know that. But when it comes to his ruining lawns and ——"

"Are you going to beat him just to cure him," asked the Mistress, quietly, "or a little bit to vent your own anger for the croquet lawn being torn up?"

The Master did not reply. There did not seem to be any apt reply to make. As usual, the Mistress had put her finger tip on the truth. Nevertheless, the Master bolstered his resolution by telling himself that women did not understand these things.

Dog-whip and punitive boot-toe were not used at The Place. From puppyhood, the collies were taught the few simple rules that must govern their actions—the chiefest of all, obedience—and they needed no physical punishment to remind them to keep The Place's law.

Thus the Master's decision to break Dawn of the digging habit, by means of a whipping, meant more than it might have implied at any other dog-owner's home.

"If you beat Dawn," went on the Mistress, in sorrowful finality, "it will break something in his soul that never can be mended. I know him better than you do. He'll never be the same dog again."

"I hope he won't. Any other kind of dog is bound to be an improvement on him as he is nowadays."

"*Please* don't do it, dear. I'd rather have every inch of lawn dug up by him than——"

"Then think of some better way of curing him," suggested the Master, the more sullenly because he knew that, as usual, his wife was right.

"I'll try to," she promised. "But——"

"But please think it up before I catch him digging again," adjured the Master. "I don't want to thrash him, any more than you want him thrashed. But he's got to stop destroying things. He's not a puppy. He's a middle-aged dog; old enough to know how to behave sanely."

Much the Master hoped his wife would have hit upon some plan for turning Dawn's ever-erratic brain from the theme of exhumation, before occasion should arise when the man himself must make good his threat by whipping the collie he loved.

Late that afternoon, his work done, the Master gathered his fishing-tackle and went down to the lake at the lawn's foot, to cast for bass. His boat drifted northward, along the shore, as he cast. Gradually it left the lawn behind and came alongside the water-edge woods at the far extreme of The Place.

Late that afternoon, too, Sunnybank Gray Dawn awoke from a snooze under the piano, his fit of depression quite gone. He sallied forth, eager to find one of his two human deities.

But the Mistress had driven over to the railroad station to meet a guest. Dawn followed the Master's trail to the boathouse. There the trail vanished. The big dog rambled aimlessly on through the sunset, in one of his favorite unofficial patrols of The Place.

Dawn knew, as should every watch-dog, the precise boundary of his owners' land. Almost every day he wandered from end to end of it, whether for exercise or from a sense of guard duty. On he moved, now, at leisurely pace, almost paralleling the line of the Master's idly drifting boat and some distance ahead of it.

As the boat came alongside the tract of woodland, sloping to the highroad a furlong above, the Master ceased for a moment from his fruitless casting, to gaze upward through the cathedral-like vista of trees. The sunset bathed the wooded hillside in amber light; bringing out each detail of even the topmost trees and bushes at the roadside, in shimmering brilliancy.

Raptly the man watched the panorama of gold-flecked greenery and soft shadows. Then, with a most non-rhapsodical grunt, he rowed hard to the near-by shore, jumped out of his boat, and began to climb the woody slope at top speed.

The magnifying and clarifying sunset light had just revealed to him a detail less picturesque than the nodding trees and the green undergrowth.

It showed him a large gray collie digging industriously in the forest mold at the foot of a giant oak, a few rods from the highroad.

Shrinking from what he had to do, yet goaded by his own loudly-voiced promise to himself and by memory of the ripped-up croquet lawn, the Master swarmed up the slope. He went as fast as might be, lest the dog finish his illicit digging before the avenger could arrive at the spot.

He need not have worried. The collie was working away vigorously and with his back to his owner, yet he was fully aware of the Master's fast approach. Also he was vaguely pleased that the man should witness the swiftness and skill wherewith Dawn was investigating a heap of loose earth he had just happened upon.

He had scented the track of human feet. Then he had followed this to a place, under the oak, where a great riffle of dead leaves hid the ground. Artistically as the leaves were arranged, Dawn smelled fresh-turned earth below them, and, as usual, he began to explore.

Up the hill panted the angry Master. In another few strides he had come alongside the dog. One hand was stretched forth to grasp Dawn by the scruff of the neck. The man glanced about in search of a stick with which to do the beating.

Then his questing eyes came to a galvanic halt and he stood with mouth ajar. Dawn had dug down to what he sought. With exploratory teeth he gripped an outjutting leather strap. Seizing this, he yanked with all his might.

Slowly some heavy object consented to be hauled forth, under the powerful leverage of jaw-grip and braced paws.

The Master stood blinking, as the hastily dug and carefully hidden hole in the mold underneath the oak gave up its secret.

A bulging leather mail-sack, slit open for some inches near the top, was the first thing to meet the staring man's view. Tied to this by a stout cord was a second and smaller, if bulkier, bag—a stout little canvas sack.

"The—the beating is postponed—for keeps, Dawn," mumbled the Master as he lifted the heavy bags. "You've a positive genius for getting into trouble, old friend. But you've got a queerer genius for turning the sourest lemon into lemonade. Come on home. I've a lot of phoning to do."

Some hours later, two men—who had been recognized as old offenders and arrested on general principles as they changed cars at Ridgewood for a Goshen express—were confronted at Croyden police headquarters by the information that the swag they had buried so carefully under a tree, within a hundred feet of where their stolen car broke down, had been recovered. Also that fingerprints on letters in the slit mail-bag corresponded with their own at New York headquarters.

The bags had been far too heavy and too conspicuous to lug, on foot, over a road along which the pursuing state troopers might be expected to track them at any moment. Hence, after a hasty council of war, the men had entered the woods. With the wide end of a broken fence rail, they had dug a grave for the treasure in the soft mold under the oak; then covering the earth with thick-piled leaves.

The hiding-place had seemed as safe as a bank. A thicket of hazel grew all around the cache. Anyone could pass within three feet of it without seeing or suspecting. There the loot could lie snug for a week or so, until it should be wholly safe to come by motor at night and cart it away. The leather sack had been slit only to verify the belief that it held registered mail and not ordinary letters.

The Mistress and the Master were at breakfast on the veranda. Gray Dawn drowsed lazily on the floor beside the Mistress, his huge body greatly and continuously impeding the waitress's efforts to circumnavigate the small table in the course of her duties. The morning mail was brought in. The topmost envelope bore the letterhead of the Inasmuch Orphanage. The Master tore it open and read aloud:

"You will receive formal acknowledgment and acceptance and the usual enthusiastic vote of thanks, and all that, in a day or two, as soon as the board meets again. But in the meantime I want you to know what a splendid thing we all agree you have done, you and your wife, in turning the federal reward over to the Orphanage. It means more to us than words can make you understand.

"Is it true that you were going to refuse the reward the government had offered for the return of the plunder, and that your wife made you accept it and turn it over to our building fund? It sounds like her.

"Now, I want to tell you two dear people something.

That reward money, added to the other contributions, gives us enough to start work on the new wing. Yes, it is to be a wing, not a separate building. It means happy accommodations for at least thirty more homeless and parentless children. Think of that!

"Do you know what we have decided to call the new wing, in honor of the way the money came to us? It is going to face the rising sun, so the earliest daylight will come through its windows.

"So we're going to name it 'DAWN Hall.'"

At sound of his name the big silver-and-snow collie banged his plumed tail approvingly against the veranda floor. Life was monstrous pleasant nowadays.

V. *THE PASSING OF GRAY DAWN*

Sunnybank Gray Dawn is dead.

He died on Memorial Day, 1929; falling quietly asleep
on his rug close beside the desk in my study here at Sunnybank and forgetting to awaken.

In his sleep his mighty heart stopped beating. That was
all. There was no pain, no terror.

Some of you knew him through my Gray Dawn stories
in magazines and through my book, *Gray Dawn*, or from
your visits to Sunnybank. Perhaps you may care to hear
more.

Not that the tales of our great blue-gray collie were
especially well told. But Dawn's odd personality managed
to crop its buoyant way through them and into the hearts
of readers. I judge this from numberless letters during the
last decade, asking about him; and from the myriad queer

94

mail parcels addressed to him—parcels containing everything from sliced chicken to candy.

He was born during a spectacular December thunderstorm in 1918. I don't care much for merle collies. But the Mistress had always wanted one, so I gave this silver-gray baby collie to her. I am glad I did. For if he had been mine I would have been only too glad to sell him for a plugged nickel, during the first year of his life, to anyone who would have agreed to take him a hundred miles away from Sunnybank and keep him there. He was that kind of pup.

The Mistress, wiser than I, claimed from the first that there was a stanchness and loyalty behind the crazy mischief in his deep-set, dark eyes. I had not the wit to see it. But I could see—everyone except the Mistress could see—that he was an unmitigated pest. For instance:

By the time he was three months old he was as big and as powerful as the average pup of twice his age. And he was vibrant with a queer vitality and persistence that led him into unending trouble and led everyone else—again except the Mistress—to lurid profanity.

His first obsession was a belief that he could catch any mole which might have the sportsmanship to play at all fair with him. As a result, Dawn painstakingly followed each and every mole furrow across our Sunnybank lawns, changing its tunnel to an open trench by dint of fast and tireless digging.

The lawns were a mess. So were such flower-beds as the mole-tunnels might penetrate, and the flower borders which Dawn chose as temporary tombs for the bones he was tired of gnawing.

95

His war against the squirrels was waged along still sillier lines. He would tree a chattering, scolding squirrel, and then would camp under the tree, barking thunderous threats at his prey; and would sit there watching and barking for the entire rest of the day, while the squirrel, jumping from tree to tree, was perhaps in the next county before the vigil was half ended.

He went on a theory that I was starving to death. Wherefore—as later did his big son, Sunnybank Sandstorm—he used to bring me horrible offerings of defunct fish he had found at the lake-edge and of gory rats he had slain in battle, and once an excessively dead skunk he had found far back in the woods. These dreadful gifts he would lay with meticulous care across my hiking boots—preferably while I was at lunch on the veranda—or, if I were not in sight, he would deposit them on the edge of my desk in the study and leave them there to await my return.

One afternoon the Mistress and I were about to start for a wedding some miles away. In the glory of morning coat and high hat I stepped down to the edge of the lake to give an order to one of the men. This while the car was waiting to bear us to the scene of the festivities, which we could barely reach in time.

Dawn caught sight of me standing there. In an excess of friendliness, he dashed down the lawn toward me at express train speed. My first intimation that he was anywhere near me was when his flying body smote me in mid-back. He and I plunged into the lake, side by side, as a result of that balance-destroying impact.

The Mistress crossed the lawn to see what had befallen.

Young Gray Dawn had left the water several seconds before I did—I had my high hat to retrieve when I got to my feet, waist-deep in the lake—and he saw the Mistress coming toward him. By way of welcome, Dawn snatched up a newly-cut thorn bush and, with this offering, he cantered over to her.

The thorns became enmeshed at once in the filmy dress she was wearing. Gleesomely Dawn galloped around and around her, still gripping the stem of the bush, while its thorns completed the wreck of the sweet white dress and swathed it tightly around its unhappy wearer.

(Yes, we were late to the wedding.)

These are only a handful of the insanely mischievous things which made me yearn to murder Dawn, or to sell him at any price, during his first year. The Mistress alone had faith in him—a faith which one day was to be proved well founded, as are most of the Mistress's ideas.

He seemed wholly without brain; wholly without promise. By the time he was seven months old he was the biggest of the collies and weighed more than eighty pounds. His coat of shining silver, stippled with black, was a thing of beauty. He was as strong as a cart-horse, as swift as a charging bull. But, to me, he seemed a wilfully blundering fool.

Then, one bitter-cold night, a little collie mother was desperately ill. I went down to the stable broodnest, where she and her newborn babies were kept, and I sat there all night, trying to keep her and them alive. Dawn had followed me to the broodnest shed. I had shut the door in his face as I went in. When I came out, at seven o'clock in the morning, there stood Dawn.

97

All night he had stood there on guard, waiting for me to come out. He had stood, not sat or lain (as the marks in the frosty ground proved), and his silver coat was one mass of hoarfrost. He was stiff and chilled. Within twenty feet of him were warm and cozy kennels. But he had not relaxed for an instant his self-imposed vigil. Eight hours he had stood.

It was my first inkling that there was more to him than the bungling buffoon I had grown to hate. While there was no sense in the vigil, there was much loyalty.

Bit by bit he began to develop the depth of heart and brain that were always to be his. Unobtrusively he was seeking in rather pathetic and often blundering fashion to please me. True, he still got into amazing mischief; but there began to be something more to him than a mere clown. The Mistress was vindicated.

An editor was visiting us. One day he said to me:

"There's a mighty good dog story in Gray Dawn. More than in any other dog you have here now. In fact, there are a dozen stories in him. I've been studying him ever since he was a puppy. Will you write me a series of Gray Dawn yarns?"

So were born my long line of Gray Dawn tales and, incidentally, my book. I did not have to fake. The dog was right there, as a model. So were a score of adventures and mishaps that could be turned to fictional use. Yet, blindly, I had not so much as suspected that there was story material in the bumptious, big, young dog until the editor had called my attention to it.

At that time my house chum and car-dog was Bobby, a big auburn collie with more brains than any other dog

I have seen. Bruce was the sire of both Bobby and Gray Dawn. The two giant half-brethren were almost of a size. Incidentally, they were friends who sought to appear as enemies.

For example, the very slightest provocation—or no provocation—would start a seemingly murderous battle between them. Snarling, they would rear in a ferocious grapple, and the fight would last for perhaps half a minute.

I suppose Bobby and Dawn must have staged at least a hundred of these dreary fights in their time. And in all those fights put together, neither one of them drew blood nor so much as pulled out a single hair. Yet, to onlookers, the combats seemed terrible. To us, at Sunnybank, they became merely a bore.

It was not that the dogs could not put up a real fight if they chose to. Each of them in his time inflicted frightful damage on other canine opponents. But in these mock fights of theirs there was not the slightest harm done.

Then at last Bobby got meningitis. He was dying. Dawn strayed into the study where I was taking care of my sorely stricken chum. At sight of Dawn on the threshold, the insane Bobby hurled himself upon him. No sham battle this, but an infuriated death attack.

And Dawn? Instead of flying gaily into the strife as always before—instead of tackling in scientific fury as when outlander dogs assailed him—Gray Dawn stood stockstill.

Head up, his dark eyes full of anguished pity at his chum's plight, Dawn neither cringed nor fled nor made the slightest effort to defend himself from the maniacal onslaught. Statue-like, he stood there, an image of grave pity, as I pulled Bobby away from the slaughter.

After Bobby's death Dawn grieved as might a human for the loss of a human friend. The crazy bumptiousness was forever gone from him. Calmly, as if by right, he stepped into Bobby's place as our one house dog. From that day he was inseparable from the Mistress and myself.

He made himself so much a part of our daily life during the next few years that we still miss him keenly at every turn—in the cars, in the dining-room, in my study, in my bedroom, in the Mistress's music-room. He was an integral part of our existence here.

One night in early December of 1928, I started out for my usual evening walk. Dawn frisked on up the driveway ahead of me. But, as it was dark, I was going to tramp on the highroad instead of going across country. And the highroads are no place for a dog in this era of speed-mad motorists. I sent Dawn back to the house and went on alone.

An hour later I was brought home, pretty badly smashed by a car that had hit me at an impetus of something above fifty miles an hour. For the next month or so I was in bed, helpless, unable to move. From the moment I was brought home, to the day I left Sunnybank for a sea trip, Dawn never once left me of his own accord. If he were taken forcibly from my room and put outside, he would smash a cellar window or thrust past some one who was entering or leaving the house, and in another half-minute he would be lying on guard close to my bed.

It was pretty and rather touching to note the great

dog's sorrowful devotion. For the first week he would not eat a mouthful. He was almost ludicrously unhappy.

When first Dr. Colfax undertook to touch my smashed side, the pain forced an unexpected and perhaps explosive grunt from me. Instantly, and with no warning at all, Gray Dawn was ravening for the throat of the stranger who had hurt his master.

Luckily, Colfax was a dog man; he understood the loyal motive of the attack and was in no way scared or offended. But it was a lesson to me to keep my teeth clenched, thereafter, no matter how sharp might be the pain of the manipulations. I didn't want Dawn to go into action again and I didn't want the skilled physician to throw over the case because of the attack of a savage collie.

Yet, always Dawn stood close beside the bed during such treatments, glancing alternately from the doctor to myself; ever ready to interfere, to the death if need be, in case I should be hurt by the deft handling of the man he had flown at.

It was so with every visitor, when at last I saw visitors. Dawn never allowed himself to doze while they were in my room. Always he lay between me and them, his eyes fixed warily on them. I suppose he thought I needed protection and he saw I could not protect myself.

His guardianship was not always a delight, though his companionship helped vastly to while away the sleepless and endless nights. For, old and staid as he had become, he was still the original Gray Dawn, with the genius for doing the wrong thing at the wrong time.

He slept on the floor by my bed, his shoulders braced

against the foot-post. Then, in the night, he would get into an altercation with a flea somewhere on his anatomy. He would scratch with mighty vigor. I would start up, with the idea that an earthquake was the cause of my bed's sudden violent shaking.

This earthquake effect, and his gift for upsetting high vases full of flowers, were his only defects as a sickroom comrade. And a single word of reproof for such misdeeds made him miserably contrite.

Up to then, for years, his nightly sleeping-place had been the rug at the foot of the front stairs. Thence, at any untoward sound, he had fared forth on a patrol of the whole house, ready to drive off any possible intruders. But during his weeks in my room he was deaf to anything and everything outside that room.

I honestly believe burglars might have gutted the whole house just then, unmolested by him, as long as they kept out of the room where I lay.

He was more than ten years old. And, during and after my illness he seemed to have aged faster and faster. There was nothing the matter with him that we or any vet could learn. But he was aging. Something was gone. Nobody knew what. At times he was as racketingly boisterous as ever. But his daily gallops grew shorter and slower.

And he spent all his spare time close beside the Mistress and myself. It was as though he grudged any moments spent away from us whom he loved. He would lie and look at us as if he were trying to fix our faces indelibly in his memory.

There were plenty of signs to warn us of what was

coming. But, because of his oxlike strength and gay spirit, I thought the end must be much farther off than it was.

Then came the evening when he fell peacefully asleep, stretched out there on the rug beside my desk.

I missed him, and I still miss him, more bitterly than a mere collie should be missed. His going took something unsparable out of my life.

"There was something with the old dog went, I had not thought could die."

Next morning, with a lump in my throat, I stood and watched two of my men shoveling the earth over him; both of them with tears running down their faces unchecked. For they had known and loved the big dog since the puppyhood days when he had tried their patience, and mine, so sorely.

I forbade any word spoken, outside Sunnybank, of his dying. I did not want reporters and camera men out here just then. Not until his death should cease to be news did I want it generally known. Most of you will read of it here for the first time.

Perhaps this rambling account of my good gray chum has not been worth your reading to an end. Nobody realizes better than I how wholly I have failed to paint Sunnybank Gray Dawn's queer character and queerer actions as they merit painting.

Belatedly I ask your pardon if I have bored you with this sketch of the last of the great Sunnybank collies.

VI. HERO

They named him "Hero." This when he was two months old and when his ruffianly barks defied the world at large, especially his closest friends. He was such a courageously aggressive little fluff of gold-brown fur and so idiotically fearless that the name seemed to fit every active inch of him. Within two days he was answering to the call of, "Hero! Come, Hero!" with gaily truculent immediateness—when he bothered to answer to it at all.

A year later, the name "Hero" fitted him as a double-width woolen blanket might fit a ladybug.

The Marriotts had been vastly proud of the rabbit-sized collie baby. But the Marriotts were vastly ashamed of the rabbit-hearted collie giant that Hero had grown into.

True, he was beautiful in coat and contour and head

and frame. But his deep-set dark eyes had not the "look of eagles" which should go with such a combination. They were mild, even cowlike of aspect. Not theirs the mingled sternness and fun which are the keynote of collie expression.

They were eyes which revealed their possessor's chronic outlook on life. In them was an infinite gentleness, and not a hint of spirit. They gave a queerly bovine cast to Hero's countenance. A dog judge would have wondered at being so little impressed by the magnificent animal, until he took time to study each feature separately and realized that the eyes were laughably uncollie-like.

"I don't mind his being gentle," grumbled Rance Marriott. "Gentleness is the grandest thing in the world. But only when it has a foundation of spirit and strength behind it. If it hasn't that kind of backing it isn't gentleness at all. It's—Lord! I don't know *what* it is. It—it's Hero!"

"But he's so obedient and friendly," protested Hilda Marriott. "He's never the least bother, and ——"

"And never the least joy, either," supplemented her husband. "If he were human, he'd be one of those boys who never cause their mothers a moment's uneasiness—nor cause anyone else a moment's pleasure. When he was a baby, I used to worry about the fights he'd get into when he grew up, and the neighborhood quarrels they were due to cause. But ——"

"I hate a quarrelsome dog!" put in Hilda.

"So do I," agreed Rance. "They're pests. But one wants his dog to be something more than a sheep. Whenever I'm walking with him and we pass the Brendas', that

105

husky police dog of Sam Brendas' comes charging out. He tackled Hero in earnest, the first time. Nowadays he does it for a joke. He sails into Hero and knocks him over and rolls him in the gutter and nips him, until I interfere. Does Hero take his own part? He does not! The first time, and ever since, he just sprawls there meekly and lets himself be rough-housed. Then when the police dog has been driven off, Hero gets up serenely and trots along with me, without an atom of shame for the way he's been licked. It's the same when a cur half his size tackles him. Hero just curls up and lets himself be thrashed."

Out on to the veranda bounded the big bronze collie, his expression almost excited—for Hero. Up to Rance and then to Hilda he capered, barking and galloping back to the front door, and returning to repeat the same performance.

"What's happened?" wondered Rance. "He looks almost alive. Is it a new game he's invented or ——"

"He wants us to go somewhere with him," translated Hilda. "See how he runs from one to the other of us and back to the hallway. Come along."

Reluctantly her husband followed his interested wife. As they started toward the hall, Hero gamboled delightedly ahead and to the top of the cellar stairs. There he waited only long enough to make certain his owners were close behind him. Then down the stairs he pattered.

"Come along!" begged Hilda, as Rance hesitated. "Let's see what it is he's trying to show us."

"A man-eating mouse, probably," suggested Rance, adding, "But, no, that can't be it. For he'd never have the sublime courage to approach a mouse, of his own accord."

The dog came running up the steps, whined eagerly, and trotted down them again. This time the Marriotts followed. At the foot of the stairs Rance turned the electric switch on, flooding the shadowy place with light.

Hero was standing proudly above a pile of soft rags in a far corner. On the rag couch lay the Marriotts' gray Persian cat, Fathma, blinking lazily up at them. Cuddled snugly against her furry underbody squirmed four tiny and varicolored newly born kittens.

Fathma was strangely non-temperamental and easygoing, for a Persian. She and Hero had been brought up together. Violating the cat-and-dog tradition, they had always been on comfortable terms, their mutual mildness serving to avert quarrels.

Now, Hero was athrill with excited interest at discovering Fathma's children. As soon as Rance and Hilda bent over the rag bed to look at the kittens, the collie rushed up the back cellar stairs to the kitchen; whence he reappeared presently, coaxing the cook down to view the newcomers.

Fathma did not resent in any way the dog's rowdyish gambolings around her impromptu nest. Doubtless she knew there was no mischief in the bovine collie. She lay there and purred, blinking sleepily; now and then licking one or another of her babies with a rough pink tongue.

That night Hero did not sleep on his rug outside Hilda Marriott's door, where he had slept ever since he was a puppy. Instead, he, the inveterate comfort-seeker, stretched his mighty bulk on the concrete floor of the cellar, as close as might be to Fathma and her babies.

"He's found his true rôle in life, at last," sneered Rance. "He's Mother's Little Helper; or The Nursery Aid! As a collie he is a grand kitten-nurse."

Hilda did not join in her husband's mirth at his own scoffing characterization of the collie she loved. To her there was something vaguely pathetic in the huge dog's absorbed interest in this family of newly born baby cats and in his air of protection over them. True, it was un-doglike and especially was it uncollie-like. But it did not seem funny to her.

That was the beginning. Every day, and practically all day, and every night and all night, Hero lay or sat or stood as guard over the litter of Persians. The cellar corner became his chosen abode. Gravely, by the hour he would survey the fast-growing kittens, sometimes touching them gingerly with his forepaw or sniffing at them.

He was in dire misery when a load of coal rattled nois-ily down the chute, and he interposed his own bulk be-tween it and the corner where the kittens were.

One day, he and Fathma had their first quarrel. Play-fully Hero rolled one of the kittens over with his nose. He was unintentionally rough. The kitten squalled in pro-test. Fathma flew to the rescue, side-swiping Hero right virulently across the nostrils with punitive claws.

The dog fled, howling, until he reached the top of the cellar stairs. There he stood, in comic dismay, slapping al-ternately at his scratched and bleeding nose, and peering fearfully down at the scene of his ill-treatment.

Step by step, at long intervals, he descended to the cellar and crept trembling along the floor until once more he was near the nest. Fear of further punishment made him shake as with a chill. But the craving to return to his duty as guard overcame his dread.

To his relief, Fathma made no attempt to renew the strife. Nor, sharply taught by that one lesson, did Hero make further playful advances toward the kittens. He contented himself with sniffing at them now and then, and in lying with his head between his forepaws, watching.

Loudly and frequently did Rance deride this new phase of the dog he had grown to despise. He took guests down to the cellar corner to behold the kittens' canine nurse. With all a collie's odd sensitiveness, Hero seemed to realize he had become an object of ridicule. He winced and cringed when laughter greeted the spectacle of a great bronze dog brooding over a nestful of kittens. But he did not desert his post. It would have taken more than mere derision to drive him from his adored little protegées.

The babies waxed larger and stronger. No longer did they content themselves with huddling in the nest. Now, with sprawling feet and unwieldy little fat bodies and stiffly erect rudimentary tails they set forth on exploring expeditions along the cellar floor.

Their eyes were long since open, and they had learned to creep. A pretty sight it was, to watch the fluffy mites crawling about the worriedly delighted big dog, while their sleepy mother looked placidly on.

One of them, in particular—a snow-white morsel of felinity whose china-blue eyes were beginning to fleck with green—picked Hero as her own chum, by the time she was able to move. She would climb over his paws or would cuddle against his chest or would play in awkward vehemence with his plumed tail.

Pleased and inordinately proud was Hero of this distinction. He would lick the kitten all over, and would lie, uncomplaining, as her sharp claws dug playfully into his sensitive tail. The other catkins did not show any great interest in him. Thus, from the start, he and the white kitten were exclusive playfellows and pals.

Fathma was a good mother, as Persian mothers go. But she was a family pet, and her place ever had been upstairs with the humans of the household. When her kittens were able to get along without her for an hour or two at a time, she would leave them with Hero and would run daintily upstairs to seek out Hilda or Rance or the servants.

When the kittens were graduated from the cellar to the woodshed and were allowed to play daily on the lawn in the spring sunshine, Hero and the white kitten had gorgeous romps together. Their friendship was pretty to watch. Even Rance Marriott grinned with grudging approval at their play.

"Of course it was just like the poor fool to pick out the kitten we're selling first," commented Rance. "I suppose Hero will mope around and look more like a sick calf than ever, when she's gone. I'm sorry for him. For he's found the one creature on earth that doesn't either bully him or despise him."

"I don't bully him," denied Hilda, "and I don't despise him. And I wish you hadn't promised Sam Brendas that particular kitten. You know how fond Hero is of her, and ——"

"And I had promised Sam his choice of the four," interrupted Rance. "I'm sorry to have to disappoint the noble Hero. Sam is sending for the kitten tomorrow afternoon. Will you have her brushed up a bit beforehand, please? And stick Hero in a closet or somewhere."

Mid-afternoon, next day, Hilda Marriott came out on the lawn, where Hero snoozed with the white kitten cuddled up asleep between his paws. Picking up the furry wisp in her arms, Hilda whistled to the dog. Happily he trotted indoors after her and his kitten pal. There, to his pained surprise, he was lured into an upper room and the door was shut behind him.

He scratched plaintively at the door, but nobody came to let him out. In a little while he heard voices downstairs—Hilda's voice and another woman's.

Readily the dog recognized this second voice. It belonged to a guest who came often to the Marriotts', a guest who lived in the house where that snarling police dog lived—the dog that mishandled Hero so unmercifully on such few occasions as they chanced to meet before Hero had time to run ki-yi-ing for safety.

Failing to gain egress from his prison by way of the door, the collie sought to amuse himself by trotting to the window and gazing interestedly down into the street. This was one of Hero's best-liked occupations ——

Hero's academic interest in the scene sharpened. Mrs. Sam Brendas had left the Marriott house and was walking down the street. In her arms she was carrying something.

As she turned the corner, Hero saw what the "something" was.

It was his chum, his pal, his idol—the tiny white Persian kitten!

Something went queer in Hero's placidly gentle brain.

The spirits of a horde of collie ancestors—collies that had guarded with their lives their masters' belongings, collies that had known gleamingly stanch loyalty to their friends—snarled fiery commands into the peaceful cosmos of this too-meek descendant of theirs.

Back to the door he ran, tearing at its panels with claws and teeth. It stood firm.

To the window he dashed. The room was on the second floor, just above the side veranda. But, for all Hero cared, it might have been on the thirtieth story of a skyscraper. It offered the only means of escape—and he took his chance.

With a great diving leap he flung himself at the glass pane. Through the brittle barrier he crashed with all the driving force of his seventy pounds and his immense muscular power.

He struck against the somewhat steep veranda roof; rolling and sliding down it to the edge; then bouncing out into space again. His falling body smote the very center of a thick and high lilac clump, just beyond the porch.

Through this barrier his weight carried him groundward; the myriad little branches and twigs breaking his fall, so that he landed on the grass with no worse hurt than a breath-ejecting bump.

By the time he hit the lawn he was on his feet and

in flying motion. Across the sward he sped, and to the sidewalk and down the street and around the corner; galloping with his glass-cut body close to earth and with hackles bristling. He knew well where Mrs. Sam Brendas lived, and whither, presumably, she was carrying his kitten friend. Not an inch did he swerve from his route.

Men were beginning to stroll up the street on their way homeward from business. These, by instinct, gave wide berth to the bleeding and savagely onrushing collie.

A dog or two came running out from dooryards, drawn by the sight of the galloper. But Hero whizzed past them, unheeding. Such of them as undertook to chase him had their labor for their pains. For no dog, save only a racing greyhound, can hope to catch up with a collie that is running at full speed.

Hero came in sight of his goal in time to see Mrs. Brendas open her own front door and disappear within the hallway. She was carrying the scared white kitten. The kitten was scared because a giant police dog had sprung up from the mat and had come toward her. With a sharp word Mrs. Brendas ordered the dog back to his resting-place and she bore the kitten indoors.

As the door shut behind her, Hero came dashing up the walk in belated pursuit. The police dog caught sight of the flying collie as Hero swung in from the street.

Avidly the bigger canine went into action, lunging to the slaughter. The police dog's temper had been ruffled by the scent of the alien kitten and by his owner's curt rebuff of his advances.

Here was a chance to wipe out that ruffle of temper —by manhandling the foolish and cowardly collie he had thrashed so often. This was to be no semi-playful nipping and rolling of the spiritless Hero. The collie had invaded the sanctity of the front yard itself and was rushing toward the sacredly guarded veranda. The insolence of his act called for a drastic and dramatic punishment.

In savage glee, the police dog launched himself at the erstwhile craven as the latter prepared to clear the veranda steps at a single leap.

Perfect love casteth out fear.

In all his despised young life Hero had not found anything, hitherto, worth losing his temper over. He had seen no need to fight. He had had no desire in his gentle heart to harm anyone or anything.

When he had been attacked and bullied by other dogs, their enmity had puzzled and pained his friendly spirit. He had seen no reason for fighting back. It had been easier to submit gently and unresistingly to their onslaughts and then to get himself out of their way as soon as he could.

But today, most emphatically, he had something to fight for. His fluffy little white playmate had just been carried into that house, and an ugly giant dog was trying to bar him from following and rescuing her. The dog, and every other obstacle, must be gotten rid of before Hero could continue his search for the kitten.

Again, into the unused reaches at the back of his brain were snarled the commands of his fearless collie ancestors —terrible warriors all—as well as the sterner orders of his more remote forbears, the wolves.

They were bidding him to fight. More, they were telling him *how* to fight; even as the instincts of herd-dog ancestors often tell an untried young collie pup how to bunch sheep and drive them.

All this, in the minutest fraction of a second, and while the police dog was charging to the slaughter.

Instead of the meekly crouching collie of their last encounter, the police dog found his charge met by a maniac devil swathed in shimmering bronze fur. Grappling, roaring, slashing, rending, the two combatants rolled down the steps together, locked in a most untender embrace.

As their falling bodies smote the flagstones of the path below, they flashed apart and to their feet, flinging themselves ragingly at each other's throats.

This was the sight which confronted Rance Marriott and Sam Brendas as, together, they rounded the corner of the street. This was the sight which made Mrs. Brendas drop the white kitten and run to the front door in consternation.

The police dog's first gust of temper had merged into murder-lust; at this utterly unforeseen opposition from the collie he had bullied and beaten at will since puppyhood. Into the fray he threw himself with a hideous zest; seeking a vital spot that he might rip open; seeking to bear down and crush and destroy the erstwhile sheeplike invader of his dooryard's privacy.

But, as a billion times before in the war history of this pugnacious old planet of ours, it is one thing to desire to annihilate and it is wholly another thing to be able to do it. Much depends on the attitude of the annihilatee. The police dog was a renowned battler, and a veteran of many bloody frays. But a fighting collie is not like any other fighter in all dogdom. And this the punitive police dog was beginning to discover.

Hero was everywhere in general and nowhere in particular. Now he was stabbing with lightning speed under the rearing enemy's forelegs, and slashing with cruel efficiency the other's fawn-colored underbody. Now he was slipping eel-like from what threatened to be a death-grip and was raking the police dog's tawny shoulder with curved eye-teeth; or he was snapping away part of an ear.

So do wolves fight. So does the lupine hereditary instinct teach many a collie to fight.

Once and again, the larger dog sought to bear Hero to earth by sheer weight and ferocity. Once and again did the collie elude the charge; and counter with deep bite or slash. Twice Hero was knocked off his flying feet. But a collie down is almost never a collie beaten.

He fell with his feet bunched under him; and by the time he hit ground he was either springing to one side, slashing as he leaped, or else was rolling compactly out of range of the frightful jaws that ravened at him.

It was a beautiful exhibition of science against bull strength. The police dog was bleeding from twenty greater or lesser hurts. Hero was all but unwounded. The police dog was beginning to breathe noisily and laboriously. Hero slashed at him, as fresh as at the start.

Roaring and foaming, the police dog drove once more for the throat. The collie ducked under the great lunging head and dug his teeth with wrenching force and leverage into the nearer of the fawn-hued forelegs of his foe. Thus does the wolf seek to cripple an antagonist by breaking his legs.

Hero got his grip; and got it fair. He held on, and wrenched; clamping his strong young jaws like a vise into flesh and sinew—toward the bone. But the maneuver left the back of his neck exposed to the dog above him. Like a striking snake the police dog's head darted forward. His mighty jaws seized the nape, grinding murderously toward the spinal cord.

Now this is a death-grip; and instinct told the collie its nature, even while acute pain and sudden helplessness surged through him. He took his one chance. With every atom of despairing power and skill, he braced himself and wrenched afresh at the leg-hold he had gained.

For perhaps three seconds the dogs remained thus, outwardly motionless. Then there was a snap, as of a twig. With a screech of agony, the police dog released his grip on the nape of Hero's neck, and strove to seek safety in retreating. But his snapped foreleg—it was two months before he could walk on it again—gave way under him.

Hero stood for a moment, panting and eyeing the victim. Then he seemed to remember his mission at that house. Up the steps he rushed, pushing past the panic-paralyzed Mrs. Brendas and into the hallway.

Thence, in another second, he emerged. Between his bloody jaws he carried tenderly and gingerly a fluff of white fur. He had found and rescued his little chum after overcoming the dragon which guarded the portal. Now he was bearing her forth from that house of bondage, and he was going to carry her home where she belonged.

Past the gabbling and stupidly marveling men Hero cantered, deaf to Marriott's belated call to him. Two minutes later he laid the kitten down gently at Hilda Marriott's feet. Then, apparently, he remembered that his master had called him and that he had not obeyed. Licking the kitten's tousled fur, once, in rough good fellowship, Hero left her there and cantered out of the house.

Meantime, both men had found their tongues, as had Mrs. Brendas. Out of the babel presently rose Rance Marriott's voice, loudly, compelling attention.

"I get the whole idea!" he declared. "Hero loves that kitten as he doesn't love anything else. He came here after it. Your dog stopped him, but he couldn't stop him for long. Then Hero went in and got what he came for. You can guy me, if you like, you people. Hero fought for her and he won her, fair. You can have your cash back or you can have any two of the three other kittens instead. But you can't have the white one. Neither can anyone else. She belongs to Hero. Is that understood?"

Sam Brendas looked up from his task of tending his police dog's hurts.

"All right," he agreed. "And we can settle the terms later on. Now give me a hand in carrying Hindenburg indoors, while Mary phones for the vet."

As Marriott came out of the Brendas house three minutes later, on his way home, a right direful figure arose stiffly from the police dog's favorite porch mat and came in gay good fellowship to greet him.

Rance stared down at his collie. Not at the cuts and other hurts that decorated his splendid body, but at the deep-set dark eyes upraised to his. Those eyes flashed with a queer light that changed the whole expression of Hero's classic face.

"The true collie look!" babbled Rance, foolishly, as he

caught the hurt head lovingly between his two hands.
" 'The look of eagles!' Hero ——"

His voice thickened in his throat. But Hero understood.
Wagging his plumed tail, he led the way out of the gate
and toward home. As they turned the corner into their
own street, a neighbor's dog swaggered blusteringly out.
This was a mongrel dog that delighted to chase Hero
under the Marriott veranda every time he could catch
him in the roadway.

In something less than half a minute, now, the mongrel
aggressor was ki-yi-ing, in astonished flight, to the safety
of his own kennel, with an ugly slash along the side of
his head and with one forepaw sprained.

"Hero!" rebuked Marriott, fondly, as he called his
frisking collie back to him. "You'd be a grand walking
companion if it wasn't that you have one bad fault—
you're too quarrelsome. Try to get over the habit of going
around with a chip on your shoulder, you—you glorious
pal of mine!"

VII. *MANY WATERS*

Red Vulcan was old. He was very old. The piling up of years had silvered his classic muzzle and had hampered his once-graceful body with much flesh and had turned his wolflike trot into something akin to a waddle.

Those same years and their accumulation of experience had deepened his wisdom even while they enfeebled his mighty strength. Gifted from puppyhood with the best mental power of the best type of collie, Vulcan's brain waxed while his other powers waned.

If he had had less uncannily keen sense and sensibilities, Vulcan would not have grieved so miserably about the gradual usurping of his place in the home and his work on the farm by his brilliantly handsome golden grandson, young King.

It was red old Vulcan that had trained King to be a

competent farm worker and watch-dog. This when King
was a harum-scarum puppy with nothing but his golden
coat and his coaxing ways to commend him.

And now, bit by bit, it was King that had become the
chum of his owners and the guardian of the house and
the handler of the cattle. The long gallops after stray
yearlings, the tearingly fast uphill runs to round up the
cows in the mountain-side pasture, the dozen forms of
exertion which once had been as child's play to the ancient dog—these things were increasingly painful and
hard.

Yet jealously Vulcan refused to relinquish them. Puffing and rolling, he would follow along in the wake of the
gaily-galloping King, on such routine duties.

Ever more and more Vulcan found it pleasant to drowse
in the sun or, on icy mornings, behind the kitchen stove.
Rheumatism sent a twinge, now and then, through his
stiffening limbs. He was good for perhaps five or six more
years of life and he was not decrepit. But he was by no
means the dog he had been. Nobody knew it better than
did he. Nor did anyone guess at his resentful sorrow in
the subtle change, and in the contrast to King's glorious
youth and vitality.

Vincent Gareth was the second largest landowner and
the most prosperous farmer in all Preakness County.
Forty years earlier he had sent to Invernesshire in Scot-
land for the brace of collies whose price scandalized his
New Jersey neighbors, but whose inspiredly skilled work
saved the labor of at least one hired man.

Incidentally, this brace of imported dogs had been the
ancestors of the famous line of Gareth collies—a strain

that had won deathless renown in shepherding trials and on the show-bench and on twenty farms.

Red Vulcan was a scion of this strain. So, of course, was golden young King, his flashily beautiful grandson. Incidentally, they two were the last of the long line.

Gareth treated his dogs well, as indeed he treated all his livestock. But he was no sentimentalist. When a dog outgrew its usefulness and when life seemed to become a burden to it, Gareth had a mercifully merciless method of putting the oldster out of its supposed misery.

More than three years had passed since such a quietus had been deemed needful. That was when Vulcan's purblind and feeble old mother, Florine, had been put to death.

Trotting homeward one morning, in that era, from driving the cows to pasture, and with the ten-month-old puppy, King, frisking at his heels, Vulcan had come to a halt on the brow of a hill that overlooked the house and the orchard behind it. For he had seen Vincent Gareth coming down from the porch with a length of rope in one hand and with a gun under his arm.

He had seen the man walk over to where Florine lay, and summon her to get up. Totteringly and uncertainly the aged creature had obeyed the call. Gareth had bent over her, tying the rope about her neck. Then he had led her, gently enough, back to the orchard and out of sight of the house. Tying her to a stump, he had patted the half-blinded face upraised to his. Then he had stepped back and leveled the gun.

Aghast, stupefied, by what followed, Vulcan had bolted back into the underbrush, the unconcerned puppy,

King, still frisking at his heels. He had hidden there, shaking all over as if with a chill. Long hours passed before he had led King homeward, and taken up again his farm-dog duties.

Left on the porch that evening, as usual, Vulcan had for once deserted his post of guard and had wandered sniffingly about the orchard until he had come to a mound of newly-turned earth. With a sigh that seemed to come from the bottom of his very heart, he had lain down close beside the grave of his dam, and he had remained there, sleepless and bewilderedly unhappy, all night.

That had been three years earlier, while Vulcan was still in his full prime. But never had he forgotten it. For one reason, it was the only time he had seen Vincent Gareth with a gun in his hands—for the farmer was not a sportsman—and for another, it was the first time he had seen Gareth tie a rope to the neck of one of his grown dogs. Those two rarities, by themselves, were enough to stamp their grim significance into the wise collie's brain.

Being only a real-life dog, and with only a dog's perceptions, he did not foresee a like fate for himself, nor understand it as a penalty of such age as was now slowly beginning to creep up on him. But never had he forgotten a single detail of the ghastly scene.

There was a bright splash in the slowly-increasing gloom of Vulcan's lot, in these latter days. Gareth's daughter, Helen, had come back from college. She and Vulcan had been inseparable chums from the days when she had romped with him in his puppyhood. Her long absences from the farm had troubled and saddened the collie. And now she was at home again and she was taking up their chumship where it had been broken off.

Helen was the one member of the household who did not seem to look on the old dog as pastworthy and who did not neglect him for King. She made Vulcan the companion of all her shorter walks. She took him along on the seat beside her when she drove to the village in the little runabout her father had given her. She loved the old dog, even as Vulcan loved her. Life was immeasurably sweeter for the collie now that she was with him again.

He did not note that Helen slackened her swift stride when he and she went walking, nor that she arranged to take her longer hikes at such times as he was not around. She humored his stiff-legged age as though he had been a fellow-human. She made all the more of him, to atone for the neglect of the rest of the family.

Of late, too, Vulcan had acquired a new friend; Vulcan who was so chary of forming friendships with outsiders. This outsider was Dick Malden, an engineer for the water company which was planning a giant dam in the upper reaches of the Reginskill. Malden boarded with the Gareths. For so busy a young man he was able to steal an inordinate amount of time to be with Helen as the days went on. Indeed, he was spending every spare moment in her society. Nor did the girl seem to resent this ever-increasing demand on her leisure hours.

Vulcan liked Malden from the first. Not that that proved anything as to Dick's character; for, contrary to the popular legend, a dog has no occult powers for discovering whether or not a human is trustworthy. But he liked Malden, and Malden liked him. The engineer had

a way with animals, and he shared with Helen her prefer-
ence for the old dog over the younger.

Then, one evening as Malden and the girl were sitting
very close together on the porch hammock, with Vulcan
lying happily at their feet, the old dog awoke from a
doze. He woke with something of a start. The low-
pitched voices which had been so caressing and so con-
ducive to his own drowsiness had changed their tone and
pitch.

With all a collie's queer intuition, Vulcan realized that
there was strife of some kind between these two humans
whom he loved and who loved him. Naturally, he was
not able to understand anything they said to each other,
and he would not have known what it meant if he had
comprehended the words. But the jarring note in them
made him look up worriedly.

"If you had told me in the beginning that you didn't
like my family," Helen was saying, stiffly, "I could
have ——"

"I didn't say I don't like them," protested Dick
Malden. "I do like them. I like them a lot. All of them.
I only said a man and his wife ought to have their own
home, even if it is only a shack, and not live with the
parents of either of them. That little house down on
Bryant Road ——"

"But dad says we can have the whole third floor here
for our own," she broke in. "And now you want to tell
him ——"

"I want to tell him what he told your mother's folks,"
said Dick. "I want to tell him that we are going to start
out in our own home instead of cadging on your family."

"I told dad we'll live here," insisted Helen. "And ——"

"And I'm going to tell him we won't," rejoined Malden, his temper fraying just a little. "I'll tell him we appreciate his offer, and all that, but that a bridegroom ought to make a home of his own for his wife and not be a free boarder in his family-in-law's. I ——"

"I never heard of anything so foolish and—and so unkind!" declared Helen, her sweet voice trembling a little. "Here they've been so dear about our engagement and made such lovely plans for our ——"

"I appreciate all that," interrupted Dick. "But I want us to have our own home, and we're going to. We ——"

"Since you're going to be a bully and refuse to do the very first thing I ever asked you to," said Helen, a sob in her voice, "I don't think we will gain anything by talking about it. I am going in. Good night."

"Helen!"

But she was gone, leaving a glumly unhappy sweetheart and a perplexedly unhappy old dog on the porch behind her.

In the morning Helen remained invisible until she saw Dick Malden drive out of the dooryard on his way to work. The girl had passed a semi-sleepless night. This quarrel had upset her terribly. She shut her brain to Malden's side of the dispute. She told herself over and over again that he was selfish and heartless in his refusal of her parents' proffered hospitality.

The fact that, deep down in her heart, she yearned to be mistress of her own home, in the little house he had picked out, in Bryant Road, did not soften her judgment of the lover who sought in such brutally masterful fashion to enforce his own wishes against her father's plan.

No, Dick Malden and she could never hope to be happy together, now that she had unearthed this revolting side of his character. Better and wiser by far to break the engagement before it was too late. Chewing relishfully on this cud of heartache, as might a child upon a sore tooth, she came to a right idiotic schoolgirl decision:

She would write Dick a dignified and very determined letter, to the effect that she had been grossly mistaken in him, and that it was plain they could not hope to be happy together, and that the engagement was ended forever, and that it would be far wiser and more tactful for him to find some other boarding-place.

This letter she would lay beside his place at the supper table; and she would eat supper in her own room, on plea of a sick headache.

The composing and writing and possible rewriting of such a letter called for a solitude and concentration impossible to secure in so busy a household. Wherefore, she resolved to go to a favorite outdoor refuge of hers and to write it there.

The Reginskill creek ran athwart the foot of the lower mowing of Vincent Gareth's farm. In its center was a long and wooded strip of island, barely fifty feet wide and perhaps a hundred yards in length. At this dry time of summer the creek was about eighteen inches deep on the hither side of the island strip, though much deeper on the far side.

To account for her trip to the secluded spot, Helen put on her waders and carried ostentatiously her rod and creel and fly-book. Inside her blouse were tucked a fountain pen and sheets of paper and an envelope. She set forth from the house and across the dooryard.

King was frisking about the yard, playing with a ball which he tossed and rolled and caught. At sight of the girl, evidently bound for a walk, he abandoned this solitary sport and gamboled up to her, avid for the suggested hike.

Old Vulcan was lying asleep in the shade of a lilac-clump. In the kitchen doorway stood Vincent Gareth.

Gareth had received his yearly tax bills that morning. The bills were unwontedly large by reason of some road improvements and of the county bonds for the new dam. He was not in a good temper. Also, he was in a mood for such economies as he could compass. He had come out to the doorway several minutes earlier. His eye had fallen on the fat old dog slumbering in the shade.

Vulcan looked even more ancient and heavy and useless than usual, by contrast to the actively romping King. The sleeping collie was a hearty eater. He was an expense, an increasingly needless expense, since King nowadays could do all the work. Moreover, Vulcan was ageing fast. It would be a kindness to the oldster, as well as a saving of cash, to put him to sleep before he should get to the stage, as had Florine, where life was a burden.

Gareth stepped back into the house, reappearing presently with his gun and a length of rope. At sight of Helen, he hid the two objects he carried behind the kitchen door.

"Going fishing, daughter?" he asked, somewhat unnecessarily, in view of her waders and the rod and creel.

"Good! Only two more days, now, till the law shuts down on trout. Make the best of the time that's left. I may join you down there, later. I've something that's got to be done, first."

Helen ignored King as the golden collie danced around her. She chirped to Vulcan as the old dog raised his head at sound of her step.

"No," interposed Gareth as the slumberer got eagerly to his feet. "I'm going to need Vulcan, here. Take King along instead, if you've got to have company. Come back, Vulc."

Wondering, yet obedient as ever, Vulcan turned about and desisted from following the departing girl. As soon as Helen was out of sight in a fold of the meadow, Gareth came forth from the kitchen and called again to the old dog. There was keen regret in the voice he sought to make so firm.

Vulcan had been settling down to another nap. At the summons he trotted obediently toward his master. Then, midway, he came to a sliding halt.

For in one hand Vincent Gareth carried a short coil of rope. In the other he held a gun.

Back flashed the great collie's memory to the day, three years agone, when he had heard Florine called in this way by Gareth, and had seen her throat encircled by the rope's noose.

Vulcan understood.

For only an instant he hesitated. Then, at Gareth's renewed call, the old dog straightened himself and strode steadfastly forward, his deep-set dark eyes fixed on the man's. If his god decreed his death, then his god's will be done!

Gareth bent, none too happily, to slip the noose around Vulcan's shaggy throat. Then he paused. A car was coming into the yard. Three men were in it. Gareth recognized them as members of the Township Commission, whose chairman had written him that they would call on him soon to discuss condemnation terms for such of his land as would be needed for inundation by the dam.

This meant at least an hour of haggling. Gareth tossed the rope down on the porch and set the gun beside it. Pointing across the meadows, he said to Vulcan:

"You can go to Helen, Vulc."

Then he went to greet his three visitors.

Still dizzy with reaction, Vulcan obeyed the gesture and the words of permission. This was a reprieve. At a pace unwontedly fast for him, yet with head and tail pathetically adroop, he cantered across the fields in pursuit of the girl. Sick with unhappiness, he was piteously eager for her loving presence.

He reached the creek just as Helen began to wade over to the island, through the shallow water. King dashed on ahead, making a tremendous splashing. Vulcan followed, using as little exertion as possible. The fast canter had winded him.

In her abstraction, Helen did not note, consciously, the presence of either dog as she climbed up onto the island and sought a tree-hidden spot where she could write her renunciatory letter unseen and uninterrupted. She seated herself on a rock and drew forth the writing materials from her blouse.

Vulcan stretched himself at her feet. King proceeded noisily to explore the island for rabbits.

Almost immediately Helen was absorbed, heart and soul, in the first rough draft of her momentous epistle. It must be eloquent, it must be infinitely sad, it must stir Dick Malden's soul and conscience to the iniquity of his behavior and to a terrible sense of the irreparable loss which was his in the withdrawal of her love from him. The writing of such a letter called for utter concentration and even for a few unbidden tears. Helen would have been furious if she had been told that she was getting a morbidly miserable delight in this first lovers' quarrel and in the punishment her denunciation and renunciation were due to inflict on Malden.

So heartless and cold-blooded are men that Dick was not giving the quarrel one-tenth the thought that Helen was lavishing on it. Somehow he could not see that the break between himself and his adored sweetheart was in any way irreparable. He was even callous and cocksure enough to believe a kiss and a few words of love could bring them together again.

Moreover, this morning Dick had been having problems of his own. The blasters were at work on a shale-bank below Lake Regin, the body of water flowing into the Reginskill. They were preparing the way for the new concrete dam which was to replace the century-old rickety wooden dam now holding that water in place. The new dam was to be not only far stronger, but many feet higher and many yards wider, than was the old, and was going to enlarge threefold the size of the lake.

Blasting is always a more or less tricky job. When it

is performed so near a water logged antique dam, like that at the foot of Lake Regin, it is even more so than usual. Shale also is tricky stuff. Nobody can tell by guesswork how far its reef may extend, nor in how many directions. A vein of it will seem to come to an end, when really it has dipped far below its apparent surface line and has continued thence at some wholly unsuspected angle.

Even the best-planned engineering sometimes goes wrong on its conclusions as to the extent of shale reefs. Dick Malden and his associates thought they had taken every possible precaution. Yet ——

A mighty and cunningly devised blast rent the shale shelf asunder. So far, so good. Malden gazed self-approvingly at the gap as the dust and the splinter-rain cleared away. But that same tremendous blast had carried its vibratory shock along the base of the bank, far beneath the surface, with as deadly a directness as if the vein were an electrified wire. It shook and wrenched the streak of rock whereon was founded the sodden wooden dam.

Under such a jolt the rotting timbers buckled. A roaring wall of water loomed above the workers. There for an instant it seemed to hang while the blasters scrambled for high ground or for trees.

Dick, standing on a knoll, saw his men drenched and overwhelmed by the cataract of newly-freed lake water. But they had gotten out of the direct path of the deluge when they had run from the impending blast. They were soaked and buffeted, but not one of them was swept away, as the vast volume of water swirled out over the surrounding lowlands and tore madly down the cleft of the

Reginskill. The creek, in an instant, was changed into a mighty river.

Malden waited only long enough to see his men were safe. Then he leaped into his car and set forth downstream at the maddest speed he could make, whizzing on the road that paralleled the creek. He was racing the flood, on the chance it overtake haymakers or others at work in some of the bottomland fields to southward.

Old Vulcan lay curled at Helen Gareth's feet as she scribbled her inspired letter, on the rock in the island thicket. Ordinarily he would have fallen asleep there and would have snored right contentedly. But sleep was not for his worried and wise old brain this morning. Too vividly he recalled the coil of rope and the gun. Too vividly he remembered the day when his mother, Florine, had been summoned as he had been, by Gareth.

Vulcan's heart was sick within him. To comfort himself in this stark life crisis, he pressed closer to Helen's feet, for her loved human support. It did not once occur to the loyal dog to avert his impending death by running away to the hills and hiding there, even though he was an expert stalker of small game and could have lived on in forest safety.

If his master had decided he must die, it was not for Vulcan to break his own life habit of stanch obedience. Fear never had entered into his gallant soul. Yet—he pressed again close to the unheeding Helen.

Of a sudden, as he lay there, Vulcan forgot his troubles. Something shot into his subconsciousness; something he could not understand; something inherited from a thousand centuries of wild ancestors—ancestors that had remained alive long enough to rear children of their own, because instinct had taught them to avoid the sudden perils of woodland and of stream.

The old dog got to his feet, sniffing the air and shivering. Then he caught Helen's skirt-hem in his worn-down teeth and tugged at it; whimpering as if in sharp pain. King, scampering around in quest of rabbits, paused to watch curiously his grandsire's odd actions. Then he went unconcernedly on with his merry hunt. Helen looked up with some impatience as Vulcan yanked whimperingly at her skirt.

"Quiet, old boy!" she said, absently, stroking his head and preparing to go on with her all-absorbing epistolary task. "Lie down. I——"

Her eye fell upon the strip of water she had waded with such ease a half-hour earlier. The strip no longer was narrow. It had spread out on the adjoining meadow and it was climbing the bank of the none-too-high island. Even while she gazed incredulously it crept higher and higher. At this rate the whole island would be awash.

She was marooned. She could not hope to wade that torrent, or even to swim it. She had no idea as to the reason for the swelling of the waters, but she knew it had cut her off from shore and might even sweep her away.

Quickly she did her thinking, and with a calm that amazed her. Taking a spare sheet from the paper she had brought with her, she scrawled three hasty lines on it. Then, still with all her wits about her, she wrapped the page in the water-proof envelope which held her flybook. Fastening the envelope, she whistled to King.

The golden young collie pranced up to her, as if sens-

ing a romp. Vulcan pushed his own unwieldy bulk between the two, his eyes upraised to Helen's face in an
agony of appeal.

"No, dear old Vulcan," Helen found herself murmur-
ing, as, with a strip torn from her skirt, she bound the
water-proof envelope to King's collar. "No, old chum.
It's too tough a job for you. It calls for youth and for
all the strength and pluck there is. And you've none of
those things except the pluck. . . . King! HOME! Find
Master. *Find* him! Quick!"

As she gave the frantic order, she pointed toward the
invisible farmhouse above the rise of meadow-ground.

From puppyhood, the Gareth collies had been taught
to carry messages in this way. King understood. And, as
ever, he rejoiced in the prospect of doing something spectacular and amusing. He wiggled with delight. Then he
dashed down to the bank. But there he came to an abrupt
standstill. For the first time, he noted the angry swelling
of the stream.

"Home, King!" called Helen, fiercely, "HOME! Find
Master!"

Recovering from his first shock of surprise, King loped
along the ever-narrower strip of bank, seeking an easy
spot for crossing. Thus he came presently to the very lowest tip of land. As there was no lower place from which
to take off, he sprang into the swirling water and struck
out for the meadow.

Fast and powerfully he swam. But the flood caught him
up with irresistible force, sucking him into its eddies,
banging him against floating logs, playing boisterously
with him, half-drowning him, knocking the breath out of

his body, the wits out of his head. His eyes bulged presently with dumb terror. His buoyancy and his zest for fight and his gay courage were gone.

Turning, and taking advantage of the slight lessening of the waters' onrush, in the lee of the island, he tried to struggle back whence he had come. A foaming cross-current helped him. Panting and gasping, he crawled ashore at the very point whence he had leaped into the stream. He crept up to Helen and crouched beside her.

In vain the frightened girl urged him back to his task. He would not so much as glance in the direction of the torrent which had buffeted and almost drowned him. As a possible rescuer, King's performance was very definitely at an end.

Realizing at last the hopelessness of trying to make him face the ordeal again, Helen untied the water-proof parcel from his collar. Vulcan had stood motionless at her side throughout the younger dog's performance. It was almost as though he had foreknown that King's courage would fail.

"No, dear old boy," said Helen, noting his eagerly questing look. "Not you. If King couldn't make it, you can't. We'll have to look for a bush that may be high enough and strong enough to hold us. I'll lift you up with me, if I can. King must take his own chances. He——"

She broke off, in astonishment. With a darting motion like a snake's, Vulcan's jaws had moved forward. He snatched the water-proof envelope from her slack grasp. Carrying it between his teeth, he crashed away through the undergrowth. Helen called to him; but for once he did not heed her call.

To the farthest upper end of the island strip he ran, even as the less wise King had sought the lowest end. Vulcan did not waste his scant strength in galloping. He ran only fast enough to keep Helen from catching up with him and robbing him of the parcel he had heard her tell King to take to Gareth.

There had been a throb in her voice as she had given that command, which had gone through the old collie like white-hot iron. He seemed to sense the need of the envelope's delivery and to connect it with their desperate plight. And he was calling on his uncannily wise brain to make up for his waning strength.

To the uppermost tip of the island he went. There, after a keen look up and down, he launched himself into the flood. There was nothing of King's earlier sensational dash about this launching. It was deliberate; all but lazy. Nor did Vulcan battle the roaring current as King had done. He let it catch him up and whirl him downstream as it would.

Yet all the time he was swimming, and swimming with a definite object. Ever he sought to edge toward the meadow which was his goal. When, for a moment, he chanced to be in a slacker rush of the stream caused by a cross-tug of the waters over some shoal, he used all his powers to move landward. Then, when a mightier rush of waters gripped him, he would let it carry him along; merely edging a few inches at a time toward the meadow.

At first glance the aged collie's bout with the stream seemed ludicrously ineffective, compared with King's sensational battle. But he was making shoreward progress, if only imperceptibly. Not one motion was wasted; not one momentary opportunity was neglected. It was a beautiful bit of navigation.

Spare himself as he would, the strain was terrific upon the fat body and its stiffening muscles and its tired heart. The flood beat him with breath-taking smashes. Cleverly though he sought to avoid the tossing logs and other driftwood, now and then such a bit of flotsam would smite him agonizingly. More than once an eddy spun his unwieldy body clean around or drew his classic old head beneath the surface.

He was spent; exhausted; in dire pain. But his wise brain shone undimmed, and his tired heart had the flaming white heroism that ignores defeat. He forced his aching muscles unflaggingly to their work. Shrewdly he took swift advantage of every chance to shift shoreward. The fat, which impeded him, also kept him afloat with more ease than a less heavy dog could have known. He bobbed in the swirl of ever-rising waters like an obese cork.

Buffeted and drawn under as he was, he would not lessen the tight jaw-grip on that precious water-proof parcel, even though its carrying sent sluices of water down his throat, and added strangulation to the rest of his torments. Wide-eyed, fascinated with horror, Helen watched his snail-like progress toward the meadow; oblivious of the water that now lapped her feet and ankles.

Then, after a century of struggle, there was rough gravel under Vulcan's clawing toes. For once the murderous current had relented. A vagrant push of it had shoved the exhausted dog against the shore a furlong south of the island. Up the bank he toiled, lurching and swaying with fatigue. Every inch of him longed to sink upon the ground and lie there. But as he gained the steep bank's summit he scourged himself into a wavering lope.

Over the rise of the meadow he went, vanishing into the fold of ground which lay between it and the farmhouse beyond. As he disappeared, Helen saw for the first time that the water was around her knees and was tugging at her. She made her way back to the last rise of the island, which still showed a few inches above the torrent. Thither the cringing and panic-stricken King had preceded her.

Past the Gareth dooryard flashed Dick Malden at his car's utmost speed. Forth from the yard came running Vincent Gareth, a sopping sheet of paper in one hand. He hailed the motorist at the top of his lungs.

In the yard behind him a half-dead old collie was slumping to the grass. Vulcan's work was done when he staggered up to Gareth, on the porch, and dropped the envelope at the feet of the man who had been about to shoot him that morning. The dog could afford, now, to take the rest his overstrained body was forcing upon him.

Dick glanced at the water-streaked scrawl. Then he leaped from the car and ran indoors. Immediately he reappeared, carrying a forty-yard clothesline and a pair of Helen's little brother's water-wings. He vaulted into the machine again, followed by Gareth; and drove it, bumpingly, at a crazy pace, straight across the meadow and toward the river.

Not until he was at the crest of the bank did Malden jump out of his car. Racing along the shore to a stout young tree some rods above the only part of the island still visible, Dick paid out the line he carried, knotting one end of it to the trunk and the other around his waist. Donning the water-wings, he dived into the water, striking out frantically toward the handkerchief-sized patch of bushy ground where Helen stood white-faced and trembling, almost waist-deep in water. Gareth grasped the line near the stump and waited.

It seemed an endless stretch of hours before the current carried Malden down and across to a spot where he could grasp a half-submerged bush and could work his way from clump to clump toward the ashen-faced girl.

But at last he had reached her, and Vincent Gareth was hauling the line's double burden carefully shoreward; while Dick's free hand fended driftwood from the woman he held in the crook of his other arm. King, deserted, plunged, howling, into the water, which bore him a half-mile downstream before it cast him up unhurt on a sand riffle.

The wedding was over. The last of the guests was gone, the guests who had escorted Malden and Helen from the Gareth home to their little new house on Bryant Road. The couple stood side by side on the steps of their cottage, hand in hand, gazing out on the sunset that bathed the whole world. Vulcan stood beside his new owners.

It was Helen who broke the brief happy silence that rested between them.

"I'm afraid dad didn't like it very much," she said, "when he asked me which of our wedding presents I liked best and I told him I loved Vulcan, here, a million times better than all the rest of them put together. I ought not to have said it, after that big check he gave me. But it was true. Wasn't it, sweetheart?"

"The truest of all the true things that ever were said," eagerly assented Dick, his hand resting tenderly on the classic old head of the collie.

Vulcan waved his plumed tail in proud delight at the man's tone and at the caress. Then, majestically he followed Helen and Dick indoors—into the house where several years of honored and loved comfort were still to be his.

VIII. *BISCUIT*

"He's a mutt, isn't he?" asked Grear, eyeing with no favor at all the yellowish and all-but-formless giant puppy that sprawled drowsily at Middon's feet on the sunlit scrap of porch. "Hundred per cent mutt, I'd call him."

"No," drawled old Middon. "You'd miscall him wrong if you was to call him that. The blood of some of the finest champions in the whole dog world is in his veins."

Grear looked down less contemptuously at the hulking pup.

"That so?" he queried. "Champions of what breed?"

"*All* breeds," succinctly answered Middon, adding, as he rumpled the big puppy's flap-ears, "That's the advantage of a mongrel—a cross-breed. If you buy a dog of any one pure breed you'll know he's got to be limited mostly to his own breed-types. A pure-bred can't go far beyond those. But a mongrel can combine the traits of a dozen breeds. That's where he has a big advantage over the thoroughbred. Now young Biscuit here ——"

At sound of his name the eight-month puppy got up from his place in the sun and stood at momentary eager attention. Then, finding he was not wanted by his master, he lay down again, this time with both heavy rear legs stretched out straight behind him. Middon pointed to the odd posture.

"Whatever other breeds went into the melting-pot that boiled down into Biscuit," he commented, "it's a safe bet one of his ancestors was a bulldog. You'll never see a mongrel lie down with his hindlegs straight back of him unless he's got a big splash of bulldog blood somewhere in his India-relish pedigree. The deepness of Biscuit's chest proves the same thing. He ——"

"Why do you call him by such a crazy name as 'Biscuit'?" demanded the visitor.

"Lots of reasons," said Middon. "Partly his color. Then because he was so easy and quick to raise, and then got so heavy, all of a sudden; and because he didn't turn out anyways as I expected him to. But mostly because I just happened to name him that, I guess. By the way, Mr. Grear, for a man who's got the costliest kennel of chows in this part of the state, you seem uncommon interested in an animal you call a mutt. If ——"

"I am," replied Grear. "Especially just now. That's why I stopped in when I saw him lying here on your steps. Want to sell him?"

Old Man Middon blinked in mild-eyed surprise at the abrupt question. Bleasdell Grear had a national repute as a breeder and exhibitor of super-quality chowchow dogs.

His kennels were all but regal. It was a shock to find such a man going about the region buying up mongrels. The visitor noted the incredulous stare, and he explained:

"My wife's sister is coming to spend the summer with us. She and her three children. Till I met those three brats of hers I used to think Herod was a blackguard to slaughter all the children in Bethlehem. Now—well, if Herod ever needs my vote to help carry his district, it's his for the asking. Most children are splendid and I love them. But these three are *not*. Every time the three kids come to see us they nag at me to let them have one of my chows to play with. Till now I've been able to stall them off. But if they're coming for all summer——"

"I get you," nodded Middon. "You want to save one of your three-figure chows from being pestered and mauled and teased to death. You want to do it by getting the kids a good husky mongrel pup, to serve 'em as a combination punching-bag and football and tug-of-war rope and unbreakable doll and so forth. Lots of folks with high-class kennels do that. They're wise. A mongrel can stand up under ten times the mauling that a ticklish-nerved thoroughbred can. Only——"

"How much?" interrupted Grear, poking at the sleeping Biscuit with his toe.

"For Biscuit? I'm not selling him."

"That means you want at least ten dollars for a purp that would be dear at two," translated Grear. "Well, I happen to like him. He looks friendly and steady and strong. So——"

He reached into his cash pocket. Old Man Middon shook his head.

"You don't quite catch my meaning, Mr. Grear," said he. "I'm keeping this pup. He's mine. That means there isn't any price on him."

Grear frowned in perplexity. His eye roamed appraisingly over the shabby little house and the hillside patch of North Jersey farmland behind it. Everything was clean. Everything was at its best. But it was a poor enough best. Throughout were marks of none-too-successful struggle against poverty.

It was because of this apparent sparseness of ready money that Grear had not haggled over a price for the cross-bred pup. Ten whole dollars would mean much to a man of Middon's penury.

"Yep," said the old man. "I'm foolish, I know. Just as foolish, likely, as you're thinking I am. Ten dollars is ten dollars. Sometimes it's a heap more. But Biscuit's my chum. If he keeps on like I've started him—well, I couldn't get anything for ten dollars or for ten times ten dollars that'd be worth as much to me as he's likely to be. He's all that keeps me from feeling pretty blue, now that I'm left alone up here. Since my daughter died it's been mighty forlorn. That's why I kept Biscuit, the time a feller down in the village offered me ten cents to take the little cuss and drown him when he was only two months old. I gave back the feller's ten cents and I kept the puppy. I've learned him a lot already, even if he isn't but a little more'n eight months old yet. See?"

He snapped his fingers. At the signal, the seemingly slumbrous puppy was on his splay feet at once, eagerly alert. Slowly Old Man Middon made a succession of gestures, all but imperceptible, yet all very evidently comprehensible to Biscuit.

In response to them the young cross-breed alternately dropped to the creaky porch floor as if dead; sat up and begged; "waltzed" in a solemn shuffling circle; lifted one paw after another off the ground; rose upon his hindlegs, then on his forepaws, with both hindlegs in air; barked twice and yelped three times; rolled over; and closed the clumsy performance by snatching a pipe from Middon's pocket and, with it in his mouth, parading across the porch on his hindlegs.

There could be no shadow of doubt that Biscuit took an egregious pride and vanity in his own repertoire of tricks, and that those tricks had been taught him by patience instead of through cruelty. No temperamentally vain motion-picture star could have postured with greater self-delight than did the shambling mongrel.

Grear nodded, patting the pup on the head and praising him extravagantly. The visitor was enough of a dog man to understand that the lonely oldster had whiled away many an otherwise desolate hour teaching his four-legged pal these simple exploits, and that the clever young cross-breed was a barrier between the old man and utter solitude.

"You win," said Grear, getting to his feet to take his departure. "If I had realized what a gifted youngster he was, I wouldn't have wasted words by asking if you'd sell him. You're a born trainer, Middon. And Biscuit is a born trick dog. You're both of you lucky to have each other. . . . Well, I'll go somewhere else to find a mongrel safety valve for those three kids. Good-by."

The old man watched his guest climb into a car and jounce down the hill road toward the village below. Middon's gnarled hand had fallen in unconscious caress on the broad yellow head of his dog. There were affection and comradeship in the touch.

Something rufous and furtive trotted around the corner of the cottage, pausing irresolute for an instant as it came out into the open, and peering down the road after the receding car. Then, as if satisfied the coast was clear, the newcomer glided, rather than ran, up the porch's rickety steps and stood in the sunshine at the top.

He was a three-parts-grown red fox; found in a hollow log, months earlier, by Middon as the old fellow was coming home through the forest. His mother had been shot or had abandoned her baby; for the tiny fox was weak with hunger when Middon chanced upon him.

Middon had carried the waif home and brought him up by hand, accustoming him from babyhood to his own presence and to Biscuit's. By dint of his natural gift as an animal-trainer, Middon had made the young fox as much a member of his household as any puppy could have been. Only when strangers were near did the fox remember he was not a dog. Then he would hide cunningly from sight, rejoining Middon and Biscuit as soon as the outsider had gone.

Mincingly he advanced toward Biscuit, now, and touched noses with the puppy, his brushy tail waving like that of a dog. Middon looked down at the two—the mongrel with his honest broad head and round brown eyes and gay openness of expression; the exquisitely graceful fox with his toothpick nose and catlike slitted eyes and hint of unkilled wildness.

"Reynard," he said, whimsically, "it's likely enough you think you're a dog, and it's certain Biscuit thinks you are. But *I* know better. And I'm afraid you'll know better, too, one of these days. All wild things do. It's only a matter of time. Look at Biscuit's face, there! Every corner of his soul and his mind is shining out of those big eyes of his. And these slit eyes of yours don't tell a single thing that's going on behind them, except when they get round and have a greenish light in them. That means you're out of temper. It's the only sign any human can go by, with a fox. But I'm going to do my best by you to make you into a decent, self-respecting, God-fearing dog, Reynard. If I lose, it'll be up to *you*. I——"

Disregarding the homily, Reynard had been patting invitingly at Biscuit with flying forepaws, luring the drowsy mongrel into one of the romps they both loved. Now they went tearing off the porch and across the dooryard, in a scampering and snapping and playfully growling mass, the clownish puppy a sorry match in speed and skill for his more elusive playmate.

"Yes," mused Middon, "a dog turns his soul inside out for his master to see. A fox hasn't any soul to show and he wouldn't show it if he had. Foxes are part cat, I guess. . . . I—I wonder how it will all work out?"

The question as to how it would all work out answered itself in due time, as will all such questions concerning the wild-born. But that was not until months had passed.

Meantime, Biscuit grew from a rangily gawky puppy to

a massively powerful dog, as large as a Gordon setter. Reynard changed less, outwardly, growing only into a graceful adult red fox, beautiful of coat.

He and Biscuit were still on tolerably comfortable terms, though their early romping chumship had not deepened into such close comradely relations as would have existed between two dogs of like fraternal upbringing.

Then, of a day, came the definite break.

Twice, in a week, a hen had vanished from Middon's well-stocked coops. The old man's chief source of livelihood was gleaned from his big flock of chickens. The loss of even one fowl was a slice from his, capital. The two lost hens had been his best layers.

Naturally, his suspicions rested at once on Reynard. Henceforth the fox was fastened to his kennel by a long chain, whence he could not break free. Biscuit was left at large. His massive honesty forbade suspicion.

Yet, next morning, another hen was gone. The morning after that, the largest rooster of the flock had vanished. Middon left Biscuit loose at night, as usual; but sat up, also, on the porch, in full view of the chicken-yard, shotgun in hand. Biscuit dozed at his master's feet. At dawn the old man's head began to nod, then to slump on his breast.

As though he realized that the guardianship of the farmstead depended now solely on himself, Biscuit got to his feet and stood glancing about him. Three or four of the earliest-rising chickens came flapping down from their perches. Two of them emerged from the small opening at the bottom of the coop door, foraging for early food.

Out they came into the rear dooryard, roaming and

questing. On the ground, some seven feet from Reynard's kennel, lay a scatter of bread crumbs from the fox's supper. Reynard himself was lying in the doorway of his kennel coop, eyes shut, head on paws. Apparently the day had not yet dawned for him.

One of the hens sighted the crumbs and waddled greedily across to where they were scattered.

Crumb after crumb she gobbled up, oblivious of everything but her own hunger. It was her last meal.

There was a rufous flash, a fluttering, and the hen spun headless on the ground.

That was enough for Biscuit. All his unformed recent suspicions and general distrust of his vulpine acquaintance crystallized at the sight. All his instincts as a watchdog and as a guardian of his adored master's property surged into action.

With a growl and a leap he sprang at the fox. Reynard dropped the slain hen, save only the head, which he swallowed. In the same set of motions he bolted back into his kennel, there snarling scared defiance at the avenger.

Biscuit lunged forward. As he reached the spot, seven feet from the fox-kennel, where flapped and spun the headless hen, he stooped and sniffed at the luckless fowl, as if to nose her from the path of further danger. But the splash of blood that was flung across his face by her death struggles seemed to convince him that she was past help.

With lowered head, he gathered himself anew for a charge at her slayer; to drag Reynard bodily out of his kennel and to wreak dire punishment on him.

The charge was not made. A shout from his master made the mongrel spin around obediently at the call.

Middon had been awakened from his involuntary snooze by the growl and the flapping. He opened his eyes just in time to see Biscuit bending over the hen, apparently having pinned her to the ground. On the crossbreed's honest yellow foreface was a spatter of newly-shed blood. The sight told its own story.

Biscuit ran over toward his master; at Middon's amazed yell. The man met him, halfway. Clutching the dog by the scruff of the neck, Middon snatched off his own thick belt. Using the buckle-end as a thong, he brought it down in a shower of cruelly heavy blows upon the mongrel. With all his wiry old strength Middon smote. The cutting buckle bit deep into the tender flesh. Never before had he struck the young dog. But this was a case for dire penalty.

Biscuit shuddered all over, as with ague. Yet he uttered no whimper nor cry to attest to the agony caused by the belt-blows. This was his god who was punishing him. True, the penalty was vilely unjust, and Biscuit knew it. But it was not for him to yowl under punishment—his strain of bulldog blood was standing him in good stead—and above all it was not for him to turn on the man he worshiped.

Well did the mongrel know why he was beaten. Well did he know whose was the blame for this crime whose onus he was bearing. Into his clean heart surged a deathless hate for the fox—a raging urge to get even for his own torture—to punish the crafty animal for whose sins he was suffering.

Reynard, meantime, lay in his kennel, his head pillowed on his forepaws, part of his face showing beyond

151

the coop aperture, his slitted eyes fast shut in seemingly dreamless slumber.

Middon smote and smote afresh, with the whizzing and stinging belt, until his old arm was tired. Then, still gripping Biscuit stranglingly by the neck, he stooped and picked up the slaughtered hen.

Even in his fierce indignation, he noted she was decapitated. But he inferred that Biscuit had killed her by snapping off her head and had been swallowing it when he was caught. That his canine chum should have killed in this wild-beast manner made the old man the angrier at him.

Picking up the hen, Middon tied the belt securely about her legs. Then he fastened it around Biscuit's furry throat, testing his knots to make certain they were firm.

There is no universally sure way to cure a dog of chicken-killing. But the most approved and usually the best remedy is to catch him in the act and then, after whipping him, to tie the dead fowl securely around his neck and to leave it there for three days. By the end of that time—especially if the weather be warm—the chances are that he will not care to go within arm's-length of another chicken as long as he lives.

There are exceptions to the cure, but they go to prove a fairly reliable rule.

Old Man Middon was not brutal. But much of his daily bread was derived from the sale of his eggs and broilers at the village butcher shop. To harbor a chronic chicken-killer was to court bankruptcy.

Also, he had grown to love this jolly and clever young mongrel of his, and it jarred the old man to the quick to

realize how far wrong he had been in his estimate of Biscuit. Any lively puppy may spring upon a fowl and destroy it, from gay mischief. But—to slay hen after hen
in silent stealth and then to secrete the bones and feathers
—to use coyote tactics in the destruction of the property
he had been trained to guard—all this savored of the
craft and unnatural deviltry of a born "killer."

For such dogs a bullet through the brain is often the
one solution. But, because he loved the cross-breed, Middon was minded first to try the effect of a pitiless beating.
and then the shame of carrying the dead hen about for
days. Should this fail to break Biscuit of the slaughter
habit, there was nothing for it but to shoot him. Middon's
heart revolted from such a course.

Biscuit had stood with head and tail undrooped
throughout the unmerciful belting which had raised red
welts on his skin from shoulder to loin. Only that ague-
like shudder of outraged feelings betrayed the anguish
of soul and of body that were torturing him.

Moveless, except for the incessant shivering, he stood
while Middon fastened the accursed fowl around his
throat. Throughout this performance, as during the beating, his honest big eyes had remained fixed on the furious
face of his god, with a startled horror that held a tinge of
heartbreak. Middon had noted the look and had steeled
himself against it.

Now, as the hen was secured in place, Middon stepped
back, panting from his own vehement exertions. Biscuit
stood looking up into the man's face, apparently oblivious
of the five-pound dead-weight that dangled shamefully
from his furry neck.

It was this moment which Reynard chose to waken from his artistically posed snooze and to step yawning out of his kennel coop. His advent was almost simultaneous with an odd thought which had just flashed through Middon's brain.

Half-unconsciously, the old man had observed that the fox was lying fast asleep in his coop, and that all the excitement of hen-killing and of dog-beating, just outside, had not wakened him. This, although Reynard's hair-trigger nerves were forever atingle at the first onset of any kind of strife.

But at last the fox appeared to have roused himself from his refreshing sleep. Waving his white-tipped brush, he minced forward to exchange a morning greeting with his master.

Middon was in no mood to pet him, or, indeed, to be civil to anyone. His heart was heavy within him at the pain he had inflicted on Biscuit and at the mute look in the dog's eyes. The man was turning away, when Biscuit created a diversion which brought him back to the scene at a jump.

Stolidly, with true bulldog heroism, Biscuit had endured his own hideously unjust punishment, though well he knew the culprit was Reynard and not himself. But when the fox came forth so smugly to receive a petting from the man he had robbed—this snapped the last vestige of the cross-breed's hard-held self-control.

With a strangled roar, Biscuit flung himself at the complacently advancing fox.

Reynard did not await his former friend's charge. With the speed of light the fox whirled and darted behind his coop, springing to the full length of the thin chain in a single bound, and hurling his eleven pounds of muscular weight against it, in the hope it might snap before the dog should be upon him.

The well-wrought chain withstood the sharp tug. But the half-rotted leather of the fox's narrow collar did not. Though it dug into Reynard's soft neck with anguishing garrote force, yet its decaying fibers parted.

The fox was free. Gasping from his brief semi-strangulation, Reynard fled at dizzy speed up the slope behind the dooryard—the slope which led to the wooded mountain above.

Few are the dogs that can keep close on the trail of a fresh fox. And the powerful young mongrel had a still greater handicap than his unwieldy size.

As he sprang for the fox, Biscuit had sought to shift his own direction. This when he saw Reynard take that aërial sidewise leap behind the kennel. Gauging the change of direction in too great a hurry, Biscuit's plunging sixty-pound weight smote glancingly against the corner of the kennel-coop.

The impact knocked the dog clean off balance. He rolled over, then scrambled to his feet and dashed up the slope in raging pursuit of his escaped foe. But the delay had given Reynard a start of nearly a hundred feet.

Old Man Middon did not call his dog back. The man did not so much as see Biscuit gallop after the fox until some moments later. At that time he caught a fleeting glimpse of pursuer and pursued, against the skyline. They were vanishing over the ridge which divided his farm from the wilderness of mountain above. It was too late then for his aged voice to carry to the dog.

The reason Middon did not see the beginning of the chase was because his eyes were fixed blinkingly on something much nearer. Biscuit had been knocked flat by his collision with the fox's coop. But the same collision had knocked the coop clean over and upside down.

There, in a neatly-gouged hollow, beneath where the kennel had stood, was a mass of feathers and of gnawed chicken bones.

The sight told its own story to the mountaineer farmer as plainly as could a page of print. It cleared every atom of the mystery of the vanished fowls. Incidentally it cleared Biscuit of any possible shadow of guilt. A chicken-killing dog does not bury the evidences of his crime, day after day, under the kennel of another animal.

To make assurance surer, Middon picked up Reynard's dangling chain and measured the distance from the kennel doorway to the spot where Biscuit had been nosing at the hen. Yes, the killing had been done well within the radius of the chain. A fleck or two of fresh blood just within the kennel door proved that Reynard had not had time to swallow the hen's head without leaving a telltale clue to the deed.

It was then that the remorsefully wondering old man raised his eyes in quest of the dog he had flayed and humiliated. It was then he caught that single brief glimpse of Biscuit and Reynard disappearing over the ridge.

"I—I can see now why he looked at me that way, all the time I was a-whaling him, so cruel!" mumbled Middon, thickly, as he winked his eyes clear of an unbidden mist that crept over them. "Gee! but I wish I had a third foot! I'd sure use it for kicking myself from here to Paterson and back. That's how it is with us humans—we punish first and we find out afterward. We lambaste the only critters on earth that's foolish enough to worship us. It's lucky the good Lord didn't give dogs any more sense than He did. If He had, they'd be too wise to love us fool humans and serve us, like they do. They'd see through us. Maybe they do, anyhow. Maybe they got natures big enough to love us, in spite of what we are. . . . I'd give a month's food and cash not to have treated Biscuit like I did."

After the way of most semi-solitary men, Middon had fallen into the habit of talking to Biscuit—though never to Reynard—as to another human. Now in the dog's absence he found with a start of annoyance that he was jabbering aloud to himself. With an impatient shake, and with a worried look toward the ridge, the old fellow pottered slowly indoors to get breakfast.

He was laying out a busy and tiring day. And he knew well he must fortify himself with food, beforehand. His self-imposed labors were to consist in hunting the mountain for his dog. Biscuit would come back home when Reynard should have outstripped him hopelessly, or should have outwitted him into losing the trail. At least, Middon knew the young dog would make every effort to come home. But he was in doubt as to Biscuit's ability to do it.

Not only would the tired mongrel be weighted down by the heavy hen that dangled from his neck, but the loop of the tough belt was more than likely to hook itself

into some tougher bush-stem or outjutting sapling stump
or low-spreading tree-branch. In that event Biscuit would
be as hopeless and helpless a prisoner as if the cleverest
of men had tied him there to die of thirst and hunger.

Not a year earlier, on a day's hunting in the lower
reaches of the mountain, the old man had come upon the
body of a handsome pointer dog whose owner had had
the folly to let him go into the field with a collar on. The
pointer, nose to ground, had run past a slanting cedar
stump which had passed between his collar and his throat,
holding him prisoner until he died.

The same fate might well await Biscuit, thanks to the
angry skill wherewith Middon had fastened the belt and
its loop to his neck.

Meantime the mongrel was straining every nerve and
thew of his powerful young body to catch the elusively
fleeing fox. Up the slope, then over the ridge and up the
steep face of the mountain itself they tore. For the first
mile Reynard held his lead and even increased it a little.

Had he been a forest-reared fox he would have fared
better in this first life-and-death race of his. For, from
babyhood he would have been accustomed to continuous
running, to tireless action of every kind—to the dodging
of enemies and the wearying quest of food.

But, from the time he was able to crawl, Reynard had
lived soft and had exercised little. His meals had come
to him unsought. His nights and part of his days had been
spent on the chain. Now he was paying the bill for flesh
and softness and inexperience.

True, he ran fast and sure-footedly. But, from almost
the first, his was not the true fox speed. To attain that

incredible swiftness of foot, one's life must have been from the first a ceaseless physical struggle for sustenance and safety.

Biscuit lumbered after; righteous indignation giving an added driving-force to his mighty young body. He was lean and he was in the pink of condition. Moreover, for the first time in all his friendly span of months, he was goaded on by a consuming rage of vengeance.

His bulldog strain kept him steadfastly in the race, despite every obstacle of broken ground; and it gave him the depth of chest needed for such lung power as the run entailed. But it was quite another ancestor—perhaps a greyhound, more likely a collie—which had endowed him with the unflagging speed that was his when his first lumbering gallop settled into a steady and mile-eating stride.

Still another forebear, a hunting dog, no doubt, had supplied the mystic scenting power which let him follow the rank reek of his quarry unerringly; at such moments as the fox was blotted from his actual view by rocks or by foliage.

Upward and onward raged the chase. The fox had swerved to right and to left, more than once, in an effort to shake off his enemy. But ever the heavy yellow head was behind him again. Ever the splay pads pattered in unerring pursuit, despite Reynard's shrewdest effort to dodge or to double.

Biscuit was too close behind to permit of successful doubling, and Biscuit's nose was too accurate to make safe a sidelong leap into the shelter of copse or tangle.

Then, giving up for the time his attempts to escape

159

through wile, Reynard breasted the mountain's steepest slope afresh, gliding easily upward over rubble and shale on which the heavier pursuer's feet slipped or were cut; flashing in and out of thickets or bramble patches whose thorns took painful toll of Biscuit's coat and nostrils.

But always the heaving and panting dog was after him, making up on cleaner footing what he lost when the going was bad.

Reynard came at last to the summit of the mountain. Far behind him stretched the miles he had traveled. Middon's cottage and hillside farm stood out like a mere fret on the distance-smoothed slope far below.

There was no time to pause and look back, nor even to fill with air his laboring lungs. Close behind plunged and panted and lumbered the mongrel; his honest brown eyes bloodshot and glazed, his mighty jaws dripping foam.

The defunct hen around Biscuit's neck whanged bruisingly against his breast and upper forelegs. Her weight grew heavier and heavier to carry. But he kept on, heedless of the impediment.

Into Biscuit's dizzy brain the ghost of some pit-bull ancestor was snarling his stanch race's never-say-die slogan. Into his thudding heart some gaily cavalier-like ancestor collie was laughing:

"Keep it up! This may be death, but it's grand fun!"

Into his achingly worn-out muscles a racing greyhound great-grandsire was pumping the mysterious coursing speed that had won cup after cup against grueling competition. Truly a mongrel may borrow from many rich ancestral treasure-houses.

Down the farther slope of the mountain, through the hush of the warm autumn day, sped the fox, silent and ghostlike as he slipped through coppice and brier-patch or wormed his way in and out of cairnlike strews of bowlder. Down the slope slithered and stumbled in pursuit the dauntless yellow avenger; now panting and snapping at Reynard's very brush, now blundering confusedly, but undaunted, a hundred feet behind.

The fox was snarling like a rabid cat, and was sobbing like a nightmare-harried child. His hair-trigger nerves were raw. Caution and racial craftiness were cast to the winds. All he thought of was to get far enough ahead of his foe to be able to pause and to draw one long breath into his tortured lungs.

Into a scarlet sumac-clump dashed Reynard, almost at the farther base of the half-unscalable mountain. Behind him staggered the mongrel.

Midway in the copse, Reynard whizzed through a low pile of leaves. From out the leaves, a set of rusty steel jaws arose and gripped him. He had set foot on the pan of a cunningly concealed fox-trap.

Forward pitched the flying red body, thrown off balance by the grip on its hindleg. With awful force the fox's skull crashed against a rock-point just in front of the riffle of leaves.

Merciful and devoid of torment was the end of the sinew-wrenching race; for that race's exhausted pacemaker. Before even the fox's numbed nerves could register to the bemused brain the fact that his hindleg was caught in serried jaws of steel, the impact of the sharp rock-jut cracked the delicate skull. Painlessly, Reynard died.

Biscuit lunged into the sumac-clump, almost at the heels of the fox. There he came to a slidingly stumbling halt. On the ground before him lay Reynard, lifeless and prone. At sight of his enemy there at his feet, Biscuit snarled afresh and drove down his dripping teeth for a back-breaking bite that should finish the fox.

Then, with his jaws a bare inch from Reynard's dead body, Biscuit drew instinctively back. Something told him that his foe was no longer a foe. The mongrel was not of the type to tear and rend the helpless. Since there seemed no longer either fight or flight in the fox, Biscuit's vengeance-lust died within him.

For a few seconds the mongrel bent above Reynard, sniffing in sad astonishment at him. Then, exhausted, Biscuit dropped heavily down among the riffled leaves; panting noisily, tongue out, mouth afoam, heart hammering to suffocation. The dead hen flopped into the leafy swirl.

Long Biscuit lay there, within a yard of the dead fox. Then, bit by bit, the dog's panting waxed less stertorous. He could breathe again without torture. His heart no longer threatened to shake his body to pieces.

Slowly, draggingly, Biscuit lumbered to his feet, the hen dangling heavier than ever. Just beyond were the heavenly sound and scent of running water. The dog was parched and racked with thirst. He made his way on uncertain feet to a brooklet a few rods beyond. There, in a rock-pool, he drank until his tongue could scarcely lap. After which he tumbled down among the brook-edge rubble and slept.

It was dusk before Biscuit waked. Again he drank deep

of the pool. Then, on legs whose springiness seemed forever gone, and carrying his abhorred five-pound burden of slain fowl, he began his climb of the mountain which lay between himself and home. He made a detour of the sumac-thicket where lay Reynard.

But, an hour later, a trapper passed that way and did not make a detour. The trapper was on his round of his fox-traps. He grunted appreciatively as he noted the smooth density of the man-raised fox's pelt.

Fox pelts, that season, sold for $11.50 each at the Paterson wholesaler's. The wholesaler cured and dressed the skins and lined them. Then he affixed ornamented snappers to them—the entire process costing him less than $8 —and sold them at his own retail fur-store for upward of $60 each.

Thus ended Old Man Middon's first and only experiment in turning a prenatally wild thing into a domestic animal. It is an experiment always foredoomed to failure.

Up the steep mountain-side toiled Biscuit, the hen still thumping against him at every stride. But now there was no need for haste. So he plodded slowly, sometimes taking advantage of easier ground or skirting thick copses and bowlder-strews.

Up he went, through the heat of the late autumn day, by dint of slowness and of sense and of rare luck avoiding the catching of his leathern belt loop in any outcrop of tree or rock. His was a stolidly determined progress homeward, not a half-blind rush. He had scope to avert possible obstacles.

But at every mile the miserable hen seemed to double in weight. More than once the fagged-out mongrel lay down to rest and to let his wrenched muscles relax their incessant grind. So passed the rest of the Indian Summer afternoon. Early dusk began to slant across the western sky.

Night fell; long before Biscuit recrossed the ridge that marked the forest boundary of his master's farm. Down the slope he blundered and slipped. Fatigue and pain were forgotten as he caught the sight and scent of home. On he pressed, eager and gay.

True, here he had been beaten unmercifully, not twelve hours earlier. Here, too, this repulsive and neck-wearying hen had been strung around his throat. Here he had met black injustice and cruelty, as reward for his own utter devotion.

But he had met them all from the man he worshiped. And it was not in the clean white heart of the mongrel to hold grudge or to sulk, just because his god had ordained to punish him.

All was forgotten—the humiliation, the ingratitude, the hot-red weals athwart his tender skin. Biscuit knew only that he was coming back to his adored master and that the parting had been homesickly long. The reunion was well worth a day of heart-racking toil such as he had undergone.

The one flaw in his rapture of anticipation was a fear lest he be not yet forgiven by Middon for the fault he had not committed, and lest his god might scold or even whip him for the day's wretched truancy.

At the thought, Biscuit's newly-wagging tail drooped. The light of happiness in the big round eyes merged into

trained dog man would have classified her as such. But to the casual observer the drooping head and frothy lips and wavering gait told only one grim and terrifying story.

Her way carried her through a pretty village at the base of a mountain which separated it from some forty miles of almost trackless hinterland country. The cry of "Mad dog!" went up. Instantly a mob of stone-and-stick-throwers was at Mavis's heels.

Never until this week had the little collie been away from home. Never had she known fear or pain. But now she was making the close and hideous acquaintance of both.

Glancing back over her shoulder, she found the village street behind her choked with a crowd of running humans. Interestedly she paused to note their approach. Perhaps Garvin, her own dear master, might be among them. But even as she halted a stone struck her with agonizing force on the shoulder. A second stone bounced off from her ribs. A pointed stick grazed her head, nicking one of her soft ears.

With a whimper of fear she wheeled and ran for her life. Behind her surged and boomed the lunatic multiple screech of "Mad dog!" Around her whizzed the flung missiles. A man dashed out of a doorway in front of her and aimed heroically a crashing blow at her skull with an ax. With a collie's wolflike elusiveness, Mavis dodged the blow, crying out in fright, but not breaking her scramblingly fast stride.

From a window another resourceful man took aim with a shotgun and pulled both triggers. The air was split by a dual roar that struck clean through to Mavis's terrified soul. The air was abuzz with a swarm of tiny leaden hornets that sang wickedly all around the fleeing collie.

There was a fire-hot sting in her neck. There were two more in her flank. Something hot and torturing raked the side of her classically-chiseled face. She was in sudden dire anguish—an agony which robbed her of what sense and coolness the mob and the stones had left to her.

Shrieking in mortal terror and pain, she swerved to the left and darted up a lane at express-train speed. Her bloodshot eyes were almost shut. Her sinewy young body was strained to its utmost panic-bred swiftness. Her brain contained nothing now but a blind yearning to put as much distance as might be between herself and these causelessly murderous humans.

Blindly she tore on, not realizing that the tumult behind her was ebbing into nothingness. She had outstripped the hue-and-cry. She had left the lane and the village itself far in her wake. No longer was she fleeing along even ground. Her whalebone muscles were putting forth their full lupine power in the breasting of the rugged mountain which divided the civilized region from the wilderness hinterland.

When at last sheer fatigue slackened her breakneck speed and when her thews no longer obeyed eagerly the command of her scourged senses, Mavis slithered to a shaky trot and peered fearfully back over the route she had come. Then she stopped her headlong flight and sank, panting loudly, in the midst of a clump of wiry mountaintop grass that grew in a bramble-and-sumac clearing.

Far below lay the civilized world, indescribably petty

and uninteresting from this great height, cut into foolish squares and oblongs for fields, pierced by the gray state road and crisscrossed by lesser yellow byways, flecked with farmsteads and blotched by ragged masses of house-clusters which were distant villages.

The gray mountain-side with its brown streaks flowed down steeply under the early April sunlight; from the summit, where Mavis panted, to the cruel village whence she had fled. On the other side, the mountain descended into miles of unbroken forest and stream and marsh and hillock and dense wilderness.

As her breath and her strength and her intelligence seeped back to her, Mavis unconsciously took account of stock. To her left lay the World of the Wild; unknown, sinister, yet vaguely alluring. To the right, whence she had fled, stretched the World of Man—the bourne which held Garvin and her lifelong home, but which also held uncountable enemies who screeched at her and tortured her and chased her right murderously.

At the searing memory of her morning's adventures, Mavis shuddered as with a chill. She was not very wise. Thus far, it had been enough for all practical purposes that she had been very loving and gentle and pretty. She felt, rather than thought. And just now she felt an irresistible terror of the world that had cast her out. Anything would be better than to return to its shouting and shooting and stone-throwing.

True, she knew nothing of wilderness life, but the longer she lay there the more its silence and mysterious calm soothed and lured her. Then, a trivial thing decided her course. As she got undecidedly to her feet, something big and brown, and tail-tipped with fluffy white, bounced out of the wiry grass and fled across the narrow plateau which crowned the mountain.

Through no conscious will of her own, Mavis flashed in pursuit. Forgotten was her weariness. She remembered only that she was ravenous and that she had eaten nothing to speak of since she left Garvin's, four days earlier.

Ordinarily she would have pursued the fat rabbit as carelessly as she was wont to chase cats. But now, something indefinable told her to swerve sharply to the left in mid-flight. A bare fraction of an instant later the rabbit swerved in precisely the same direction.

Mavis's swift jaws closed deftly on her prey. Followed a rapturous meal which thrilled her as never had she been thrilled by her uninspiring daily meals at home.

Her choice was made. Her new life was begun. In a wilderness peopled chiefly by creatures smaller and weaker than herself, food was plentiful and safety was assured. Earliest spring was on the hills. Nature was coming to life and a wolf-descended collie was reverting to nature.

A dog even less sensible than Mavis would scarce have starved, there in the mountains, during the lush months which followed. There was food and to spare. As the season advanced, provender grew more plentiful. And this was well, for, as the season advanced, Mavis waxed less expert in her newly-learned ancestral trick of living on the land.

No longer with express-train swiftness and eel-like twists could she run down her prey. No longer could she outstrip fleet hares, nor, ending a "stalk" in a flying leap, could pull to earth a rocketing pheasant just as it launched itself in air.

Daily she was slower and more unweildy. Now she must content herself by a wily creeping up on unwary baby rabbits or by digging out families of field mice or other non-elusive game. Luckily for her, the wilderness contained enough of these easy captures to keep her from want.

Then, on a night she made her way wearily and draggingly to a leaf-strewn hole under a windfall tree—a nest she had sought out and found after days of subconscious search. In her teeth she bore a skunk whose defensive powers she had braved for the sake of the ease wherewith he could be overtaken. She did not desire, just then, to eat this malodorous meal, nor, indeed, to eat anything at all. But instinct had whispered to her to bring it along to her lair.

The next morning's rising sun shot a single exploratory ray into the hollowed space under the windfall. The thin bar of light played caressingly on Mavis's fluffy and burr-matted coat as she lay there exhausted. It played, too, upon three squirrel-sized baby collies that nuzzled in squirming greediness against her soft underbody.

Garvin had set high hopes on these babies of Mavis's and of Champion Brownmount Marvel. And now there were but three of them. All three were many miles beyond their unhappy owner's reach, out on a trackless mountain-top.

A collie puppy is the easiest animal to raise—or else he is the hardest. There is no way of foretelling which he will be. Also, Mavis was decidedly a novice in the ways of motherhood. For this reason or for any of a hundred other reasons, two of the three tiny collie pups ceased to nurse before they were a day old, and slipped quietly out of life.

Mavis nosed them over and over, helplessly, several times, as they lay there so cold and unresponsive to her croonings. Then, acting again on the mother instinct which demands that the broodnest be kept clean, she followed another immemorial canine custom. Sadly she got rid of the lifeless incumbrances by the simple and sanitary process of eating them.

After which she concentrated all her maternal efforts on nourishing and caring for her one surviving infant.

This third baby—a male and of rusty-brown hue—had no intention at all of following the mortuary example of his litter-mates. Not only did he refuse to die, but daily he grew stronger and livelier and bigger as he absorbed the entire food and care which nature had ordained for a full family of pups.

In a month the baby ceased to resemble a wet squirrel and merged into a fluffily shapeless thing, as large as a rabbit. In another fortnight, he was gnawing industriously, with pin-point teeth a quarter-inch long, at the tenderer parts of such forest game as his mother bore home to him from her brief foraging trips.

Also, by this age, he had ceased to creep; and was walking clumsily with fat legs asprawl, from one end of the windfall lair to the other and even out onto the open space in front of the prostrate tree. With about as much grace as a broken-wheeled three-ton truck, he gamboled with his gentle little mother, charging at her and tugging one of her tulip ears after another, or growling in fierce falsetto as he made believe bite the white paws that patted at him.

By the time the baby was two months old he was weaned and was eating raw and tough meat which would have killed a kennel-born puppy. At three months he did his first stalking, wriggling up behind a field mouse, his fat stomach close to earth, then leaping on his prey and seizing it. The fact that Mavis had caught and killed the mouse, a mile from the lair, and had brought it thither for her baby to tackle, made no difference in the pup's elation at his own prowess.

But in another month or so he was stalking and tracking on his own account. The lush summer was ending. The mountain creatures were fat and lazy from much good fare. Thus, his first essays were easier than they would have been in leaner times. Yet quickly he was learning the uncanny swiftness and craft and forest instinct of the Wild.

Big he was, and strong, far beyond the average of his age and breed. Like all pups which have been born in the wilderness and have never known man, he had the furtiveness and the precocious wisdom of a wolf.

On a day in late November he ranged high on the mountain, tracking a bevy of partridges with vulpine skill. Mavis, as a rule, hunted with him. But today she had been lured downhill in chase of a rabbit which lost itself in some rock crevices. The scent of another rabbit led her farther downhill to the very base of the mountain. There the rabbit broke cover and dashed frantically toward the highway, a mile north of the village where Mavis had been stoned.

Mavis followed, downing her prey a scant hundred feet from the road. There the sharp and once-familiar sound of a whistle made her forget her victim. So, from earliest puppyhood, her adored master, Garvin, had been wont to summon her. She looked up. A car had stopped at the road edge. A man had clambered out. As he whistled he hurried toward her.

For a moment Mavis shrank back, for flight. Then scent, as well as sound, told her who this human was. With little shrill cries of joy she galloped up to Garvin, dancing around him and slapping at his legs with her flying paws, then leaping high on him and striving to lick his face.

Delighted at his rare luck in chancing to see his lost pet as he had been motoring past, Garvin gathered the happy dog in his arms and carried her to the car. There he held her between his knees while his chauffeur drove homeward. Once or twice she struggled, as if to escape. And ever she looked up in worried entreaty into her master's face. Not being a reader of canine minds, Garvin had no means of knowing she was imploring him to drive back and get her puppy, too.

Thus did Garvin find his well-loved collie, and thus did Mavis lose her better-loved puppy.

Keenly and wonderingly did the deserted pup miss his little mother. He coursed the mountain until he found her trail. He followed it down to the fields and thence to the spot where it was mixed with the unfamiliar man-trail.

There abruptly it vanished. Nor could he pick it up

again, cast about as he would. From the moment Mavis's trail met the man-trail all trace of her was lost. Vaguely the pup associated her disappearance with this rank man-smell. In his heart was born an instinctive dislike and fear of the scent.

He took up the burden of life again, solitary and desperately lonely. He was a companionable and friendly youngster. Never before had he been lonesome, but now he was the only creature of his kind in all the tumble of hinterland that was his home. There was nobody to romp with; nobody to cuddle up to in the windfall lair on cold November nights; nobody to hunt with.

Yet, apart from mere loss of companionship, the pup was none the worse off for his mother's disappearance. He had learned to hunt for himself long before now.

Indeed, thanks to the forest upbringing, his tracking instincts and his deftness in the catching of game were far more finely developed than were those of his house-born dam. He could outhunt her and he could outrun her and outstalk her, young though he was. Nature had taught him forest secrets withheld from the more domesticated Mavis.

Through the late fall and the early winter plentiful food was his for the finding. True, it was hidden higher in the hills and farther from civilization than earlier in the year. But this was to the pup's advantage. For the remoteness of his food-stock kept him far and farther from the more frequented foothills and the hither side of the mountain, during the two months when those stretches were ranged by hunters and by their dogs.

Far off, now and then, he would hear the muffled roar

of a shotgun, or a vagrant breeze would bring him a faint whiff of the dreaded man-scent. But in his winter hunting-grounds he saw no humans or dogs.

He was busy as the hunting season waned. No longer was it as easy as of old to catch a stomachful of nourishing dinner at the price of a ten-minute quest. True, he still had all the food he could eat, but it took him all his time to catch it.

With January the hunting season closed. Game, which had been scared far back among the hills, now came again instinctively to its former haunts. And once more the pup ranged the hither side of the mountain, from crest to plain. There was food enough to keep him strong and healthy, though not enough to keep flesh on his wolflike ribs. Yet he weathered the winter with comparative ease, on to the time of returning plenty and of warmer nights.

At eleven months the pup was twenty-seven inches tall at the shoulder. His weight was sixty-four pounds of fleshless muscle and bone. His coat was unbelievably thick and luxuriant, thanks to the bitter cold of the winter months. It shone like burnished bronze.

It was about this time that he met his first dog, other than Mavis. A runaway mongrel hound, coursing the lower reaches of the mountain in search of rabbits, stopped with a growl and a show of teeth as he beheld on a rock in front of him a magnificent young giant of a collie.

The puppy was well pleased to meet this fellow-dog. Always at the back of his friendly brain had smoldered that sense of loneliness and of longing for chumship. Here at last was a chum!

The collie wagged his tail and came wriggling forward

in gay greeting, seeking to touch noses with his new friend. But the hound would not have it so.

He was morose of spirit, at best, and he was a renowned fighter. Here was a pup, patently inexpert in warfare, such an opponent as the big hound loved to harry into howling submission and to bully and worry and mishandle.

As the collie frisked forward, awiggle with eager welcome, the hound snarled and lunged. The puppy jumped back with a little gasp of pain. The hound had nipped him excruciatingly on one of his tender ears, and then had lunged for the throat, ripping away a handful of snow-and-bronze ruff-hair.

This was not the kind of romp the pup had looked forward to. But worse was to follow. Before he could recover from his pained astonishment, the hound had hurled himself upon him, digging punitive teeth in the young shoulder and ravening there with raucous growls, bearing the amazed puppy to the ground.

The hurt, the unfriendliness, the shock, did something queer to the collie's sunny temper. Of a sudden, as he cringed under the uncalled-for assault, there was a red-hot surge in his brain, an electric thrill through his whole whalebone-and-iron body.

The warrior spirits of a thousand fierce ancestors—wild dogs, wolves, fearless collies—snarled battle orders to this dumbfounded descendant of theirs. Through no volition of his own, the puppy went into action.

The hound was boring gleefully for the big youngster's throat and underbody, when all at once the rolling and

unresisting collie changed into a canicidal maniac, with
the strength and ferocity of a tiger.

Up from the ground sprang the pup, righting himself
and shaking off with ridiculous ease the other dog's grip.
Then, fight as he would to defend himself, the hound was
borne earthward beneath a furry and furious avalanche.
He did not rise again.

Boys, playing truant from school, found him next day
lying there with his throat torn out.

The puppy had learned several things. He had learned
that his own kind was not friendly and that his only hope
of safety was to attack before he should be hurt. Also, he
had learned that there is a terrible joy in battling, and
that he could more than hold his own with a fellow-crea-
ture as heavy as himself. In brief, he ceased to be a loving
and lovable puppy and became a wild beast.

Through the spring and early summer odd rumors
reached the farms and valley hamlets:

Three different dogs—two of them large—had sneaked
off from home at various times to course game through
the hills. All three were found, soon or late, killed and
mangled.

Boys, ranging the foothills and lower mountain-side,
declared they caught a fleeting glimpse of a gigantic and
bronze-hued creature that must be a wolf at the very least.

A six-months-old calf had not only been slain by night
in one of the hillside pastures, but its body had been carried or dragged straight up the mountain, past a point
whence the trackers could follow it no longer.

A man, rounding the spur of a crag (in search of a
strayed cow which never was found), saw a flash of shin-

ing bronze fur and heard a wolfish growl as something vanished from a ledge of rock just in front of him.

From end to end of the valley ran these tales, gaining much flesh at each retelling, and supplemented by the customary half-hundred impossible stories of still more impossible things done by the mysterious monster of the mountain.

Folk bought new locks for their hencoops. They kept their more valuable cattle in the home lots instead of letting them stray at will on the hills. The Grange took up the matter of an organized search and of offering a reward. But the stories which were reported were so manifestly lies that sensible men doubted there could be any grain of foundation in them.

In every rural neighborhood baselessly fantastic sensations are forever finding birth. Witness the innumerable newspaper reports of wild men and of stray leopards and of haunted houses and the like.

To Garvin, fifteen miles down the valley, came at last the wild rumors. Garvin laughed, but only with his lips. His mind was busy.

Mavis had escaped from the Brownmount Breeding Kennels on the day she was to have been sent home. She had reverted to the wild. For more than half a year, presumably, she had dwelt somewhere among the hills back of the roadside field where he had found her.

What more possible than that this supposed monster might be her pup—hers and Champion Brownmount Marvel's? There were no wolves in that region. Moreover, no wolf or other large and devastating brute has a waving and shimmering bronze coat.

Without a word of his real purpose to anyone, Garvin packed his camping outfit and announced that he was going up into the mountains somewhere or other for a month's rest-cure. He was a veteran woodsman; and he was wont to bury himself in the hills for a few weeks every year or so, to steady his nerves and to recover the habit of keen appetite and dreamless sleep. So not even his own family wondered at his sudden plan.

For two nights Garvin stayed at a village inn, while he spent his days in scouring the mountain-side for a good camp site. At last he found what he wanted, high on the shoulder of the mountain, in a rock-curve, and fifty feet from a spring. On his second night at the village a new "monster" story was brought in. After he had interrogated both people concerned, Garvin sifted down the much-twisted versions to the following facts:

A man and his wife and their six-year-old little girl had picknicked halfway up the mountain. After lunch the man and his wife had taken a nap. The child had strayed farther up the steep slope, picking flowers. She had lost her way among the rocks. Therewith she had set up a lusty bawling which had reached the ears of her dozing father. The father had run uphill to find her.

Meantime, as the lost child wandered weeping among the rocks, a huge and bronze animal had appeared from nowhere. He had trotted up to her and had whimpered and had licked her wet face and tried with all his dumb power to comfort her. So far did he succeed that she ceased crying and put both her fat little arms around his shaggy throat and hugged him, while he continued to wag his tail and to lick her face and to whimper encouragement to her.

Just then her father appeared around the edge of the rocky gully. He saw his lost daughter and, close beside her, a giant and gaunt brute. From her earlier wails the man inferred that the huge creature was attacking her. So, snatching up three huge and jagged stones, he hurled them with all his force at the animal.

One of them struck the monster glancingly on the head, making it stagger and all but fall. Recovering itself, the beast had glared at the onrushing man for an instant and then had launched itself, ravening at his throat.

The man threw up one arm, instinctively, to guard his jugular. The monster's teeth shore past coat and shirt sleeve, through skin and flesh, clean to the bone. The man reeled and fell at the impact. The child, fearlessly, tugged at the brute's ruff as it bored in at the prostrate man. As she threw herself in front of her fallen father, the monster wheeled and vanished ("melted away," the man swore) among the rocks.

The father described the wild animal as something like a monstrous dog and something like an equally monstrous wolf and not exactly like either. He was certain, he said, that it would have devoured his baby if he had not arrived in the very nick of time.

Garvin heard and nodded. His last doubt was gone. This was a collie. More, this was *his* collie, the champion-stock pup he never had seen but which he vowed he would make friends with. Next day he began his camping month.

Not by chance had he chosen that inconveniently high

THE WAY OF A DOG

and distant spot on the mountain shoulder for his camp; nor even because it was so near to the only spring within several miles. He had chosen it because, in a patch of mud at the spring's edge, he had seen hundreds of five-pad footmarks, all of a size.

Here, at least sometimes, the big wild collie came to drink. Nor would he come so often if his lair was nearer to another spring. Thus, in all likelihood, the dog made his headquarters somewhere within a radius of a half-mile, at most, of the camp site.

Garvin was content. Instantly he began his quest. This was easy to do, since the quest's sole duties consisted in doing nothing at all.

Back from an absence of several days, the collie jogged toward his lair under the windfall where he had been born. Always he came back here, soon or late, no matter how far afield his hunts might take him, nor how long a time they might last. Perhaps it was sentiment which made him return to his birthplace. More likely it was mere custom and the fact that it was a bare hundred yards from the best and deepest and cleanest and coolest spring in the whole county.

For half a week he had been gone, working the marshes, twelve miles deeper in the wilderness. There, at this season, young woodcock were plentiful. So were muskrats and mudhens. It was an ideal hunting-ground if one did not go there often enough to make its habitants overwary.

To the marshes he had trotted in grumbling anger, from his encounter with the stone-hurling picnicker and

186

the sobbing little girl. Now, replete and tired, he was glad to turn home.

As he breasted the farther rise of the mountain crest and came to the summit, he stopped short in his tracks, his hackles abristle, one corner of his lip upcurled. A gust of night air brought him the reek of wood smoke, and through it the strong and unmistakable man-smell.

Head down, the collie moved forward again, this time as silently as a trail-following timber wolf. A furlong farther on he stopped again.

There, in a rock curve, between him and his lair, twinkled the gold-red eye of a camp fire, illuminating a brownish tent and a pile of duffle-bags and some workmanly cooking utensils. Beside the fire sat a man, idly smoking a pipe and peering into the blaze.

Long and disgustedly the collie gazed. Once and again a soundless growl was borne, deep down in his throat. Never before had he been close to a fire. Also, except for the stone-thrower, this was his first good look at any human. His adventure with the stone-thrower had added much to his instinctive dislike of men. Through the smoldering ire at his heart twitched a thread of sharp curiosity, mingled with something less definable.

At last he moved backward until a pile of rock hid him. Then, in a wide detour, he sought his lair. Much he was tempted to travel all night, if need be, and to put as many impassable miles as possible between himself and this human. But, somehow, the fire held a queer allurement.

Then at his heart tugged something else; that same indefinable thing he had felt as he peered at the man beside the blaze. Wherefore, against his own forest instinct, the collie went to his windfall bed, there to lie awake for hours inhaling the mingled odors of fire and of man which the night wind brought to him.

Next morning at daybreak another and wondrous appetizing scent blended with these. Never before had the dog smelled frying bacon, nor indeed cooked food of any kind. But it drew him, step by step, toward the camp. Finally, behind a shoulder-high rock he stopped, crouching, eager.

The human was eating, not thirty feet away from the collie. When he had finished his meal, Garvin took up a dozen strips of the redolent bacon and flung them in as many different directions. One of them sailed over the rock behind which crouched the collie.

The dog leaped sidewise with the speed of a striking snake, as he saw it coming. Then, inch by inch, he neared it, on the leaves there, just beyond him. He circled it, then sniffed and rolled it over with his nose. A touch of his tongue told him it was warm and salt and savory. In a gulp he swallowed it.

At once he made a stealthy trip, guided by his nose, to where every other bacon strip had been tossed—except two of them which were in plain sight of the man beside the camp fire. He would not risk exposure by snatching for these, heavenly as was the taste of the new fare.

Ever he kept one watchful eye on the man. Garvin was sitting very still in front of something that flashed and shimmered in the growing day. The thing was a three-faced shaving-mirror, of glass that enlarged and made clear each near-by object it reflected.

As the man's back was to the dog, the collie risked lifting his head clear of the clump of brush behind which he was hiding. The man did not turn, nor did he move at all. But he called, very quietly:

"Jock! Jock! Jock!"

At the first sound the collie slipped eel-like out of sight. But the voice did not change, nor did the man move. Again and again the name "Jock" was repeated in that same coaxingly friendly tone, about which there was something vaguely attractive.

Perhaps a hundred times Garvin repeated the call. Then, in a natural and half-argumentative key, he began to recite the Declaration of Independence. He did not know it all, of course, but he repeated, thrice, the parts of it he did know. Then, softly, he sang a crooning old song. After which he called "Jock!" another score of times.

The collie listened, sometimes curling his lip wolfishly, sometimes with the muscles of his tail involuntarily twitching. In front of him was the twinkling fire. The air (and his stomach) was full of the divine savor of bacon. A human voice—a born dog man's voice, at that—was talking and singing, and then was repeating, over and over, a very simple sound, whose timbre and diction were even then becoming familiar to the listening collie, through endless iterations.

It was all very wonderful.

Garvin continued to focus the half-hidden and furtive collie in the triple mirror, until he thought the day's lesson had lasted long enough. Then he arose and yawned.

Instantly, at the human's first motion, the dog shrank out of sight.

But at dawn next day the call of "Jock!" stirred the

collie from his nap in the windfall lair. He started up.
Instantly to his nostrils came a scent so ravishing as to set
his mouth awater. Garvin was frying liver.

To nineteen dogs out of twenty, the taste and the smell
of fried liver are irresistible. Jock was one of the nineteen.
Slowly, skirting the open spaces and moving with lupine
craft, the giant collie crept to his vantage-place of the
previous day. There, between two narrow gaps of rock he
saw, and was seen, in the mirror.

Garvin was at breakfast. Between mouthfuls the man
called now and then: "Jock! Jock! Jock!" Then, as by
chance, he tossed over his shoulder a small lump of something brown-black. It fell just on the near side of the two
rocks. There it exhaled not only the aroma of cooked
food, but its own particular scent.

The collie hesitated, fidgeting and wavering. The man
had his back turned and made known his presence only
by that intermittent call of "Jock." The collie flashed out
of his hiding-place at a speed that defied the eye to follow
it clearly. While he was still in swift motion he snatched
up the liver and melted back behind his rocks.

The food was transcendently delicious. Still hot, it
reeked with grease and salt and with the true liver flavor.
This was a trillion times more palatable than was the best
raw kill.

Now, the man was calling again, coaxingly: "Jock!
Jock! Jock!" Apparently the "Jock" sound told of wondrous food, and of many more things. The collie peeped
out. The man had not turned. But, clumsily, over his
shoulder, Garvin flung another little lump of fried liver.

This time the liver fell midway between the camp fire

and the rock. It would be rank foolhardiness to go so far in quest of it. Yet the cry of "Jock!" and the odor of cooked food were monstrous seductive. Step by step, after a long wait, the collie sneaked toward the morsel. In a rush and a backward dash he secured it and carried it to the rocks.

No more did the man call him. The day's lesson was at an end—the lesson which taught the collie that "Jock" and food meant the same thing. This human apparently was setting no trap for him.

That day, during Garvin's desultory rambles through the woods around his camp, something half-invisible slunk behind him, following him everywhere, yet ever ready to flee. The collie did not know why he followed the man. He did not want to. Nor did he know why, at night, he did not go to his lair, but lay just outside the radius of the camp fire and watched while Garvin ate and talked and sang.

Garvin did not speak the magic word "Jock!" as he ate and talked, that evening. But next morning the collie was roused from a light snooze by hearing it. With it came anew the adorable odor of frying food. This time the dog came to within six feet of the indifferent and mirror-gaz-ing human, to annex a handful of pork scraps Garvin threw just behind him.

A week passed before the collie would creep up to the hand thrust out with fried liver in it. Even then he did it only because Garvin's back was turned and because Gar-vin had called, "Jock!" without moving, for a solid half-hour.

But, night after night, that week, the dog had lain, flat

to earth, in a thicket close to the camp fire, ever watching the human and reveling in his pleasant voice, and luxuriating in the glow of the flame.

Cooked meat, firelight, human presence, and human voice!—They were mysteriously alluring, but not yet alluring enough. Things were happening inside the wild creature's brain, it is true; things which stirred and drew him strangely. But the instinct of the wild and the memory of the picnicker's stingingly flung rock were even stronger.

Then, one morning, the dog followed the man as usual on the latter's lazy mountain-top stroll, finding odd pleasure in the walk. Garvin strode along the top of a five-foot ridge of rock; stumbled cleverly, and fell prone at the bottom of the tiny ridge.

Carefully as the fall was made, Garvin skinned one knee and barked his palms in executing it.

The collie started back as the man tumbled. Then he saw Garvin did not get up, but that he sat with his face in his hands, crying and moaning.

Garvin had been torn badly by a handful of shrapnel in France, and had not uttered a sound as it was cut out of him. Yet now, remembering the incident of the picnicker's child, he wept loudly and dramatically.

For some time he continued to cry, with all the pathos and misery at his command. Then, just as he was giving up the experiment as a failure, a cold nose touched lightly his clasped hands. A softly warm pink tongue lapped timidly his face.

Here was a chance—a preëminent chance—for him to seize the sympathizing dog by the throat, and to chain him and muzzle him, and to lead him back, shuddering and struggling, to captivity. But that was not Garvin's object. He wanted the dog's soul far more than his mere body.

One of his hands shifted, as he wept lamentably, and his fingers rubbed the collie's rough ears.

The dog pulled back from the caress, growling. Garvin wept the louder. As the worried pink tongue licked him again, the man stroked the collie's silken head. Ten minutes later the dog was enduring, shyly yet with secret delight, this petting of his head and ears. Yet, as Garvin rose and moved toward him, he dashed away.

That night the man was sitting by the fire, his mirror propped in front of him. Occasionally he called softly, "Jock!" A cold nose shoved itself into his cupped palm, then withdrew with scared alacrity. Garvin dropped a bit of fried liver into his palm and held it as before, crooning, "Jock!"

Presently the liver was lifted lightly from its resting-place. Then a tongue licked the empty hand. Turning ever so slowly, Garvin saw the dog sitting beside him. As he turned, Garvin talked. He laid his hand on the classic head, then passed it down the withers and the bur-tangled back.

The dog shivered violently. But this time he did not dart away.

"Jock," crooned Garvin, "you belong to *me*, now. Not because I own you by law, but because you're my chum. Because you have learned the collie's heritage of cooked food and comradely talks and walks and human companionship. Because you'd be lonelier than ever, if I left you now. But nobody is going to catch you, Jock. You don't go back to civilization till you follow me there of your own accord. That won't be yet, Jock. But every day and every night the cord that grips you to me is growing stronger. I can wait. You're a dog, now, Jock. Not a wild animal. Not a 'monster.' And you and I are friends."

At every slightly accented repetition of his name the collie wagged his burr-matted plume of a tail. It was mysteriously and impellingly pleasant to be talked to in human language and to hear the newly-familiar word "Jock" so often. Already he had learned to associate that food-accompanied word with himself.

"If you were safe up here in the hills, Jock," said the crooning voice, the next morning, at breakfast, while the magnetic hand continued to stroke the shoulders and head of the half-hypnotized young dog—"if you were safe up here, I'd leave you to the free life you're used to, even though you're the finest collie I ever set eyes on and even though I've sworn I'll make a pal of you. But you *aren't* safe, Jock. There are queer stories about you. Presently some reward-seekers or a crowd of monster-killers will begin to comb the mountain for you. Soon or late they'd get you, if they had to use poison or bone-smashing traps to do it.

"So, I am going to humanize you, Jock, and take you home with me. But I'll make a bargain with you. When the time comes, Jock, you won't have to follow me to civilization unless you do it of your own free will. I shan't leash you or carry you. That's fair, isn't it, Jock?"

The dog stretched himself, fore and aft, in true collie fashion. Then, deliberately he lay down, curling himself

194

close to the man's feet, his head against Garvin's boot. For an hour the two remained thus; Garvin talking intermittently, now and then stroking the dog's head and once or twice giving him a scrap of fried meat.

Then Garvin got up, and began his usual aimless morning hike through the mountain-top weeds. This time the collie did not stalk him, unseen, but trotted proudly along, in full sight, finally making a scurrying rush into a thicket and emerging with a half-grown rabbit between his jaws.

This offering the dog laid gingerly at Garvin's feet, looking up at the man with a newly-born adoration of chumship.

That night, after the two had shared a glorious meal of stewed rabbit, the collie stretched himself to sleep across the narrow doorway of Garvin's tent. He had found his god—the god he would serve and follow henceforth, right blithely, to the end. Happier and more fortunate than are we humans, he could commune with his god, face to face.

Garvin, on his hemlock-bough bed, muttered half-aloud to the drowsy collie:

"A handful of liver, to win your attention, Jock—then a handful of patience to win your trust—then a handful of fake distress and of common dog-sense to win your worship, Jock! People would have laughed their silly heads off at me, Jock, if I had told them I was coming up into the wilderness to catch a dangerous monster with no better weapons than those.

"I'm going to bring home the grandest big-game trophy in the world—and the grandest pal, Jock. Good night, old chum!"

The plumed tail smote the ground thumpingly. Then, with a restless shift of his mighty body, the dog laid his head athwart Garvin's nearest foot. Thus pillowed for the night, Jock grumbled in perfect contentment and fell asleep.

ing softly under his breath and trying to lick her flower-face.

"There is the answer," repeated Mrs. Venner. "And there is Moron's permit to go on living here. He worships Baby, and she cares more for him than she cares for anything and everything else. It would break her heart if we sent him away."

"He must be a wonderful protection for her," assented the guest. "And they make a lovely picture, cuddled together there. Sense or no sense, he would guard her with his life, I know."

"Yes," grated Rufe, smarting still at the loss of his chick, "it's a fine joy to realize that. At our picnic, last week, Baby rolled off the bank into the lake. The water wasn't deep enough to drown her, of course. But as far as Moron was concerned, it might just as well have been. He thought it was a glorious good joke. He danced around on the bank, barking and wagging his fool tail and grinning, while little Rex here jumped in and pulled her ashore. Then when he saw us praising Rex for it, Moron jumped into the water and retrieved a very dead cat and brought it to us, so he could get some praise on his own account. Yes, he's a grand protection for Baby. About as much protection as her Teddy-bear. He's sure one gorgeous specimen of doghood!"

Rufe clumped off to bury the slain pheasant chick. The others drifted across to the rose-gardens beyond the house, the setter at Dirck's heels.

Moron gazed after the departing group. He would have liked to join them, even as every normal dog rejoices in sharing a walk with humans. But he knew he would not be welcome, and that he would be made keenly aware of his unwelcomeness.

Only with Berenice did he feel he was on terms of more than strained sufferance. And the familiar tone of Rufus Venner's speech had had no need to be reinforced by use of his nickname in order to tell Moron he had been the object of one more opprobrium. For the dog inherited all a collie's innate sensitiveness and intuition, without an atom of a collie's innate wisdom.

Well did he know that nobody at the Venner house liked him. Well did he know that blame was ever waiting to crash about his ears—blame for whose causes he had not the remotest knowledge. Rex would do something, for instance, which won affectionate approval from these queer humans. Moron would try, pathetically, to duplicate the praised exploit—as just now he had done in capturing the chick—and he would be made to feel he was boundlessly worthless; as indeed he was.

It was a strange and a pathetic situation, all around. It had been such a situation since first the Venners had realized that Moron's lack of dog sense was inherent and was not the mere foolishness of early puppyhood. Daily it was growing worse.

The average dog, with the gift to understand that he was disliked and scorned, would have withdrawn into himself or would have turned ugly or hopelessly cowed. But Moron was not an average dog. His whole buoyant nature called out for friendship and approval. Though every failure crushed his sensitive spirit, yet always his spirit rebounded in a wistful hope of doing better next time.

He seemed perpetually in the attitude of realizing that the world is an unspeakably rotten place to live in, but hoping against hope that suddenly some miracle may make it become pleasanter.

He had been dully hard to train in even the simplest teachings of house-brokenness and obedience. Not that he did not make pathetic effort to master his owners' teachings, but that his defective brain simply would not grasp such teachings. Hopefully, cringingly, blunderingly, super-friendlily, he lived on; his one friend the fluffy baby, his one welcome from her.

In face of fifty discouragements, he persevered in his dull way, in the effort to learn the Law and to win approbation. Each discouragement daunted and bewildered him and made him miserably unhappy. Yet he lacked the sense—or the callousness—to cease permanently from trying.

It was three mornings after the episode of the pheasant chick that Dirck Venner patted Rex applaudingly on the shoulder when the little setter flew at a tramp that slouched up the kitchen path and drove the intruder harrowingly out through the gate into the road.

Moron, from the nursery window upstairs, beheld with envy.

Ten minutes later the Venners' clergyman—a college classmate of Dirck's and an intimate friend of the household's—turned in at the front walk and came up the steps. The front door stood open to the cool of the early summer morning. The clergyman came into the hallway, in response to Dirck's hail from the library.

With a snarling rush Moron flew downstairs and flung

himself ragingly upon the visitor. The clergyman threw up an instinctive hand, barely in time to save his throat from the raking white teeth. But his cassock was rent from neck to hem by the ravening jaws.

"Why, the dog's gone mad!" exclaimed the visitor, fending Moron off as best he could, while Dirck came rushing out into the hallway. "He's seen me a hundred times and he never went for me before. He ———"

Dirck seized the collie by the neck, and forthwith administered to him a savage beating which made the luckless Moron's every bone and nerve ache. But the punishment's shameful agony was fiftyfold more terrible to the sensitive heart of the dog than to his rugged body.

Often had he been scolded. Several times he had been slapped or struck or ordered out of the house. But this was his first actual beating. Stupid as he was, yet he had wit enough to know the man was wreaking hot temper and a sense of outraged hospitality upon him, rather than giving a judicial chastisement.

Dirck flung the shuddering and anguished collie from him, a well-guided kick propelling Moron out through the open doorway and down the veranda steps. Then he turned in apology to his chum. But the clergyman forestalled Venner's attempt to speak.

"I think," he said, coldly, "that there are better ways for a man to show his inferiority to a dog than by kicking him. Also, perhaps there are better ways of venting one's dirty temper than on a brute beast that can't resent it. If I can stand having my clothes torn by the poor dog, don't you think you could have eased his punishment with a shred of common justice? Not that it's any of my business."

"I suppose you're right," panted Dirck, winded by the violence of his exertions. "It's the first time I ever kicked a dog. But the cur is getting unbearable. This is just the climax. A human idiot that is unbearable is sent away and put under restraint. I can't see why an unbearable idiot dog must be allowed to stay here. Every time I plan to get rid of him my wife begs him off because Baby loves him so. But I'm getting pretty close to my limit of endurance."

"From the wild-beast way you mishandled him just now," suggested the clergyman, "I should say you had gone several miles past your limit—or any other merciful man's limit. I'm sorry if I'm offending you by this kind of talk, Venner. But there are two things that always get under my skin. One of them is a frightened child and the other is a cruelly treated dog. That poor tortured collie hasn't the faintest idea why you half killed him. So it did him no good to be pummeled and kicked so unmercifully. It did you more harm than it did him. The smashing of self-control is just about the most hurtful thing that can befall any man. I seem to have been luckiest of the three, for my cassock can be mended or replaced. You and Moron have both lost something that can never be wholly replaced or mended. Think it over, Dirck."

The clergyman was wise and far-seeing. But in his impromptu sermon he had made one important error. He had said Moron had no idea why he had been so cruelly beaten.

Very well indeed did Moron know why. He knew it as

soon as his poor bewildered wits could grasp any thought other than the terrible thing that had befallen him.

He gathered himself up at the foot of the steps, chattering and shaking with nerve-rack, his body one aching mass of pain, his breath clean kicked out of him. Instinctively, blindly, he sought shelter, bolting under the veranda through a gap in the lattice-work, and crawling into the farthest and darkest corner.

There he lay, moaning, shuddering, gasping, his thick brain awhirl, close to collapse. Horror made everything a blank, except the torment of his physical hurt and the anguish of his memories of the furious man who had hammered and kicked him.

Bit by bit, there in the cool darkness and silence, he began to calm down. The shivering no longer was incessant. The hoarse panting grew quieter. His dull mentality began to work again, first in visualizing his punishment, then in groping for its cause.

Thus it was that Moron grew to understand why he had been beaten. He had attacked a man who had come into the house. Apparently that was a mortal sin. For it he had been nearly killed. Rex had been praised for driving a tramp out of the grounds. But the tramp had not come into the house. Therein lay the difference. It was a fine thing to fly at anyone on the grounds, but it was wrong to attack anybody who had gained the sanctuary of the house itself.

This was the first time a punishment's reason had been comprehended by Moron, and it had taken a brutal whaling to start his understanding of it. But now the basic facts were wholly clear in his befuddled mind.

At last, worn out with pain and fright and misery, he fell asleep.

It was dusk when the big collie awoke. He was awakened by the sound of Dirck Venner's voice calling him. At the call, Moron scrambled stiffly and achingly to his feet and made glad progress toward the gap whereby he had entered the space under the veranda. For this was the voice of the dear master he loved and whom ever he was seeking so vainly to placate and make friends with.

Moreover, the voice, just now, had no tinge of the usual impatient disgust which ran through it when addressing the collie. Wherefore, Moron scuttled delightedly toward the gap, his haste making his sore back hit bumpingly against the veranda boards. Dust and cobwebs were showered down on him from the impact, adding to the disreputableness his coat already had attained from lying so long on the damp mold.

Then, as he reached the gap, the dog hesitated. To memory came the beating that had been his at the hands of this man who was calling him. He fell to trembling. But, as Dirck called again, long training enforced the call. Cringing to the very ground, Moron crawled out from under the porch and up the steps to where Dirck was waiting.

In the dusk, Venner could see only the outlines of the crawling collie. But those told enough to strike the man afresh with shame at his own brutality toward the helpless animal.

All day Dirck had been trying to keep at white heat his indignation against the fool dog, and trying not to remember what the clergyman had said and what his own conscience indorsed. At last, he had admitted to himself he had been wrong. Thus he had sought for Moron. Failing to find the collie, he had come out onto the veranda and called aloud for him.

Dirck and Mrs. Venner were on their way to a somewhat formal dinner dance. Venner had dressed early. Now, in the panoply of evening attire, he was spending the two or three minutes before the car should be due, in trying to make amends to his ill-used dog.

Moron's terrified attitude, as he crept up the steps, struck Dirck to the heart. He had frightened and tortured the collie. Yet obedience was goading Moron into coming at his call. There seemed something infinitely honest and loving in such an approach. Venner spoke gently to the dog cowering at his feet. Then he stooped and petted the shivering head, there in the dim twilight, talking kindly to the collie and petting him encouragingly.

Moron thrilled in an access of delighted relief at knowing himself forgiven and at such signs of affection as had not been his in many a sad month. Ecstatically he responded to the tenderness, by leaping up on Venner, petting at the man's snowy shirtfront, rubbing against Dirck's immaculate white waistcoat.

Around the curve of the drive came the car which was to bear Dirck and his wife to the dinner dance. The headlights poured a vivid glare upon the collie; revealing him as a mass of dust and grime and cobwebs and moist earth.

Dirck glanced in swift apprehension from the dog to his own raiment. One look at his erstwhile white waistcoat and whiter shirtfront and at his carefully-pressed evening clothes made him yearn to repeat the morning's punitive performance.

Setting his teeth, he turned away from the lovingly dancing Moron and hurried indoors to repair his ruined costume as quickly as might be. If he had done a weak and wrong thing that morning, in venting his lost temper on his helpless dog, assuredly he was controlling himself now, under fifty times as much provocation.

Wholly unaware of his master's swift change of mental attitude toward himself, Moron scampered gleefully indoors after Dirck, still gamboling about him, until Venner reached his own room and entered it, slamming the door in the blithe collie's face. Whereat, Moron trotted off to the nursery to see Berenice, from whom he had been absent all day and whom he was beginning to miss.

Always the collie slept across the threshold of the nursery door. Mrs. Venner declared he chose such resting-place with a view to guarding the baby from possible harm. More cynically, Dirck used to say it was because the rug there was softer than the others in the upper hall, and that the dog, moreover, could be certain of at least one person falling over him in the dark.

Tonight the house was unusually quiet. Mr. and Mrs. Venner were at the dance. Rufe had gone up to camp for a week, taking Rex with him. The maids were at the movies, all except Berenice's nurse. The nurse had a toothache and was lying on the couch in the nursery. The nursery door had been shut by her against Moron when she saw his condition of utter griminess.

So the big dog lay drowsily on the rug outside the closed door, half awake, half dozing.

Late in the evening he lifted his head from his paws and listened alertly. A sound, too low for human ears to have caught, but plainly audible to him, came from somewhere downstairs. Moron got up quietly and went to investigate.

The noise he had heard was made by a bit of silver falling to the floor in the dining-room. Moron reached the door of this room, only to find it shut. From within he could hear distinctly some one moving about with quick and stealthy steps. Instinctively the dog's hackles bristled and his lip curled. Far down in his furry throat a thunderous challenge-bark began to form.

Then, with sudden sick recollection, he thought of his punishment for assailing a man who had entered the house that morning. The bark died unborn. Moron had no mind to risk another agonizing trouncing for this cause, nor of wrecking the heavenly new-found friendliness between Dirck and himself.

His hackles subsided. He stood there, wagging his tail, watch-dog instinct merged into civil curiosity.

A man had gotten into the dining-room, through one of the easily-opened long windows looking out on the garden shrubbery. This as soon as he had assured himself nobody was on the ground floor. For the next ten minutes the intruder busied himself in assorting and appraising the somewhat valuable collection of table silver kept in the sideboard drawers.

The drawers' locks were as easily forced as had been the window-fastenings. Deftly the intruder separated plated ware from sterling, dropping the latter into the capacious bag he carried. He dared not risk going upstairs, where a night light in the nursery implied that some scream-addicted servant might be on duty. But he was well content with the haul he was making. It was a pleasantly profitable night's work.

A soft sound outside the dining-room door brought him to his feet. The sound was not repeated. The man decided it must be his imagination. Yet, bothered thereby, he tiptoed to the door and peered through the keyhole into the dimlit hallway.

There, just in front of him, stood a huge collie.

The burglar shrank back. Next to an irate householder with a knife, the average professional thief dreads most to encounter a vigilant house dog.

But this dog was not barking. He was not even growling. Indeed, his plumed tail wagged in friendly greeting.

The man opened the door. In stepped Moron, courteously inquisitive but in no way threatening. Petting the friendly collie on the head, the thief went on with his work. When he had quite finished he grinned down at the dog. After which he took a blank place-card from a serving-table drawer and scribbled on it in pencil. With a bit of string he affixed the card to Moron's collar. Then he picked up his heavy loot-bag and departed as he had come; the dog following him politely to the window and watching him make his furtive way through the shrubbery toward a lane at the rear of the grounds, where waited a lightless car.

Long after midnight, Dirck Venner and his wife returned home. Moron came out into the hall, at a gallop, to greet them. Dirck shoved him back as the grimed body launched itself affectionately toward the slab of white shirtfront.

"Look!" exclaimed Mrs. Venner. "He has a note fastened to his collar. Perhaps one of the maids put it there, knowing he'd come to meet us. He ——"

"At last we find a use for the sagacious Collie, then," scoffed Dirck, the spoiled-clothes memory still rankling. "He is invaluable, as a letter-box. And his tongue would be first rate for licking stamps, too. Who can deny, now, that everything on earth has its use, if only one will look long enough for it? He can ——"

A little cry of horror from his wife interrupted the man. Mrs. Venner had untied the card from the merrily wriggling dog's collar. Now she read aloud the scribbled words thereon:

"You sure got one fine watch-dog and I wish all folks had the same kind. It would make my work easier and not so lonesome. He was nice company for me and he wagged his tail instead of his jaws. That is the kind of a dog to have. You got some nice silver, too. Only I wish so much of it wasn't plated."

What with policemen and detectives and reporters, the Venners did not get a chance to sit down to breakfast, next morning, until after ten o'clock. It was then that Dirck for the first time trusted himself to speak of Moron. He was urged thereto by a sight which ordinarily would have brought a smile of kindly amusement to his set lips.

Out on the side lawn Baby Berenice was playing. In rompers, she was disporting herself on the shaven and bone-dry grass. With her, as ever, was the big golden collie, clumsily romping, yet with a curious gentleness marking his every motion. Never, in their wildest playing, did the dog forget his own strength and the baby's helplessness.

The spectacle set Dirck Venner's hard-held temper asmolder.

"Dear," he said, glumly, "I don't want to rub it in or to say anything to rile you or make you unhappy. But I've had all of that abominable cur that I can stand. Last night was the climax. It's made us the laughingstock of the whole place."

"But ——"

"I'm going to get rid of him," went on Dirck, unheeding. "That's final. I won't give him away, for there isn't anybody I have enough of a grudge against. I can't sell him, for even if I took a plugged nickel in payment for him, I could be sued for obtaining money under false pretences. There's just one thing to do. After breakfast I am going to take him for a walk in the woods, out yonder. When I get to Pancake Hollow I'm going to put a pistol bullet through his head and tumble his body down the gully. It will be a quick and painless death for him and a mighty relief to everyone in this house. Baby will soon forget him. I'll buy her another dog, right away. One with a rudimentary idea of sense, this time."

Mrs. Venner made no reply. Following the direction of her husband's glance, she gazed sorrowfully out of the open window at the scene on the sun-swept lawn—the laughing baby and the protectively big collie playing together so happily.

For a full minute both the Venners watched the child

213

and the dog; without speaking. Venner was trying to hold firm to his lethal resolution. His wife was trying not to cry.

Baby Berenice was growing tired of the romp. Also, the sun was hot and hotter out there on the shadeless patch of lawn. A few yards away was a clump of shrubbery. Around the base of the clump was a tangle of flowering plants. It would be fun to sit there in the shade and pick flowers.

Accordingly, she made her way on stubby and none-too-sure little legs across the intervening dry turf. Her parents watched her toddling progress. Moron got up from a luxurious roll on the grass and trotted after her.

As the child came within the belt of shade and stooped to gather the nearest cluster of flowers, Moron drew to a dead halt, stiffening all over. Fool as he was, he shared with other collies the wolf ancestry which whispers sometimes to its descendants the secrets of the wild.

To the dog's keen scent came a faintly sickening odor as of crushed cucumbers. To him, with it, came a nameless hereditary fear. And now the story told by the odor was reinforced by a gruesome buzzing sound from amid the flower tangle.

Berenice was troubled by no instincts at all. Hence she advanced fearlessly, reaching out for the flower-spray. Then a new playfellow came in sight from among the snarl of flowering undergrowth. The baby laughed aloud and bent to pat the newcomer.

In the mountain, behind the forest which fringed the lower end of the Venner grounds, weeks of hot drought had dried the rock pools and trickles. The reptile denizens of the rock-ledge heights had been driven downhill and toward civilization by the goad of thirst.

One of these mountain-dwellers had pursued a rat through the hither reaches of the woods. He had run the rat to earth in the very middle of that shrub-clump, before daylight, and had killed and devoured his prey. Then, curled low in the flower tangle, he had slept. Wakened by the thud of awkward little feet approaching his resting-place, he sounded his buzzing alarm and reared himself for murder.

From the lips of both the carelessly watching Venners broke a gurgle of speechless horror as they saw their baby lean chucklingly forward to pet the uplifted triangular head of the rattlesnake.

Dirck leaped through the open window; landing on all-fours, staggering up and rushing toward the clump. His wife sat dumb and stricken, her eyes staring wide at the impending tragedy.

Moron was close behind the baby as she stooped toward the snake. He had some vague impulse to shove her aside. Yet that weird woodland lore of his ancestors told him there was no time and that the snake could strike infinitely faster than he could shove.

Not a month earlier the dog had been in dire disgrace for biting in two a pheasant chick. At that time Venner had shouted angrily, even as Venner was shouting now. It would mean another hideous beating, at very least, were he to commit this same fault again.

Yet if he did not, death would be the portion of the laughing baby he adored. There could be no question of choice between these two dire evils. The collie lunged forward past the child, moving with the speed of light.

Mrs. Venner saw Moron leap at the snake; even while her husband recovered his footing and started across the lawn too late to be of any use in averting the little girl's death.

The dog had wasted no time, yet he was all but too slow. For even as he pushed Berenice aside the snake struck.

The twin syringe-fangs missed the pudgy little hand by less than an inch. They found their goal in the furry cheek of the dog.

Back drew the triangular head for a second lightning-swift stroke. But forward flashed Moron's head at the same time. The collie's scissor-teeth gripped the serpent behind the neck and closed savagely.

The rattle-tipped body writhed and thrashed about in the grass even while Moron was spitting out the envenomed head he had bitten off.

Then the dog turned to see Dirck Venner bearing down on him.

Moron had endured a torturing punishment for a far lesser offense, barely a day earlier. Also, he had just incurred death—and he knew well he had incurred it—for the baby he adored.

As the gasping and mouthing man rushed toward him, Moron turned and fled.

This time he did not make for the shelter of the veranda gap. His wolf ancestors were shouting grim secrets into his slowly-working brain. One of these secrets was that a Wild Thing must turn to the wilderness to die. Death was in the venom that even now throbbed, blazingly painful, in the collie's cheek.

To the near-by woods galloped Moron, heedless of Dirck's loud cries to him to return, heedless of Dirck's lumbering pursuit.

The dog did not slink away, as at other times, with crest adroop and intucked tail. Sweepingly he ran, head up, plumed tail flying as in gay challenge.

Ever he had feared piteously the dislike and the scoldings of the humans whom he loved with such wistful yearning, and whose love he could not win. But he did not fear this death he was to face in the depths of the forest yonder—the forests where once his wolf ancestors had ranged, and whither their inherited teachings were bearing him now.

Through his own dizzy excitement and remorse, Dirck Venner noted subconsciously this glorious transfiguring of the erstwhile cowed animal. It was not that the collie was fleeing in terror from him; but as though Moron heard and joyously answered a call from Something infinitely stronger and more compelling.

The great dog had cast aside the encumbering scared wistfulness and the pathos and stupidity that had clothed him.

Glorified, majestic, his golden coat aflame in the morning sunlight, he sped eagerly into the welcoming green arms of the forest and to what waited there for him.

XI

* *

TREASURE TROVE

* *

The big collie was making a gallant fight of it. Nesta thrilled to the battle, though she had no knowledge of dogs and equally little interest in them or in anything else. It was a glorious struggle he was making; this shaggy mahogany-and-white brute.

Nesta had watched the entire scene. She was walking along the River Road, in the frozen slush of the muddy byway, when first the rabbit flashed across her path and scurried out on the frozen surface of the stream. Hard at bunny's heels galloped a half-grown hound puppy.

Out upon the treacherous early March ice the pup followed his fast-escaping prey. Then, thirty yards from shore, a patch of rotting channel ice swayed and cracked and disintegrated under the young hound's bumpily scrambling feet. Through the gray expanse appeared a patch of black water, in whose middle the pup floundered helplessly.

Once and again the puppy reached the broken edges of

218

the water-hole and strove to lift himself up to safety. But ever the decaying channel ice crumbled under his wildly clawing forefeet and he slumped back, his whole head submerged. The current, too, was seeking to draw him under the unbroken ice beyond. Nesta shut her eyes.

Then something brushed harshly past the girl. A collie had come upon the scene from nowhere in particular and was dashing across the firmer shore ice toward the exhausted puppy. The little hound saw rescue coming and he redoubled his own useless efforts to resist the tug of the current and to climb up the splintered edges of ice at the edge of the hole.

Silent, wind-swift, the great collie sped. As he neared the ragged gap the ice began to bend and crack under him. He came to a sliding halt at the edge of the hole and braced his white feet, leaning far forward to catch the frantic puppy by the scruff of the neck and to draw him out of the water.

Before his jaws could close on the wriggling victim the ice had given away under him. The gap was larger than before. In it now two dogs instead of one were struggling.

The collie secured his hold on the pup's neck. With an effort that carried his own head and shoulders far out of water he swam to the edge of the hole and fairly thrust the hound upward, over the edge.

Perhaps here the ice was less weak than at the point where both had fallen in. At any rate, it did not break under the puppy's forefeet. With a last effort of strength, the little fellow clawed his way to the surface of the ice and dashed off at top speed for shore.

The impact of the youngster's jump drove the collie's

head far under. He came up beneath the ice. Whether by instinct or by luck or by brain, he swam upstream a yard or so. Once more his head appeared in the gap; dripping and gasping. To the edge of the hole he swam, at the place where the puppy had clambered to safety. But his own weight was far greater than the hound's. The ice broke under him as he heaved himself up. Down he went, far below the surface; only to rise and strike out for another point.

Thrice, he had lifted half his tawny body over the edge and was drawing up his hindquarters, when the rotten ice collapsed with him. The fourth time he came up more feebly, yet undaunted, his white paws cut and bleeding. He swam from end to end of the gap as though seeking some firmer spot for his next effort.

It was then that Nesta Breen, through no volition of her own, found she had left the road and was hurrying out onto the frozen river toward the hopelessly battling collie. Common sense bade her turn back. But the awful hope in the dog's eyes, as he saw her come to his help, outweighed sanity.

Yet she kept enough presence of mind to stoop and up-end a long plank which some boys had left lying on the ice when they had been seeking bonfire material. It was very heavy and it was somewhat imbedded. But she wrenched it free and she staggered onward with it, shoving it ahead of her.

Nearing the gap, she placed the plank in front of her on the ice and crawled, face downward, along it. The rotting ice crackled and heaved. But, thanks to the distribution of leverage, it held. Presently she was able to reach forward to the dog.

The collie had swum close to her side of the gap. As she reached out, he made one supreme effort to lift himself over the edge. The ice crumbled again under him. But this time Nesta had firm hold of his ruff. The ice groaned and chuckled and bent as she pulled him toward her.

Right valiantly did the dog second her efforts. Scrambling, heaving, writhing, he drove forward and upward as she tugged him to her.

And now both of them lay on the wide plank; panting and worn out.

Presently, inching her way, Nesta began to retreat toward shore, still on the plank. Even after she had come to the landward end of it she continued to lie face downward, arms out, and to work her way toward the bank in that fashion, until she felt beneath her the thicker and rougher ice on which she had made the first part of her short rescue-journey.

Then only did she venture to stand up and to make the rest of the few yards on foot. She was sick and shaken and dizzy. But most of all she was astounded at herself and at this insane thing she had done. She could not understand it.

Throughout the shoreward trip the collie had forborne to follow the example of the puppy by scooting to the safety of dry land. Instead, he had accommodated his pace to her snail-like motions, remaining close at her side. Once, as she hesitated, he leaned down and licked her tense hand, whimpering softly.

The water was freezing on his shaggy coat; he was bleeding from ice-cuts on paws and chest. He was still panting and tired from the terrific exertion. But his care seemed to be wholly for the woman who had saved him from death.

Through her own daze of self-astonishment Nesta observed this. She caught the look of utter worship and gratitude in his deep-set dark eyes. It gave her an odd feeling of happiness. And again she fell into a wonder at herself.

The collie had seemed gigantic as he had flashed past her to the rescue of the drowning puppy. Yet now, with his bronze coat dank and sodden with water, he seemed as lean as a greyhound.

The puppy had scuttled away as soon as he had gotten out of the water. But the collie did not stir from the girl's side. Up into her face he was looking with adoration. A wry smile twisted Nesta's lips.

"You're wasting your time," she told him, unconsciously speaking as if to another human. "I got you out of the water. That's all I can do for you. There's no sense in your hanging around me any longer."

As she spoke she resumed her fast homeward walk. The collie's plumed tail had wagged appreciatively at her tart words, whose purport meant nothing to him. Now he fell into step at her side, once more accommodating his pace to hers, thrusting his cold muzzle lovingly against her palm. The touch startled Nesta, so tender was its caress and so full of trusting affection. She stopped short, eyeing the dog bemusedly. Then she said, with more sharpness:

"Go home! I don't want you. I told you there's nothing more to be gotten out of me. A man wouldn't have needed to be told that twice. In fact, a man *didn't* need to. You're only a dog, so you're stupider than he was. Go home!"

Steadfastly the collie gazed up into her face as she harangued him. His look gave her a queer feeling that he was not deceived by the closeness of her words, but that he read past them into the lonely soreness of her heart. The fantastic notion would not be laughed away. Moreover, as she moved on, he trotted again at her side.

"I don't like dogs," she told him, grumpily. "I don't want you with me. *Go home!*"

As before, she felt he was disregarding her command because he read past it and because of the unhappiness in her heart. He seemed to yearn to be of comfort to her. She shrugged her shoulders and walked faster. Presently she stopped before the gate of a bungalow deep in a shabby lawn.

"I live here," she said, turning on the collie. "Now that you have seen the house, perhaps you'll be as wise as the man I told you about. He called here only once after we had to move down to this place from the Terrace. Once was enough."

She opened the gate and shut it behind her, hurrying up the frozen walk. With no effort at all the collie cleared the three-foot picket fence and dropped into step again beside her. On the veranda steps she paused.

"I'm a fool!" she announced to the dog. "If I weren't, I'd drive you away with a stick. And if *you* weren't a fool, you wouldn't wait to be driven away. Come in, if you want to."

She unlocked the front door and passed into the warm living-room. An elderly woman glanced up pleasantly at her from a chair beside the fire. At sight of the collie standing with waving tail on the threshold, the woman by the fire stared in blank astonishment.

"Ernesta Carrickford Breen!" she exclaimed. "You haven't—you surely haven't been wasting any of your tiny income on—on a dog?"

"No, Aunt May," answered Nesta, "I only wasted a chance of drowning. Nothing as precious as money. I pulled him out of the river. He fell in, trying to save another dog from being drowned. I don't know why I bothered to fish him out. But I did, and he seems to think he belongs to me. I didn't ask him here. He came."

"But you're never going to keep him? Why, a great big brute like that eats as much as——"

"As the people who forget to come and see us since we went broke? Perhaps he does. But he's ever so much more welcome to it. I never thought about keeping him, till you spoke of it. But I *am* going to. If he'll stay. . . . Did you ever read 'Les Voyages de M. Perichon'? But you wouldn't be likely to. It's French. And everything French is immoral. It's a story of a man whose life was saved and who got sick to death of being grateful to the hero who had saved him. He grew to hating his rescuer. Then he saved some one else's life—or he thought he did—and he became so fond of this second fellow that he gave him his daughter. He——"

"How silly!"

"Yes," agreed Nesta. "Isn't it? Because it's true psychology. I think people are always gratefuller to those

they give everything to than to the people who give everything to them. Anyway, an hour ago I wouldn't have taken
a dog for a gift. I never felt any sort of interest in dogs.
But—well, for a moment or two this collie and I were
in pretty real danger together. And if it hadn't been for
me he'd be floating down the river now, under the ice.
I'm—I'm going to keep him, Aunt May. I like him. He's
so different from people."

For the first time in a long year Nesta Breen found
something to be keenly and non-morbidly interested in.
Despite herself, she realized she had a real affection for
the great dog she had saved. In her gross ignorance of
canine nature, the collie's quickness of brain astounded
her.

For example, she had no way of guessing his name.
After trying in vain to make him show recognition of such
hackneyed appellations as Towser and Tige and Rover
and the like, she named him anew. She chose "March,"
from the month wherein she met him.

Then, studiously, she set to work to teach him the new
name, expecting to have weeks of time and labor in making him respond to it. To her amaze, he learned it in less
than a day.

In like manner he picked up with bewildering speed
and much enjoyment every simple thing she tried to teach
him. Already, she found, he had been trained as a house
dog, and to lie down and to shake hands and to perform
other ordinary feats. He was wise and gentle and unob-
trusive; eagerly playful when she was in the mood to
romp with him, yet ready to lie quiet for hours at her
feet while she read or wrote or mused.

A dog man would have classified March merely as a well-trained collie of high type, with all a true collie's brain and pluck and gentleness and humor. But to Nesta he seemed the embodiment of everything marvelous. Her first careless fondness for him grew to a devotion. He was her inseparable comrade, indoors and out; her guard and chum.

The lonely girl's heart expanded under his companionship. Her hard-acquired youthful bitterness softened strangely under March's splendid normalcy. She ceased to brood so morbidly over her misfortunes.

Once, in a fit of ill-temper, she struck March sharply across the head. He did not cringe, but looked at her with a grieved amazement that cut her to the heart. Nor did he hold grudge for the unjust blow. Nesta wondered afresh at the boundless fund of forgiveness that is part of a dog's nature—and for which he has such ceaseless and pitiful need in this world of wrath-swift humans.

But when a loafer on the highroad kicked at March as he and Nesta were coming home from a springtime tramp through the hills, the collie flung himself at the man in such fury that Nesta could scarce restrain him from revenging the affront by tearing out his assailant's throat. Remembering his reception of her own unmerited blow, the girl marveled afresh and with a strange sense of shame.

Unwittingly, it was she and not March who was receiving an education during these pleasant months of companionship. If she was able to teach the dog, clumsily, a few new accomplishments, he was teaching her many far more worthwhile lessons which she did not even know she was absorbing.

One morning in early summer Nesta and March were swinging along the River Road, the dog trotting some yards ahead. A cloud of dust heralded a motor-car chugging laboriously toward them down the stretch of unsurfaced byway.

As always, the sight of the distant car made March drop back to his mistress's side. Once or twice, during their first walks together, she had summoned him back to her, on the approach of a car, lest he be run down. But almost at once he had learned to come back without command when a car hove in view.

This morning Nesta drew to one side of the road to avoid the oncoming motor's dust. The dog ran back to her in the wayside grass, standing statue-like beside her. The car lurched onward over rut and bulge. It was passing the girl and the collie when its passenger, a stout man on the rear seat, called to the chauffeur to stop. By the time the machine was at a standstill he had jumped out onto the road and was hurrying back toward Nesta.

At the hasty approach, March moved forward and stood alertly between his mistress and the stranger. The dog made no overt move to attack, but his hackles bristled ever so slightly, and his deep-set eyes were stern and questioning as they followed the intruder's advance.

A single glance told Nesta that the stout man was nobody she knew. So, with only the mildest curiosity she awaited him. But as he came closer, March growled softly, far down in his throat, and took a warning step forward.

The man stopped with ludicrous suddenness. Apparently he was enough of a dog expert to read the quiet menace aright. He stood there, in silence, for an instant, studying every line and aspect of the collie. Then, lifting his hat in a gesture which held only the most rudimentary civility, he demanded of Nesta:

"What dog is that?"

"It is my dog," she made answer, voice and eyes level, in spite of a sinking in her heart.

For months she had had an undefined fear lest March's owner might some day appear and claim him. It seemed impossible that the possessor of such a marvelous chum would not scour the whole world in search of him. But as time went on and nobody declared ownership, her fears had lightened. Now in a rush they crowded back upon her.

"He is mine," she repeated, turning away as if to continue her walk.

But the man spoke again, this time with still less semblance of civility.

"One minute, please," he said, stepping after her, and then halting with great suddenness as March spun about and faced him with a more pronounced growl and a show of white eyeteeth. "Late last winter, I was driving along this road, on my way home from New Haven. We had a blowout. Vile road, then, as it is now. I left a valuable collie dog in the tonneau while I got out to help my chauffeur. The dog slipped his collar and jumped out after me. I didn't see him do it, but I found the collar and leash when I got aboard. I suppose he wandered off and you found him. Yes, that's the dog."

For a panicky moment, Nesta was tempted to turn and

228

fun, calling March after her. But she stood her ground, the flush of exercise dying from her face, yet her eyes and mouth as steady as ever.

"You are mistaken," she said, carelessly. "This is my dog. I am sorry you lost yours, but ——"

"He wasn't mine," corrected the stout man. "If he had been, he wouldn't have run away from me. I wouldn't have had to tie him in the car. That kind of collie sticks by his master. He ——"

"If you don't even claim he is yours ——" began Nesta, in polite contempt, as she made as though to turn away once more, "I ——"

"He belongs to a cousin of mine," said the man. "My cousin bought him from an English kennel; and had him sent to a handler, to take on a circuit of the American shows. He had won his championship in England before he came to this country. Won it at eighteen months. He completed his American championship at the New Haven show, this year. He is International Champion Harrow-gate Peerless. His kennel name is 'Squire.' My cousin paid thirty-five hundred dollars for him in England. His American championship makes him worth an easy five thousand dollars. This dog here is one of the greatest collies on either side of the Atlantic. He ——"

"This dog of mine?" queried Nesta, innocently. "I'm glad you like him. But I thought you were talking about an English collie that ——"

"Same dog!" snapped the man, annoyedly. "I can take oath to that. I could swear to him, among a thousand. I saw him at the Madison Square Garden show—West-minster, you know—in February, and again at New

Haven. I made a close study of him, both times. My cousin had to go to Europe, the morning of the New Haven show. So he asked me to take charge of his dog after the show, and bring him home. My cousin lives at Paignton, about a mile from me. About five miles from here. I got the dog from the handler and tied him in my car. I've told you how I lost him. Pretty position I was in when my cousin got back to America and found I'd let his thirty-five-hundred-dollar dog get away! I've advertised all over and hired a dog detective and hunted everywhere. And now here I blunder on him by sheer good luck! I——"

"You seem determined to think—or to pretend to think —that this is your dog," interposed Nesta, a trifle wearily. "I have told you he is mine. I think that is all. Come, March!"

"*Squire!*" called the man.

At sound of the name, March quivered and turned about.

"March!" said Nesta, softly.

Instantly the collie wheeled and ran to her, thrusting his nose into her hand and wagging his great plume of a tail.

"You see," commented Nesta, as she moved off.

"I see!" retorted the man, hotly. "I see he recognized his kennel name when I spoke it. He ——"

"You saw he answered the name of 'March,'" corrected the girl, with amused tolerance. "If he showed interest when you called him, it was because you stepped forward as you spoke. I really wouldn't advise your coming any nearer, Mr.—Mr. ——"

"My name is Vanden," supplemented the man as she hesitated. "I'm acting in this for my cousin, Mr. Derek Royce. This is his dog. And," stubbornly, "I saw he recognized his name of 'Squire.' Not that I needed any more proof. I know every inch of him. There are a hundred collie-fanciers who saw him at his American shows and who can swear to him. I suggest you give him to me and save trouble."

Nesta did not reply. The last part of Vanden's speech had gone unheard. Her attention had stopped short and jarringly at Derek Royce's name. She stared stupidly at the stout man. He repeated, more truculently:

"I suggest you save yourself trouble by giving him to me at once."

"Certainly!" retorted Nesta, a gust of rage sweeping away her momentary daze. "Certainly. If you want him, take him. *March!*"

At the anger and appeal in her voice, the big collie stiffened. Facing Vanden, he crouched slightly, his lips upturned from his white tusks, his eyes ablaze, his mighty body tensed as for a spring. At the mute threat, Vanden took a hasty backward step, his hands raised instinctively to protect his throat. Nesta laughed in nervous excitement.

"If he's yours or your precious cousin's," she taunted, shrilly, "take him! If I give the word, he'll take *you*! Dog-stealing isn't a safe outdoor sport, when March happens to be the dog. If you want him, take him. This is the last time I shall give you the chance to. And if you follow me or try to get him, I'll say only one more word to *him*.

That word will be enough. Now, do you want him or don't you?"

Vanden looked worriedly at the dog. March had begun to move stealthily toward him, in a sinuous motion that carried a world of menace.

"Call him back!" said the man, thickly.

"Good!" assented Nesta. "Come, March!"

She walked away, fast, March bounding along beside her. Vanden stared long and ragingly after the two. Then he turned upon his chauffeur.

"Drive me to the post-office," he commanded, "and then to one or two of the shops. It ought to be easy to find who she is and where she lives. There can't be two women in this dump of a suburb, with such a dog. Anyone ought to be able to tell me who——"

"I can tell you, sir," said the chauffeur, "and save you all that trouble. She's Miss Ernesta Breen. Lives down on the Wyckoff turnpike, about two miles south. Used to live up on Park Terrace, till her father died. Folks thought her dad was worth all the cash in the Treasury. But he died just about flat broke. She and her aunt went down to a cheap bungalow of his, to live. They——"

"How in blazes d'you know all that?" asked Vanden, in surprise.

"I knew it when I drove for Mr. Royce," answered the chauffeur, "before I came to work for you, last autumn. He used to be at her house a lot of times when she lived up on the Terrace. I only drove him there once after she moved down to the Wyckoff pike. He——"

"H'm!" mused Vanden, his face clearing. "That ought

to make it easier. Let him go there, himself, and get his dog. It's past *me*. I'll tell him about it when I go home."

Nesta was hurrying on with March, planning an elaborate detour whereby she might reach her bungalow without being trailed by Vanden. Yet, even as she made the detour, she realized its futility. The man could find out who she was. Anyone in the neighborhood could tell him. She and her magnificent dog were familiar sights on the roads and in shops.

She winked hard, to keep back the tears. For the first time, she realized how dear the collie had become to her and how much of her lonely and loveless and embittered life he had come to fill. She had no doubt at all that Vanden had spoken the truth about him. Nor did it surprise her to hear that he was one of the most famous and high-priced collies in America. Always she had known he was the most wonderful and lovable dog alive.

But she knew, also, that Derek Royce would have no trouble at all in proving possession. He would take away this chum of hers, even as once before he had taken away all that made her life worth while.

She could visualize the stout man's losing of March, back there in the late winter. She could see the collie waxing restless at being tied in a car and among strangers; his slipping of the irksome collar during the long wait while the tire blowout was repaired; his noiseless spring to the ground and his wandering aimlessly down the road until he chanced to see the drowning hound puppy.

It was all as clear as day; just as this new development was as merciless as the rest of life.

"March," she said, presently, talking as ever to the

collie as if to a fellow-human—"March, they're going to try to take you away from me. They shan't have you! *They shan't have you!* Do you hear, March? You belong to *me.* I gambled with death for you and you're the only friend who never went back on me. Nobody's going to get you away from me, March. We'll fight this out, together, you and I."

Her words meant nothing to the collie, save the frequent repetition of his own name. But her voice told him she was wretchedly unhappy. Whining under his breath, he nuzzled her hand and laid his head against it, peering up worriedly into her sorrowing face. There was comfort in his eager sympathy. She petted his classic head and buried her little hand confidingly in his ruff.

"They're not going to take you from me, March," she repeated, this time with a new hope. "I don't know how I'm going to prevent it, but I *am.* It would be bad enough if you were going to a stranger, but you'll be going to the most despicable man who ever lived, March. He made me think he cared for me, once. And he made me think I cared for him. We weren't engaged, March, but I was sure we were going to be. Then Dad died and all the world fell down around my head. And when I crawled out of the wreckage, March, I was in the bungalow, with just enough to keep alive on.

"He came to see me there. Just once. That was all. He never came again. I don't even know why he came there that once, March, unless it was to quarrel horribly with me and to make that an excuse for never coming near me again. But he let me see he had no use for me, now that I hadn't any money or any position or any friends. He was just like all the rest of the people I had known. Only, they hadn't pretended to care for me, as he had. No, March, you're *not* going to him! I'd sooner shoot you. We'll fight this out, we two."

The fight began sooner than Nesta feared. As she and March were walking through the bungalow's patch of rose-garden, after lunch, a car stopped at the gate. Nesta looked up, nervous and apprehensive. Derek Royce was coming across the tiny lawn toward her. Already he had cut off her retreat to the house.

Her hand on March's ruff, she faced him, white, deadly, resolute. She was braced for anything.

"How are you?" Royce greeted her, seeming not to see that she ignored his half-extended hand; then speaking to the dog with a cheery: "Hello, Squire, old boy!"

This time March did not stiffen nor curl his upper lip as when Vanden had approached him. Instead, he viewed Derek with friendly courtesy, waving his tail in salutation. True, he did not seem overjoyed or excited at encountering his long-lost master. Yet he was politely glad at the meeting.

Little as he had seen of Royce during the time the collie had spent at the handler's, yet March had come to like him—to like him at least well enough to bear him in pleasant memory for the several months since they had met.

March's gratitude and devotion had gone out in a rush to the girl who had saved his life. She was his goddess, his one object of worship. Yet he was willing to be civil to this former acquaintance of his.

Nesta saw his amicable greeting of the loathed Derek.

235

Her heart sank within her. Her miserable gaze strayed to the car at the gate. In the tonneau lounged Vanden, his thick fingers idly toying with a dog collar and leash. The action, and all it implied, set the girl's temper ablaze.

"My cousin told me he met you and Squire on the River Road this morning," Royce was saying, "so I ran over to see if the dog was really the one I lost."

"He isn't," Nesta made answer, her voice curiously muffled. "He is *my* dog. And you aren't going to take him away from me."

For an instant Royce did not reply. He was looking from the girl to the collie. March had discovered a highly dramatic hop-toad in the grass of the rose-garden. With pricked ears and head on one side, he was following gravely the toad's frightened hops. Then, with abrupt change of theme, Derek said:

"When I went away from here, the last time, I told myself I should never come near you again. I didn't care to go through another such evening or hear things said to me that you said then. I've spent a solid year trying to forget them and to forget you. Then, today, when I found a legitimate excuse to bring me back, I came to you as fast as I could. I'm afraid I am a rather poor apology for a grown man."

"I am afraid that is the kindest thing you can say of yourself," she returned, adding, "And now, will you please go?"

"No," refused Derek, "not quite yet, if you don't mind. I have been doing a good deal of wondering, this past year—especially at night. Somehow, the nights are so much longer than they used to be. Then, yesterday, in my woods, I found a sparrow that had gotten caught by one wing in a mesh of vine-tendrils. He was half dead with pain and fright. I set him loose. But as soon as I touched him he pecked furiously at my hand. I understood why. He was so terrified and harrowed that he thought the whole universe was his enemy. He——"

"I am not interested in ornithology," she intervened, "or in poetic speculations as to the heart-throbs of sparrows. Will you please——?"

"That made me wonder if I hadn't found the key to something else," pursued Royce, not heeding the snub nor indeed seeming to hear it. "I remembered how bitter you were when a crowd of worthless parasites dropped you, after your—your misfortune—and how you got to looking morbidly for slights, even when there were no slights to find. You were sick with grief over your father's death, and you were incredulously angry over the way some few toadies had treated you afterward. And you got to thinking the whole universe was like those toadies. So——"

"May I ask you once more to——?"

"No, not yet. I called here when things were at their worst and when you were most on the lookout for slights. You blazed out about some mighty good friends of mine who weren't in that toady category at all. I defended them, I remember. It made you still angrier. You turned on me and hinted that perhaps *I* might care to drop away, too, since I could stand up so eagerly for other people who did. It riled me to have you think such a thing about me. That started our silly red-hot quarrel. I suppose I said a lot of rotten things, and I know you said things that made me vow I'd never see you again. . . . The sparrow pecked at my hand when I was saving it from the vine tendril. I wasn't angry at the sparrow, because I understood what it must be suffering. Then I got to wondering how I had been such a fool as not to understand why you ——"

From the gateway was issuing a most prodigious racket.

March had followed the erratically hopping toad across the grass to the gate, where the toad ended the merry chase by slipping into a hole under a post. Vanden, from the tonneau, had viewed with keen interest the slow approach of the collie.

Into the stout man's brain seeped a really brilliant idea. He saw his cousin, apparently arguing the dog's possession with the flushed-faced and indignant Nesta. How simple to end the whole dispute by lifting the collie into the tonneau and bidding the chauffeur drive off! Royce could get a taxi from the village station to take him home. On his arrival he would find his recovered prize dog securely fastened in his kennels. Possession was nine points of the law.

While March was engrossed with his toad-trailing, Vanden got to the ground, collar and leash in hand. With great swiftness for so large a man, he swooped down on March from behind; seizing him with one hand by the nape of the neck, and lifting him bodily over the fence.

Skillful was his grip, and it rendered the thunderously growling dog impotent to bite or to escape. It was this growling that attracted the notice of Royce and Nesta. By common consent they started for the gate at a run. Vanden heaved the dog aloft to thrust him into the tonneau. The man's toe stubbed against the corner of the gatepost, throwing him off balance. He thrust out both arms, instinctively, to right himself. The collie tore free from the loosening fingers.

Scarce had March touched ground when he was at the man who had sought so roughly to kidnap him. He hurled himself roaringly at Vanden. The latter, his balance still uncertain, leaped back to avoid the onslaught. He slipped and fell with a crash on his back in the roadside ditch.

Like a furry avalanche March was after him. For an instant Vanden lay helpless; his fat throat exposed to the ravening jaws. Nesta, running at top speed, essayed to call off the avenging brute. But horror sanded her throat to dumbness.

Then, almost in mid-air, the great dog checked his charge. He halted and stood irresolute. His foe was down and no longer could defend himself. March ceased his attack on an enemy who had been rendered impotent and prostrate. He stood gazing down at the dizzy Vanden, making no move to renew the charge. Vanden had the sense to lie where he was and to say no word. He was a veteran dog man and he knew collie nature.

"Good sportsman, Squire!" applauded Royce, vaulting the fence and catching the unresisting dog by the ruff. "Good *clean* sportsman! You're too clean to punish him when he's down and out. Get up!" he went on, far less approvingly, to his cousin. "Get up and climb back into the car. Why on earth did you do such an abominable thing?"

"And now," said Nesta, trying to speak calmly, "will you please let go of my dog and go away? I ——"

"*Her* dog?" snorted Vanden, scrambling back into the

safety of the car. "*Her* dog? We can get a hundred reliable witnesses to prove ———"

"Shut up!" ordered Royce. "We can't do anything of the kind. From your description, I thought maybe this dog might be Squire—my Champion Harrowgate Peerless. That's why I came here. Well, I came on a wild-goose chase. I didn't get—I didn't get *anything* I came for. The dog looks a bit like Squire, but it isn't Squire. I never saw this dog before. So ———"

"You're crazy!" shouted his cousin, aghast. "Why, *I* saw Squire time and again! I can swear to him."

"He was my own dog, and I saw him much oftener than you did," declared Royce, "and I can testify this isn't the dog. We've made fools of ourselves by coming here after him. I never saw this dog before, I tell you. Miss Breen, will you try to forgive my intrusion if I promise never to repeat it? I congratulate you on owning such a fine collie. . . . Good-by."

He got into the car, ignoring his madly sputtering cousin and forbearing to meet Nesta's wide-staring eyes. As the chauffeur made ready to start, Derek heard a stifled little voice begging, tremulously:

"Will—will you please come back here—just a minute?"

Unbelievingly Derek stared down at her. Then, drawing his breath in a quick gasp, he was on the ground and following her tremblingly into the garden. As soon as they were out of earshot from the car, Nesta turned to face the voicelessly eager man.

"Take him!" she said, in the same muffled little voice, her eyes on March, who was standing protectively beside her. "He's your dog. You lied. But it—it was a beautiful lie. I lied, too, when I said he was mine. And it was a disgusting lie. You—you and March—I mean, Squire—you two aren't going to be the only clean sportsmen in the world. I've—I've been learning something— from *both* of you."

"He belongs to you," cried Royce, his face alight with a wondering hope. "I won't take him—without *you*. I ——"

"Derek Royce!" sobbed the girl, her hands tight clasped in his, but her tear-misted eyes focusing on the fat figure in the car. "Derek Royce, did anyone ever tell you—you have the most ATROCIOUS taste in cousins?"

XII

* *

HIS COLLIE

* *

Anyone who cares for action pictures—for the type of "chase scenes" so dear to cinema pioneers—would have been mildly thrilled at the fast-moving procession which whizzed its way across the Brayle lawn that afternoon.

Well in the lead—but with his lead ever decreasing—flapped and flew and ran and squawked a Rhode Island Red rooster. Large and magnificent was he, and ordinarily of a pompous trend. He had won a first prize at the Madison Square Garden poultry show a few months earlier. He had won award after award at lesser shows.

Just now his dignity had fled to the winds; and he was fleeing well-nigh as fast—but not quite fast enough.

Behind him across the green lawn flashed a red-gold streak of incredible swiftness, which resolved itself into a flamingly vivid, beautiful young collie dog. The dog was galloping gaily along, stomach to earth, plumed tail outflung. His jaws were wide and anticipatory.

A few rods behind the collie, and losing ground on the

dog even faster than the latter was gaining it on the luck-less rooster, rushed a thirteen-year-old boy in khaki.

Close behind the boy came puffing an obese giant. He brandished a malacca cane. Far to the rear and farther outclassed in the matter of speed ran a slender middle-aged woman, who was wasting breath she could not spare in appeals to the man.

Broad was the lawn. The race continued from the vine-girt veranda at one end of it almost to the high-road at the farther end. Then, in a light-swift series of fate-swats came the climax.

The rooster had all but reached the high privet hedge that fenced the Brayle lawn from the road. He gathered himself for the fluttering rise which should carry him over the privet to safety. But he was a fraction of a second too late.

As the rooster left ground, the young flame-colored collie caught up with him. In mid-flight the dog's double row of white teeth snapped sharply together. The rooster tumbled against the privet, his head bitten neatly off by that single sideways slash of the dog's lupine jaws.

Having won the race, the collie paid no further heed to his victim, but turned to meet the khaki-clad boy who was bearing down on him. From the very outset of the chase the lad had not ceased to yell "Morven!" at every jump. But Morven was still too young and too slightly trained to forego the joys of chicken-catching merely be-cause his loved young master was shrieking to him.

Once the collie had glanced over his galloping shoulder at sound of his name. But he had seen Manfred Brayle following him in a semblance of eager participation in the pursuit. Indeed, farther behind were Manfred's father and mother, also appearing to share his zest in catching up with the rooster. Deeming that the multiple shouts were a form of encouragement, Morven had put on all the speed his lithe young body could master. And at the last he had run down his prey.

He turned to receive the applause his fine performance had merited. Mouth agrin and dark eyes bright with mischief and tail awag, he ran up to Manfred. But even as he ran his quick collie sensitiveness told him something was wrong. These people—his master and his master's parents—did not have the look of folk who are preparing an ovation. The thick malacca cane Mr. Brayle was swinging aloft carried with it a vague menace to the dog that never yet had been struck.

It was Morven's first opportunity to catch a chicken. During the six months he had been at Braylewold he had spent some time, now and then, in strolling around the high wire inclosure wherein were lodged the prize-winning Rhode Island Reds that were the joy of Mr. Brayle's heart. Morven bore them no malice. But they chanced to be the only chickens he had seen in his own year and a half of life. They interested him.

Then, this afternoon, as he had been lying on the veranda at Manfred's feet, while Mr. Brayle read aloud, the rooster had worked a way through a torn spot in the wire pen and had come stalking around the side of the house. Morven had trotted over to investigate the fowl at closer quarters, animated only by the whimsical curiosity that is a collie's birthright.

The rooster had not awaited his coming, but had

squawked and had started to run away. Playfully Morven had given chase, even as the average dog will follow any one or anything that runs. The rooster had put on speed and had helped himself along by flying.

Back in the atavistic mists at the base of Morven's brain had wakened age-old memories of wild fowl that fled thus from his wolf ancestors and the glad thrill of the pursuit —a pursuit on whose success depended the hungry hunter's dinner.

Through no volition of his own, the collie dashed after. Ancestry told him where and how to seize the bird. To him it was a deliriously merry game. He was glad to see his human friends had condescended to take so active if so futile a part in it.

But now a doubt sprang into his heart, and the gay mischief died out of his deep-set eyes, to be replaced by perplexity.

Manfred Brayle caught his dog by the ruff and flung himself in front of the wondering collie. Quick as was the boy, he was barely in time. For his father was upon them both, stick poised.

Mr. Brayle did not waste words. All the indignation in his soul found vent in a crashing blow he aimed at the chicken-slaying Morven.

Such a blow might well have broken the dog's back, for the malacca cane's wielder was a giant in bulk and in strength, and his arm was goaded to greater force by the wanton killing of a rooster that had been his brag and his delight at a dozen poultry shows.

Down whirled the cane. But it found a mark other than Brayle had planned.

Manfred had swung the collie behind him, but had had no time to get himself out of the stick's way. The malacca smote the boy glancingly, missing his head and face, but striking his left shoulder with a force that spun him half-way around and knocked him to his knees.

His mother cried out in terrified appeal. But the collie wasted no time or effort in vocalization. Silent, terrible, he launched himself at the giant who had struck his adored young master.

Manfred's grip on the dog's ruff was torn loose by that savage leap, yet it was strong enough to deflect Morven's charge. The ravening jaws missed Brayle's fat throat and merely raked the breast of his silken Palm Beach suit, rending it from lapel to hem.

Brayle gurgled with fury and struck again at the dog. But once more Manfred had caught the collie by the ruff and shoved him aside. The boy was sick with pain from the slantwise shoulder-blow. But, without waiting to scramble to his feet, he had thrust his raging collie chum free from the downward swishing path of the cane.

This time the stick missed both boy and dog, but its ferrule banked against a stone with such force as to crack the shiny malacca from end to end. It was Brayle's favorite cane.

Before the angry man could do more than drop the useless stick and catch hold of his own numbed and tingling arm, his wife had reached the group and had thrust herself fearlessly between her purple and infuriated husband and the snarling Morven and the sick-white boy.

Manfred had regained his grip on the dog's ruff. But there was no need for restraining Morven now. The high-

246

bred collie would not for his life's sake have attacked Mrs. Brayle or any other woman. Since she had come between him and the man who needed punishment so direfully, and since Manfred was yanking him back from the task of avenging, there seemed no further use to struggle and to growl.

"Dear!" Mrs. Brayle was panting. "Oh, my *dear*! What are you doing? You might have killed him. He ——"

"Killed him?" sputtered Brayle, misunderstanding her fear for the stricken boy and glaring at Morven. "*Killed* him? That's what I'm going to do. The miserable brute has killed my best rooster—the best Rhode Island Red ever bred in this state! I ——"

"I'll pay for the rooster," pleaded Manfred, getting dazedly to his feet, but still keeping between his enraged father and the collie. "And I'll tie him around Morven's neck for a couple of days. That'll cure Morven forever of chasing chickens. He'll never do it again. He didn't mean any harm, Dad. He ——"

"Be quiet!" stormed Brayle. "The cur will never kill another chicken. You're right about that part of it. Because I'm going to shoot him myself. I'm going to do it as soon as I can get to the house and load my pistol. Take him to the stables; I'll be there in three minutes."

"*Dad!*" pleaded Manfred, wildly, as he sought to remember he was thirteen and a Boy Scout and that tears were babyish. "Dad! You'd never do *that*! Why—why he's my chum and—and everything—and I bought him with the money I'd saved myself and with Uncle Jim's birthday check. And I've taught him to shake hands and lie down and everything, Dad! And he's the best pal any one ever

247

had. Oh, Dad, he didn't *mean* any harm! *Please* don't ——"

"Be quiet!" ordered his father again, his face losing its purplish loose-lipped look and setting in the bone-gray pallor of deep-rooted anger. "Take him to the stables, as I told you—unless you want a flogging, too. Wait! It isn't on the free list to own a mutt that kills things better than himself. Take him to the stables and tie him there. Then go to my bedroom and get my pistol and the box of cartridges from my top chiffonier drawer, and bring them to me on the porch. That's the least you can do to atone for your filthy dog's mischief. Go! *Quick!*"

The boy was staring, panting and unbelieving, up at the wrathful man. It was his mother who intervened. No longer was she crying; suddenly she had grown very calm. Nor did her voice tremble as she spoke to her suffering boy.

"Do as father says, Manfred," she bade him. "Take Morven to the stables and tie him there. Then go and get the pistol and bring it down to the veranda. Go, dear."

Her voice was quiet, as always it was when she was terribly in earnest. Somehow, now, it impressed Manfred more than did Brayle's mouthed thunderings. They were both against him—against him and his dear dog. There was no hope. There was no appeal.

Manfred tightened his grasp on Morven's ruff. Slowly, and still in pain from the blow, he moved away toward the house and the stables behind it.

"No tampering with the cartridges, either!" shouted his father after him. "I shall look at them carefully, remember. Walk faster."

Manfred did not reply. Neither did he quicken his slow pace. Brayle made as though to take a step after him, fists clenched, but his wife's hand was on the man's arm.

"Harry," she said, in that same curiously quiet voice, "you are not going to bully him into hurrying; when he thinks every step brings his beloved dog nearer to death. Let him alone. And you are not going to shoot his dog, either, Harry. Understand that, please. *You are not going to kill him.*"

The fuming man checked his impulsive step toward his departing son and the collie. There was no pleading in his wife's steady voice; no fear, no argument. She spoke with a soft firmness that splashed against his white-hot fury like flung ice-water. Muttering, grumbling, he stared down at her set little face. Before he could answer her she continued in the same measured steadiness:

"When you are yourself, you are the splendidest man in the whole world, Harry. But when you get into one of these wild-beast rages of yours you are unspeakable. I have told you that before. At such times you ought to be in a padded cell and not left at large to torture people who can't defend themselves against you. Were you too blind angry to know that you knocked Manfred down with that horrible cane of yours? If it had struck him full on the head, it would have fractured his skull."

"He—I didn't—he got in the way——"

"Yes," went on the woman, a tinge of iced steel in her soft voice, "he got in the way. Why? To save his dog from being beaten to death with that club. He risked his own life—yes, his *life*, Harry—to save an animal that depended

249

on him for safety. If he hadn't done it, by this time the dog would be lying here screaming his life out with a crushed backbone. He———"

"Serve the brute right!" flared Brayle. "He———"

"Yes, I know. He followed the instincts of so many high-spirited young animals. He chased a chicken and killed it. That is how his ancestors in the forests kept from starving. Morven had never been told to leave the chickens alone. He had never had a chance to learn they mustn't be killed. The time he ran down that woodchuck and killed it after a hard fight, you patted him and you praised him. How was he to know the difference?"

"He———"

"Manfred cares more for that dog than for anything else in the world except you and me, Harry. If you had killed Morven, what memory of you would the boy have? Always he would think of you as the tyrant who battered his helpless chum to death. No matter how much you might have tried to make up to him for it, that memory would last out his whole life. He wouldn't think of you after you're gone, as the kind and friendly father that you are, most of the time. He would remember you as a howling and purple maniac, hammering and trampling his precious little dog to a pulp.

"And all for what? Because the puppy followed his instincts. Because you had praised him for killing a wood-chuck that had been doing damage to the vegetable-garden, and because he supposed he would get the same kind of praise for killing this other strange creature. Is that the kind of justice you want Manfred to grow up to believe in—the justice of brute strength and cruelty? Is it?"

Brayle's face was working. With all his might he sought to retain his indignation at the slayer of his prize fowl. But, now that sanity began to seep back, he found himself recalling the boy's face as the swishing cane blow had sent him to his knees—the writhen lips that would utter no sound of pain; the tight-controlled voice that begged for the life of his dog pal—the devotion to his imperiled collie, which banished all thoughts of his own sharply hurt shoulder.

"You're right!" grunted Brayle, in sulky surrender. "But ——"

"But Manfred is waiting at the house now in worse agony of spirit than any grown-up could know. He is waiting for the executioner to come and murder his pet— the executioner who made him take part in the killing by getting out the pistol and cartridges for it. That last was a bit of *finesse* almost worthy of an Apache torturer, Harry. Are you going on with the execution? I have said all I am going to say. If I haven't been able to save him from you, and if I haven't been able to save *you* from the insane cruelty that you'll regret so bitterly and so uselessly, then there's nothing more I can do. Well?"

"You're right," muttered Brayle sheepishly. "You're right—as you've got a way of being. I'll go up and tell him the execution is off. Poor kid!" he added, quickening his pace. "He must be feeling rotten unhappy. I'll go and put him out of his worry."

As an amendment to this idea, he raised his voice and

made the afternoon silences re-echo with his son's name. But there was no reply.

Manfred went with lagging feet toward the stables. His heart was dead. No longer was he holding Morven's ruff. The collie was padding happily along at his side, now and then trying to comfort his master's misery by shoving his nose against the boy's tight-gripped fists and by looking worriedly up into the blankly miserable face.

At last—a long last—Manfred spoke.

"He isn't going to shoot you," he said, speaking to the collie as to another human. "He isn't going to shoot you. And there's only one way to keep him from doing it. I've figured it all out. If you stay here, I can't stop him from killing you. And you won't go away without me. I know that. Besides, I don't want to stay here with two people who are mean enough to want you to die. I guess there's only one thing to do. And we'll have to do it on the jump."

The dog whined, troubled at the misery in his master's dead voice.

"Besides," added Manfred, "you'd never stand aside and see *me* killed, Morven, old boy. Why, down there, just now, when dad whaled me, you jumped in to stop him from it and to try to bite him. You knew you wouldn't have a chance against him. But you did it all the same. Well, I'd be a pretty poor sportsman if I didn't do as much for you, wouldn't I?"

He was walking faster now. Rounding the side of the house, he went in at a rear door and ran up to his own room, Morven trotting at his heels. In a closet hung his Boy Scout camping kit, ready for a week's hike that was scheduled for the following month. Manfred got it down and slung it over his shoulders. Then he went to his bureau and took out a battered little tin box. It contained the cash he had saved for his "salt" during the proposed hike and his monthly allowance, just received, and a stray bill or two that he had tucked away during the six months since he had used up all his previous savings in the purchase of Morven.

Stuffing the money in a pocket of his khaki trousers, he scribbled on an envelope-back with a pencil:

Morven isn't going to get shot. He and I are going away so you can't kill him.

This he stuck in his bureau looking-glass, where his mother found it an hour later.

Downstairs and out of the house the boy hurried with his dog. As they made their top-speed way across the meadow behind the stables, Manfred heard his father's voice shouting his name. He ran the faster.

Like many another Boy Scout, the runaway had learned to think and to plan for himself. Thus, he was not running blindly from home, with no prospect of preventing his parents or the local police from overhauling him before night. His scheme was worked out.

With other boys of the neighborhood he loved to wander through the mile-distant train-yards, and even to hide in unfastened box-cars for short stolen rides up the line. He had a more than rudimentary knowledge of freight-train routes and habits, and he knew on which tracks the soon-to-depart freights were wont to stand. He had learned, too, with all a boy's elusiveness, to dodge yard inspectors and brakemen. Thus, when he reached the yards a little before sunset, it was almost as much by skill as by luck that he was able to make his way undetected to a line of empty box-cars and to find one whose sliding door yielded to his inquiring tug.

Up he wriggled, after a hasty glance in both directions. He snapped his fingers. The collie sprang up through the aperture and landed beside him on the car floor. Then, once more looking along the track, Manfred slid shut the door.

In almost complete darkness he and the highly interested collie stood listening for a possible yell of admonition from a yardman. The car was redolent of onions. Empty sacks littered the dirty floor.

But it was a haven of refuge. And in a few hours at most the train was due to start. It mattered little in what direction it might be bound, so long as it would carry the two refugees far enough afield to escape Brayle's wrath.

Then, just as Manfred groped around for enough sacks to make a comfortable seat, he heard the striking of a match. A corner of the car was illumined. Morven growled. The boy laid a restraining hand on him.

In the lighted corner sat a right disreputable figure—a man who came nearer to the comic-paper conception of a tramp than do most of his road brethren. Scanning the two newcomers, the tramp got to his feet.

"Well, well, well!" he chuckled huskily as he touched the match fire to a bit of candle from the bundle beside him. "Our young hero is runnin' away to sea, ain't he? Took the faithful purp along, to make him into an old sea-dog. Well, well!"

He advanced. Again Morven growled. The collie did not like the look or the scent of this derelict. Collies have reduced snobbery to a fine art. They have scant fondness or respect for ill-dressed strangers. Manfred stood his ground. Two boys of his acquaintance had met a tramp during a stolen box-car ride and had been robbed of every penny they had with them. He remembered laughing at their hard-luck story of the experience.

"Now, sonny," resumed the tramp, slouching forward, "if you're runnin' away to sea, you want to do it right. They won't take you aboard if you've got cash in your clothes. So shell it out. Or do you want I should frisk your pockets for it?"

Young as he was, Manfred had sense enough to know that his sole chance of staying alive and of keeping his dog alive, until he should land a job of some kind, consisted in the wise hoarding of his scanty stock of money.

Perhaps if he had had only himself to consider he might not have dared to defy this grown man at whose mercy he seemed to be. But the throaty growl of his dog and the tensing of Morven's shoulder muscles under his fingers gave him his inspiration.

From his pocket, with his free hand, he drew his scout knife. With his teeth he opened its wide blade, his other hand still gripping Morven.

"At just one word from me," he said fiercely, giving back not a single step, "my dog will be at your throat. While you're busy with him, I'll do *my* share with this knife. I sharpened it yesterday. How about it?"

Grinning, the tramp took another shuffling step.

"Morven!" gasped the boy sharply. "*Watch* him!"

Though he held the ruff, yet there could be no mistaking the snarl of eager response from the collie, nor the straining at his master's detaining hand. Like all his tribe, the tramp was morbidly familiar with canine temper. In this taut and growling collie he read genuine bluffless menace, even more than in the steady eye and steadier knife hand of the boy.

"Aw, take a joke, can't you?" he sniffed, plaintively, as he recoiled toward his corner. "I wouldn't harm you none. I was just foolin'. I ——"

"You're going in the wrong direction," interrupted Manfred. "Back up to the door and then get out of it."

As he spoke, he loosened somewhat his tension on the ruff. Morven lurched forward, teeth bare.

"Out!" repeated Mantred. "I'm not sure I can hold him much longer. Clear out!"

Mumbling lurid undertone blasphemy, the man shambled to the door, found its catch and swung outboard as he slid the panel a foot or two to one side. On the edge of the car's threshold he essayed to bawl a belated defiance. Manfred let go of his dog. Morven sprang for the partly opened doorway. It was slammed hastily in his face. Boy and collie had the box-car to themselves.

It was perhaps an hour later that the train gave a rackety jolt, then another, then began to move. Slowly, rumblingly, the line of box-cars joggled into motion.

From his pocket Manfred Brayle took two dog biscuits that he had snatched from the top of his bureau as he left his room. Giving one to Morven, he began to dig his own strong teeth into the other.

"This is all the supper we're due to get, Morven," he

told the contented dog as they snuggled luxuriously down among the piled sacks. "We'll talk about breakfast when we come to it. There's worse grub than dog biscuit, I guess. They're made of whole wheat and dried beef, Morven. That's good enough food for anyone—when there isn't anything else."

Many hours later Manfred was jounced out of a pleasant sleep by the clattering and bumpy halt of the freight train. He went to the door and opened it wide enough for him to peep out. Day was coming out of the east, and the gray world was chill with the dawn wind. Mist hung over the farther hills. Birds were waking.

"We've been moving pretty steady for nearly twelve hours, Morven," announced the boy. "I figure we've gone as far as we need to. We may not get such a good chance to jump clear again all day. Come on."

Unseen, the lad and the collie slipped to the track side of the switch where the freight was waiting for a mail train to pass. Once clear of the tracks, they struck across a field and came to a road. It was a byway, and Manfred followed it idly. Presently it passed through a mile of woodland, fringing a narrow river. Then it merged into a county road. A mile or more beyond clustered the first houses of a town.

A grocery store at the town's hither edge was opening for the day when a Boy Scout in hiking clothes strode in, followed by a big red-gold collie.

"We're camping back yonder in the woods," the lad told the yawning grocery man, "and I've come for more supplies."

He did not explain that "we" comprised only his dog

THE WAY OF A DOG

and himself. The grocer, well used to the occasional Scout camps in the neighborhood, readily supplied the list of foodstuff dictated to him by his youthful customer. The boy seemed to know just what to buy and was very evidently at home in his commissary rôle. Another visit, this time to a hardware store, furnished a rough cooking outfit and some simple fishing-tackle.

An hour later, in the woods at the river brink, Manfred and his collie were reclining beside the remains of their first campfire, drowsily full of ill-cooked but tolerably wholesome breakfast. Then came an hour or two of busy ax-work among the evergreens and the building of a bough tepee and the arranging of the kit and the supplies beneath its primitive roof.

Followed a fortnight of forest idling. The dog was gloriously happy, the boy fitfully so. When Manfred was fishing or swimming or when he woke on his balsam-bough couch to the glories of a springtime daybreak, he was able almost to convince himself that he was not miserably homesick for his mother. At less exhilarating times the mental effort met with scant success.

He was living by the day and taking no special heed for the morrow. While his carefully rationed supplies should hold out, there was no immediate need to consider the future. He could drift. Day by day the drifting waxed less novel and more heartsick.

But for the loyalty Manfred felt he owed to his threatened dog, the boy would long since have gone home —though he had not the faintest idea how to get there or indeed in what part of the country he might be. Yet, being at an age when youth still believes implicitly in the promises of adults, he was certain his father would keep his infuriated pledge to shoot Morven. And that was something Manfred intended to avert, even if he himself should never again see the home he yearned for.

The collie was a delight to the lonely youngster. Thrown wholly on Manfred's companionship and leading the forest existence that collies love, the dog was daily becoming more and more humanized, more and more a perfect pal to the lad he worshiped. He seemed also to be trying to do his share toward the woodland food-supply. For thrice he came back from reconnoitering trips bearing tenderly in his mouth half-grown young rabbits, which formed a delicious variant on the fish-and-bacon-and-flapjack fare of the camp. A fourth time he spoiled his record as a provider of toothsome edibles by bringing proudly to his master a slain skunk—which had died gamely, fighting with its only available weapons.

Then of a hot morning the last pinch of flour and the last thin slice of bacon were gone. The supplies must be renewed. Manfred sought out the corner of his kit where he had cached his sparse roll of bills.

Field mice had been using the hoard for the lining of their nest. Of the carefully hidden money nothing remained but a handful of shredded and chewed greenish paper.

"Morven," said the boy, solemnly, as the collie nosed the scent of the departed mice and nuzzled carelessly the bits of gnawed currency, "do you know what this means? It means I've got to find a job. I've got exactly eighteen cents in change. That won't buy us anything at all. In the books, when a fellow goes to a store and asks for a job, he gets it.

Then by and by he becomes a partner and he marries his boss's daughter. I don't care much about that last part of it—but it's up to me to get the job."

After a bath and a careful brushing of his forest-marred khaki suit, the boy fared forth with his dog along the county road to the near-by town. He passed the shops where he had bought his outfit and made his way to the more thickly settled business section. At last he stopped before the local bank.

"Wait out here, Morven," he bade his chum. "Maybe they don't let dogs in banks. But in the books it's generally the hard-fisted banker who gives the young hero a job. We'll try here first."

Obediently Morven stretched himself out on the stone pavement close to the bank door while Manfred went bravely in.

Twenty seconds afterward the collie was struggling with useless vehemence to break free from a net that had been cast deftly over his head and body from behind. The town dog-catcher was making his daily rounds. Here was a dog with neither leash nor muzzle—fair game for the man who received one dollar from the local officials for each and every such catch.

After inquiring vainly for the president of the bank and haughtily refusing to state his business to the teller who questioned him, the bronzed little boy in stained khaki was advised by a gray-clad watchman to get out of the bank before he should be thrown out.

Manfred stalked haughtily from the somber building; vowing to come back there when he should have made his fortune in some other job and buy the whole institution just for the pure pleasure of discharging the watchman and the insolent teller.

Then on the outer steps he paused and glanced worriedly about him. Morven was gone.

He whistled. He called the dog till he was hoarse. He made the rounds of all the neighboring streets. Then he began to ask questions. His very first query brought information. A street urchin had seen a big red dog nabbed by the dog-catcher right in the street in front of the bank, and slung into the pound wagon. The same urchin was able to tell him the way to the pound and to add with unctuous relish that it was dandy fun to watch the big iron cageful of dogs soused into the river on Saturday mornings.

Running at crazy speed, caroming off from passers-by, butting blindly into a policeman and then ducking under the bluecoat's detaining arm, Manfred made his way to the pound. The dog-catcher had just returned from his sorry tour. Six new-caught wretched dogs were in the deep wooden pen, where a score of earlier arrivals snapped and growled at them. In the midst of the canine rabble, like a captive monarch among ragamuffins, stood the bewildered Morven.

At Manfred Brayle's shrill shout, the collie cast away his way of perplexed misery and ran to the edge of the pit to welcome his rescuer. Up into the boy's drawn face peered the dog, vibrant with happiness at the reunion. His eyes and his demeanor told far more clearly than any words that he had boundless faith in his master's powers to get him out of this pestilential place.

The look of utter happy trust went clean through Manfred's heart.

"How much do I have to pay to get him loose?" he demanded, shakily, of the bored attendant.

"Two dollars," was the answer. "One for the pound fee, and one for his license."

"I can earn that in just a few days," said Manfred. "If you'll let me take him with me, now, I'll promise to bring you the money the first minute I can get it."

"Lots of kids say that," observed the attendant, walking unconcernedly away. "But the law says if the cash ain't paid in twenty-four hours, the dog has got to be drowned. Get away from the edge of the pen. He's making the rest of 'em all excited, the way he jumps up at you. They're liable to bark for an hour, now—and I got a headache. Chase!"

Two entire dollars! And in twenty-four hours! The boy wandered forth into the pitiless sunshine, dizzy and sick at the prospect and at memory of the collie's look of absolute faith in him. Then came reaction.

He had read of pawnshops. There must be one in this abominable town. If he ran back to camp and gathered all his Boy Scout equipment and his cooking things and his extra shirt and brought them to a pawnbroker here, surely he could get much more than two dollars for them.

Back to the woods he legged it, through the stifling heat, at a dead run, skirting the business section in order to have fewer traffic delays. Breathless and weary he rushed into his snug camp. Then, as on the steps of the bank, he paused in mute horror.

Tramps or woodsmen or light-fingered hikers—he never

knew who—had happened upon the bough shack in his absence. Everything had been cleaned out with much thoroughness. Not a garment, not a utensil, remained. But for the clothes he stood in, Manfred was destitute.

And, if two dollars were not forthcoming, inside of twenty-four hours Morven must be jammed into an iron cage and be drowned in the town-polluted waters of the very river wherein he and his master had bathed so jollily!

Two dollars! Manfred thought of his parents. But even if he could get word to them—had not Mr. Brayle vowed to kill the dog, and had not Manfred's own gentle mother endorsed the vow by sending him to do his father's cruel bidding? Small chance of help from either of them or from anyone on earth! All at once the world seemed hideously large and he himself infinitely small and alone.

Then, setting his teeth, the boy started at a jog trot back to the town. He had no plan. But in a place of that size there were many dollars. Surely, in a whole day he would be able to get hold of two of them!

Into his racked mind came a fantastic newspaper story he had read—the story of a desperate man who had raised money for his starved family by selling his body to a hospital.

Perhaps in this town's hospital they would be willing to pay him two dollars for his own tired little body and would let him live long enough to ransom Morven and to turn the collie loose in the friendly woods where he could forage for rabbits and the like.

It wasn't much of an idea, but it was the only one Manfred could think of at the moment. Apparently jobs were not quite so easy to get in real life as in those improving success-books he had read.

Near the bank he sighted a policeman; the same one who had grabbed at him as he ran to the pound. Up to the patrolman went the boy and tugged at his sleeve. As the man turned around to face him, Manfred asked:

"Can you tell me the way to the hospital? I ——"

"I can tell you the way to the police station," interrupted the officer. "That is, if you're who I think you are. The description fits you fine, barring some extra dirt you've been gathering on you. You ducked me once before," he added, to explain his collaring the anguished boy. "Now, then, speak up and tell me what name you call yourself. And don't you lie!"

"My name's Manfred Brayle," answered the captive, crossly. "And I don't lie, either. You've ——"

"That'll be all," the policeman stopped him. "Come along peaceful-like, and don't make no trouble."

In a daze Manfred let himself be led ignominiously through the street. In a daze he was stood up before a dignitary behind a desk in a dim station front room. In a daze he was led to a large rear room—not a cell—and was locked in.

Perhaps it was an hour, perhaps just a few minutes, he sat there. Then the door opened for only ten or eleven inches and something came in. Mincingly, doubtingly, it wriggled through the narrow opening. Then it sniffed the air and caught a glimpse of the small boy slumped low in the big chair.

With a yelp of ecstasy Morven flung himself at his master; capering wildly around the chair and patting the inert body with flying white forepaws and seeking to lick the dull face. Roused with a wrench from his exhausted apathy, Manfred seized the recovered collie around the shaggy throat; and forgot to be a Boy Scout or a mature job-seeker or anything else except a weepingly astonished and over-rapturous child.

Then his father was standing in the doorway. Not the wrathful parent of two weeks back, but a man whose eyes were suspiciously wet and whose lips worked convulsively. Manfred tightened his hug of the collie's wrigglingly furry body.

"You're not going to kill him!" he declaimed, in tearful defiance.

"If he waits for me to kill him," said Brayle, unsteadily, "he'll die of old age. It's *you* who ought to be killed for frightening us so and making us so miserable. No, it isn't, either. It's *I* who ought to be shot; for starting the whole thing, that day. I behaved like a wall-eyed fool. But I think I've paid for it, son—and it's taught me more than I'll ever be able to forget. I think *you've* paid, too, from the look of you. Your mother's paid heaviest of all; and she hadn't anything to pay for. That's the way with mothers, I suppose."

He cleared his throat, then continued with elaborate briskness:

"A tramp was arrested. He tried to get off easy by telling about a well-dressed boy and a dog that stowed away in a box-car. We wired, and found you weren't on board when the train got to Paterson. So we've been combing the country between. Yesterday the police here got word of a Boy Scout with a collie who bought some things a

while ago in this town. They wired me and I came on.
The police had your description. One of them told me
you had just gotten away from him and run toward the
pound. He said you didn't have Morven with you. So I
put two and two together and I went to the pound."

"*Dad!*"

"He was there. I bought him free and came uptown to
the hotel with him. I was starting out to look for you
again when they phoned me you were here. That's all.
Coming home?"

"I—I guess I've been an idiot, Dad. And ——"

"I've heard that a fellow's first step upward is when he
revises his list of the world's great men and gives himself
a lower place in it than he used to think he had," answered
Brayle, gathering the worn-out little body tenderly in his
arms. "That's what you seem to be doing, right now.
That's what *I've* been doing every minute for the past
two weeks. So maybe we're both headed for greatness.
Let's phone home and tell mother so. Come along,
Morven!"

XIII. THE BIOGRAPHY OF A PUPPY

Sandy's first earthly sensation was of groping blindly, hungrily, squirmingly, against his mother's furry underbody; along with five similarly squirming and hungry and helpless canine atoms.

He weighed little more than a pound. He was blind. He could not walk. He could not stand. All he could do was to cluck like a hen and to squirm and to eat and to sleep. That was his life. He looked like a plump rat of no especial color.

When the babies were barely two days old, one of Sandy's brothers ceased to eat; and began to make queer intermittent shrill sounds that grew fainter hour by hour.

"A squeaker!" grumbled the Master as he and the Superintendent stood above the litter. "We'll give him a drop of paregoric and bundle him in hot cloths and do all the other things. But it won't be any use. A newly-

267

born collie puppy is either the easiest or the hardest animal on earth to raise. Some of them couldn't be killed by an ax. Others of them wouldn't live if they had three doctors and seven trained nurses working over them. The longer I breed them the less I know about them."

The pitiful little "squeaker" died—a rat-sized and no-colored and futile morsel of doghood which might have grown into an international champion or into a life-saver or into the only chum of some solitary man or woman or into a sheep-killing scourge. All those potentialities, and a hundred more, had lurked within his tiny brain and body. All had been wiped out by a single twinge of colic.

Lime-water had been added liberally to the dam's food, to avoid this very thing. Yet it had happened. In dog-raising, the only flawless bit of Revealed Wisdom is: "*Anything can happen.*" But this is the story of Sandy; not of his less lucky brother.

At twelve days, Sandy had begun to look less like a plump rat than like a plump rabbit. His vague color had settled for the time into a gray-pink, with blackish blotches here and there. At twelve days, too, his closed eyes opened for the first time. Two of the other pups already had their eyes open; two more had not.

Few of the countless absurd theories about dogs are more false than the belief that their eyes open on the ninth day. Far more often they open anywhere from the eleventh to the fourteenth.

Sandy could see his surroundings, such as they were. He was housed in a room, some seven feet long, by a yard wide. A foot-high board cut off the far end of this room into a yard-square "broodnest," whose flooring was cedar shavings over which a soft old blanket had been tacked. Here Sandy had been born. Here must he stay for another week. Then the board would be taken away and he and the other puppies would be at liberty to crawl clumsily all over the small room.

For days thereafter he did not make any particular use of his new gift of sight. His acute sense of smell was enough for him. It told him, in pitchest darkness, just how and where to find his mournful-eyed red-brown mother, Sunnybank Victrix. Her crooning little call was all his flattened ratlike ears troubled to hear.

His days and nights were taken up in eating and in sleeping. Nature was putting growth and strength into him in this immemorial way of hers. For he had an incredible lot of growing to do. A normal-sized man, making such proportionate increase in a single year, would become taller and broader than the Statue of Liberty.

Long before Sandy made the least use of his beady eyes they had caught the troubled attention of the humans at Sunnybank. For Sandy's eyes were a brilliant pale blue, shot with occasional brown splotches—the eyes of the typical "blue merle" collie. His sire, Sunnybank Gray Dawn, was a gigantic blue merle; yet he had dark-brown eyes. In this, his baby son, the merle traits cropped out in the blue eyes as well as in a tendency toward the silver-gray coat of his sire.

But the coat was more yellow than gray, giving it a ludicrous pinkish tinge. Years later it was to be mahogany brown, flecked with silver—luxuriant, glorious. But in puppyhood it gave no sign of its future beauty.

In brief, Sandy was one of those chromatic misfits, a

"sable-merle" collie; with all the physical faults of both his parents, without the physical perfections of either. Such a dog cannot hope to excel in the show ring or to command a high price as a pet. He is a loss.

Luckily, Sandy had not the remotest idea he was any different from his handsomer brethren and sisters; though he had reached the age when he and they could romp awkwardly and slowly, growling in falsetto excitement as they rolled around the soft broodnest in baby mock-war-fare.

When he was three weeks old he had an annoying ex-perience—his first of many. His education began. The Master came into the broodnest an hour after the puppies' mother had been sent out for a run. He carried carefully the well-scalded top of a baking-powder tin. It was full of warm milk into which part of an egg had been beaten.

Setting the tin on the floor, the Master picked up one of the five pups at random. The pup happened to be Sandy. Putting the little fellow on the floor in front of the milk, the Master thrust Sandy's nose into it.

The nose was not kept there longer than the fraction of a second, but long enough to cover it with warm milk. It was a sticky and disagreeable sensation. Sandy resented it. He tried to wriggle free. Then he sought to cleanse his milky nose by washing it with his tongue. To the hungry baby's surprise, the milk tasted good.

By the third day thereafter he was able to crouch in front of the tin and to lap gawkily at its contents. Much of the milk was spattered broadcast and much more rolled off his unaccustomed tongue. But more and more of it, every day, went down his throat. Within a fortnight he could drink milk like a veteran and could even begin to chew the bits of soft and soaked bread in it.

But he preferred to dine as always he had dined since the day he was born. There was too much effort and too little result in the tedious lapping. Here, however, came his second annoyance; this time a real grievance.

His big and gentle mother, Victrix, no longer summoned him to her furry side with that sweet little crooning sound. Indeed, she pushed him away when he sought to nuzzle against her. When he refused to take the hint, she growled, and then snapped dramatically at him.

Her strong jaws could have shorn the fat baby in two. But Victrix took good care they should not so much as pinch him. Her only object in the show of ferocity was to scare him into relying on his food-dish alone for dinner. After a few such rebuffs, Sandy ceased to grieve wonderingly at her new crossness toward him, and he learned the lesson her snaps and growls had sought to teach.

It was not that Victrix loved him and her other babies no longer. She would fly ragingly at any other dog that loitered past the broodnest or that nosed inquisitively at her young. But she was giving him his first lesson in self-reliance.

Then came a day when the five puppies and their mother were transferred into a space far larger than the Kansas prairies. To human eyes their new home was merely a shaded wire inclosure, perhaps thirty feet long by twenty feet wide, with a low dish into which fresh water was forever trickling, and with a green-painted kennel house raised a foot or so above the ground, a sloping runway connecting its entrance with the earth below. But to Sandy the spaciousness of his new abode was limitless.

The five pups, on fat legs which still were a bit shaky, explored slowly and marvelingly every inch of the vast territory. Hours a day were taken up in the exploration. Then as the summer waxed hotter they found why the long kennel house was so far aboveground. Under it there was soft and cool earth in which to grovel. A faint draught of air was passing continually through.

Here, a puppy could wallow deep in the dim-lit coolness and defy hot weather, only dashing clumsily out to greet such humans as might pass. For the first few weeks of his life Sandy had been kept in a temperature of eighty degrees. Warmth and dryness are chiefest of the secrets for keeping newlyborn animals alive. But now that he was two months old his coat was beginning to grow longer and thicker and fuzzier, and the cool of his earthy day-bed was refreshing.

From the time he and the others could waddle in the broodnest, they had learned to look forward to the visits of the Mistress or the Master or of any of the Sunnybank workmen. From the first, they found it pleasant to be petted and talked to.

Now that they were living in the puppy-yard, guests were brought out, every few days, to look at them and to pet them. For this was one of the Sunnybank theories: From babyhood, all puppies were taught to accustom themselves to be petted by strangers and to understand that humans are friendly. Thus, none of them fled in terror to a far corner of the yard, as do so many puppies, at sight or sound or scent of unknown people. None had the

272

faintest trace of fear or bashfulness. Out they would troop, as gaily as a comic-opera chorus, when any human neared their yard.

Sandy was first of the five to catch scent or sound of such visitors. He it was that led the awkward gallop to the wire fence. He, too, it was that inherited most strongly of them all the battle-secrets of his wolf-ancestors.

Puppy play is an unconscious imitation of canine warfare. Sandy excelled in this. While the others were content to romp clownishly and purposelessly, he used brain and heredity in the sham battles.

Early he caught the knack of throwing his opponent off balance by a shoulder-shove, and then to raven playfully for the throat by the time the other puppy had fairly touched ground. Early he learned the ancient wolf-trick of feinting for the throat and then seizing a foreleg in pretended breakbone grip. Early he learned to lunge over an adversary's head and to catch him by the base of the brain.

He was not in the least quarrelsome. Never did he start any of the occasional hot little fights with which the pups punctuated their play. But, once attacked, he put into active use every inherited trick he knew. Always he won. Never, after the battle, did he bully his victim or hold a grudge.

The Master used to stand by the hour to watch this incessant play. He was looking for something. At last he found it. One day, he said to the Mistress, who was watching the puppies with him:

"I've picked the dog I'm going to keep. I didn't plan to keep any of this litter, but I've found what I want. It's that little pinkish-yellow lop-eared chap; the one you call 'the pink puppy.' He wouldn't be worth a dollar to any professional breeder. But he has brain and he has pluck and he has heart and he has poise. Besides, he has a queer individuality that is all his own. He has more personality than the rest of them put together. Some day he's going to be our house dog. I'll have him registered as 'Sunny-bank Sandstorm.' We'll call him 'Sandy,' for short. I'm going to sell all the others. They're beauties, every one of them. Sandy is the only poor specimen in the lot. But I'd rather have him than a dozen prize-winners."

So it was that pup after pup of the five disappeared from the shaded yard, as buyer after buyer came for them. Soon Sandy alone was left. Twice, people who care more for the inside of a dog's brain than for his mere show-points, asked, half-shamefacedly, the price of the blue-eyed and gangling Sandy. Always the Superintendent's answer came:

"There isn't any price on him. He's going to be the Boss's own dog."

But it is one thing to pick out a puppy for one's "own dog," and quite another to make him into a dog worth having for one's own. There is the same difference as between saying that a halfgrown boy has a strong legal bent of brain, and in giving that same boy a $50,000 lawsuit to handle. With even the most promising pup, there is much to teach before he can qualify as an ideal house dog. Nor is the education a mere matter of weeks or even of months.

Left alone in the puppy-yard, when the other pups had gone, Sandy consoled his solitude by fierce battles with the huge old hiking shoe which the Master had tossed in there for him. It was Sandy's favorite toy, and he used to worry it and gnaw it and tussle with it by the hour. He didn't know he was acquiring thus the scent of the Master's steps, by constant gnawing of his cast-off footgear; nor that he was toughening his jaw muscles on the stiff leather and giving needed exercise to his forty-two teeth. He thought he was playing. But he was learning.

At four months he was taken out with the grown collies, on the shorter of their two daily runs. It was rough pastime. For as he sought to join in their romps he would be knocked down a dozen times a day. The big dogs did not mean to hurt him. They did not even admit him to their gay rompings. But one or another of them, unintentionally, would brush against the youngster and bowl him over.

Again he was learning. He learned that when the Master called or whistled, the grown dogs always came galloping, at the summons. Imitatively, Sandy did the same. He was discovering that when the Master whistled or called, it was the correct thing to come scampering up to him.

Besides, he was growing to like the Master more and more. It was fun to be allowed on these runs with the older dogs and to share with them an occasional bit of biscuit or other titbit from the Master's pocket.

Even as the newcomer in a boys' school likes instinctively the instructor whom the other and older fellows like best, so Sandy was learning to like the Master. He was learning to come at call, even while he thought it was all a game.

275

But presently things began to happen which, for a time, made him loathe and fear this Master whom he had liked so well. The man seemed to be selecting Sandy as the butt for incessant and cruel teasing. For instance:

At first, toward the end of the daily scamper, the Master had picked Sandy up and put him back in the puppy-yard. But one day he did not pick up the youngster. Instead, he ordered the other dogs into their yards and then stood in the puppy-yard's open doorway. He called Sandy to him.

Now this was like ordering back into the school-house a child who is in the midst of play. Sandy had been having a beautiful time, gambolling around with the big dogs. There were a million delightful things to do around the grounds and in the lake. It was slow, to be cooped up in a yard, with only a torn old shoe to play with. Sandy was not minded to go in.

True, the Master was calling him. But that meant little enough. It was all right to come, on call, when he and the others were out on their walk. But what was the sense of obeying when obedience meant imprisonment? The idea was absurd. Sandy trotted off.

But the voice of the Master followed him; insistent, compelling, monotonous. It seemed almost as if the voice had a thin string fastened to it, drawing the puppy toward the yard. Sandy stopped trotting. He looked back at the Master with an ingratiating smirk. He wagged his tail merrily. But still the Master stood beside the yard gate, and still he called. Sandy took a few steps toward him. The voice became encouraging, friendly, coaxing.

But there was the yard and there was imprisonment.

Sandy stopped. The voice did not stop. It kept on calling, quietly but insistently. This performance began to get on Sandy's nerves. He galloped off. But again he stopped. He could feel the voice pulling him mysteriously backward. He approached, this time, to within ten feet of the gate; only to scurry away.

Over and over were the retreat and the mincing advance repeated. Sometimes the puppy ran almost out of hearing. Sometimes he came within arm's-length of the man. But always he would sheer off from entering the prison-yard. Once or twice he lay down, turning over on his back and waving his paws and rolling his eyes. But ever the voice hammered quietly away at him. Ever its steady iteration of his name pestered and teased him more and more.

The Master was not a patient man. Fifty puppies or more he had broken to this supreme obedience test, and always he dreaded the temper-fraying ordeal of it. He yearned unspeakably to let some of his impatience creep into his monotonous voice; and even to grab the wretched pup by the scruff of the neck and sling him bodily into the yard.

But such loss of self-control would be too expensive a luxury. It would wreck forever his hope of establishing between himself and Sandy the perfect association he was striving to form. There was nothing for it but to assume a serenity he did not possess; and to keep on calling the stubborn youngster—to break the young collie's will, by human patience.

For a solid half-hour the somewhat ludicrous scene continued. Then, with a sound between a gasp and a sob, the puppy ran into the yard.

Instantly Sandy found himself the recipient of as much patting and extravagant praise as if he had saved fifty heroines from drowning. A handful of gorgeously desirable animal crackers accompanied the praise and petting.

Sandy's nerve-rack fled. He realized that he had done a most remarkably brilliant thing in obeying the order to go into his yard. He grew ecstatically pleased with himself. Nor, ever again, did he refuse to enter the yard at command or to obey the Master's call. He had no taste for a repetition of that eternal will-breaking, patient voicing of his name and the incessant gesture toward the open gate.

Sandy had learned something more. He had learned that human will-power is greater than the dog's. It was a lesson which taught him much, without smashing his self-respect or his spirit. True, the Master might have given the pup a terrific beating for not entering the yard at command, and might then have kicked him into it. But in doing so he would have snapped the delicately forming bond between himself and his dog, a bond which one day would be stronger than forged steel.

A collie's mental and psychic mechanism are ten times as sensitive as are the works of a $2,000 watch.

Perhaps there are better obedience tests than that of ordering an unwilling and playful puppy into his yard. But the Master knew of none. It had served its purpose, satisfactorily, for many generations of Sunnybank collies.

During the next week or two there were long woodland rambles, alone with the Master; walks that were a prideful delight to the puppy. Then recommenced that seemingly nagging ill-treatment on the Master's part.

On a walk, for instance, Sandy was not allowed to run free, except during the homeward half. For the first half he was equipped with an uncomfortable soft collar, to which was attached a leash. For a while, collar and leash were torments. Then, bit by bit, the puppy learned that if he kept at a certain pace and did not tug nor hang back or get between the Master's feet, the leash did not tease him at all. Already he had grown used to the once-vexing collar.

But, barely had he learned to "lead" when a new imposition was invented. As he trotted ahead of the Master, on his leash, he would hear the sharp order, "Heel!" At the same time the leash would draw him quietly but irresistibly backward until his nose was on a line with the man's heel. There seemed no sense at all in this.

Then Sandy thought out a crafty way to avoid the uncomfortable haul on the leash. When he heard the command to "heel," he dropped back instantly without giving the leash a chance to pull him. For some reason, this ruse was rewarded by praise as extravagant as had greeted his entering of the yard gate. Sandy discovered again that he had done something brilliant. Thereafter the call of "heel" was eagerly looked forward to, in order to show off his new trick.

Torment after torment resolved itself, in increasingly brief time, into a mere game; ending with the achieving of some brand-new accomplishment which called forth praise and animal crackers. Presently Sandy found himself eager to learn. He grew to recognize each successive kind of teasing as the mere preliminary to another delightful trick. He began to look forward to such preliminaries, and to strain his intelligence in the mastering of their meaning.

But the world was full of queer and incomprehensible laws—laws that were so easy to break, so hard to remember!

To shake and rend a disreputable burlap bag found behind the stables—this was permissible. The pastime was even viewed by the humans with amusement.

But to try the same merry game with the music-room tiger-skin rug:—this brought down on Sandy a fearsome scolding and a day's banishment from the house. Yet, where lay the difference?

To gobble hungrily his dishful of bread and milk, in the kennel-yard, was lawful. To assail with the same zest a luncheon dish that had been set down for a moment on the dining-room serving-table:—this was a black crime, and punishable as such. Why?

To pursue a stable cat up a tree was a legitimate sport. To rush harrowingly at Tippy, the Mistress's fluffy gray Persian house cat, as she drowsed on a living-room couch: —this was fiercely forbidden. And so on, for a score of instances.

Bewilderment after bewilderment, blunder after blunder, marked the first month or so of Sandy's apprenticeship as a house dog. More than once the Master despaired.

Here was no super-puppy, as had been Sunnybank Bobby; knowing by strange instinct the things that may or may not be done, and needing only a single lesson in any accomplishment in order to acquire it for life. Here was no such blameless dog as had been Bruce, Sandy's glorious grandsire, without a flaw of body or of mind; nor as old Sunnybank Lad, who had learned with the same unbelievable quickness and half-human intellect as had Bobby himself.

No, Sandy was in some ways just an average collie pup, and to be labored with as such. Only when the Master noted afresh that stanch look in the pup's pale-blue eyes or an occasional instinctive display of steady nerve or of fine brainwork, did he realize he had been right in his early judgment of the young dog.

There was an utter absence of fear, too, in Sandy and a lack of the crazy bumptiousness which marks the average lively pup of his age. Besides, he had a way of thinking things out for himself; and of devising games which he played with solemn ingenuity.

His chief joy, for a time, was to carry magazines and newspapers from the veranda table to the lawn and there to tear them to small fragments. It was hard to break him of this. And by the time the breaking was done he had discovered a new and far more fascinating game.

The time was spring. Along the lake shore at the foot of the lawn lay an occasional very dead fish. These fish became the joy of Sandy's life. He did not eat them. But they had a most alluring fragrance, a fragrance which he transferred to himself by rolling on them.

But the pup seemed to realize that this was a selfish pleasure, at best, and that it ought to be shared with some one he loved. Accordingly, he would scour the lake shore for perhaps a half-mile until he came upon a stranded fish of sufficient deadness. This he would pick up tenderly; resisting the urge to roll on it. He would carry it intact to the Master, wherever the latter might chance to be.

Oftenest the horrible gift was presented while the Mistress and the Master were at breakfast or at luncheon in a vine-shaded corner of the veranda. If the wind chanced to set in the opposite direction, the Master's first knowledge of Sandy's presence was when the puppy would lay the fish carefully across one of the man's boot-toes, then stepping back with happy pride in his human god's certain rapture at the token.

There was hurt wonder in Sandy's pale eyes; as sizzling rebukes, instead of praise, followed upon the gift. Slow was he to grasp the fact that such a delectable morsel could be less welcome to the Master than to himself. Day after day he would search diligently along the shore for such full-flavored presents and bring them duly to the Master.

It was a long and discouraging process to make the generous pup understand that the fish were not desirable and that it was against the Law to bring them up onto the veranda or into the house.

For by this time Sandy had formed the habit of bringing the Master a dozen presents of various kinds, every day. He rummaged in the stables until he found the rubber boots used by the men in washing cars or dogs. Thoughtfully chewing the foot off one of these boots, he bore it to the Master and laid it at his feet. Or it would be a bone, whence the meat long since had been gnawed; or a car-cleaning rag or square of chamois, or a defunct mouse.

The lanky young giant of a collie spent hours a day hunting Sunnybank for any trophy which he could lug to the Master. Then, one noon, he found a genuine prize.

He cornered a big and vicious rat, behind the stables and attacked the rodent with much enthusiasm. He was not battling for himself, but for the man who was his god.

The rat nipped Sandy again and again on lips and underjaw, but the pup did not flinch. Presently he was able to drive his white teeth into the back of the hotly-fighting rat and, with one shake, to end the duel.

The Master was at lunch on the veranda. Something plopped soggily down across his feet. It was a large and newly-slain rat. Sandy, with eagerly wagging tail, stood there; his mouth badly bitten and scored, but his eyes bright with happiness. He had fought and he had killed and he had brought his kill to his god. What mattered a bitten mouth?

The Master was in a quandary. He dared not scold or punish Sandy; lest the puppy think he was chastised for killing a rat. Such a course would make him worthless, henceforth, as a rat-catcher. So the pup was praised and petted for the deed. The Master took up the rat by the tail and carried it far out into the garden and buried it there. Somehow, he did not feel a desire for any more lunch, so he went into his study to begin his afternoon work.

Half an hour later he heard a shuffling sound just outside the study. He opened the door. There on the threshold, and crusted with fresh garden-earth, lay the defunct rat.

Sandy had tracked the Master's steps to the garden. He had located the rodent's grave and had dug up his grisly trophy. He had carried it to the study's shut door—as near as he could get to the Master—and he had left it there.

Next day the Mistress brought back from the village with her a large and truly magnificent white canton-flannel dog. By the gift of a canton-flannel elephant, years agone, she had taught Gray Dawn, Sandy's sire, to desist from bringing her a series of gruesome offerings, such as fish and rats and chewed shoes.

The white-flannel dog was presented in due and ancient form to Sandy. The puppy was enraptured with the softly bitable plaything. He carried it everywhere. He brought it to the Master at all and sundry occasions. He would lay it on the lawn and then seek to terrify it by rushes and fierce barks. He would growl over it as over a bone. He would toss it high in air or worry it, or go to sleep with it between his paws.

To his delight, the Master joined in his alluring games with the flannel dog. For instance, the Master would toss the toy far down the lawn. Sandy would dash after it and bring it triumphantly back, laying it, at command, in front of the man's feet. This he would do delightedly, again and again.

Sandy had not the faintest idea that this was a new bit of education and that he was learning to retrieve. But by means of the flannel dog he taught himself to follow any flung object and to bring it back to the Master, dropping it at the latter's feet. To Sandy it was only a jolly game.

Next began a game a little less jolly, but still interesting—a game in which the flannel dog also shared. Sandy was told to lie down. The precious flannel toy was placed between his forepaws. Then came the order, "*WATCH* it!" The Master would move away. As Sandy jumped up to follow, he was bidden to lie down again; and the toy was put once more between his paws, with the same incomprehensible command.

Gradually it dawned on the collie that this flannel dog —and incidentally any later thing left thus in his care— must not be deserted; but must be watched over, zealously, until relief should come.

His latent sense of scenting was brought out in a still more enthralling game. The Master would hide the toy and then tell Sandy to go and look for it. Almost at once Sandy learned to cast about for the familiar plaything—even as fiery little Sunnybank Wolf, in bygone years, had learned in like manner to find any given object which the Mistress or the Master had touched.

The crash of thunder had no terrors for Sandy; though at its roar Gray Dawn and one or two others of the Sunnybank collies would crowd close to their owners and stand thus, trembling, throughout the storm. Nor did the report of a gun arouse in Sandy either fear or excitement. The Master had not been wrong, at the first, in gauging the quizzical calmness at the back of those pale-blue eyes of his. The puppy feared nothing. His nerve was iron-steady.

To Sunnybank came an apparatus which interested all the dogs. It was an automatic lawn-sprinkler. Inquisitively, they would stroll toward it; until a swish of water from one of the nozzles chanced to catch them in the face. Then, in offended disgust, they would withdraw.

But to Sandy the sprinkler was a blend of plaything and mortal foe. He would charge it gaily, undaunted by the pounds of cold water which its high-power hose hurled against him. Half-drowned, he remained for minutes at a time close to it, biting the sparkling water jets and trying to shake them to pieces. The harder he shook, the more heavily was his head deluged.

One day the hose was running, just before its adjustment to the sprinkler. An inch-thick stream of water gushed from its nozzle for something like twenty-five feet. Here was Sandy's chance to tackle the enemy-plaything at its liveliest. He rushed it from every conceivable angle, while it drenched him to the skin and all but knocked him over.

Then he stepped back and studied the water, with his head contemplatively on one side. He was thinking— thinking as logically as any six-year-old child. He saw that the strong stream of water all issued from a single small hole at the end of the snake-like hose. Very good. That, then, was the source of the stream. That was the point whence to attack it if he wanted to put it out of business. Sandy went into action.

With a leap he was at the foe. He caught the nozzle of the hose firmly between his jaws and shook it. The nozzle was pointing straight down his throat. An inch-thick stream, powerful enough to travel twenty-five feet, was banging against his gullet. Gallons and gallons of hard-driven water were tearing their way down his throat.

Strangled and half-blinded, Sandy let go. Back he went, out of reach; coughing and spluttering. There he sat down and continued his studies of hydraulics, from a point of safety. The thing had not thrashed him. He wasn't anywhere nearly through with it. But it had caught him at an irresistible angle and he had had to withdraw for further planning.

Inside of a minute he had worked the problem out. He could not quell the stream by biting it, nor by catching the tip of the nozzle. Both those methods had been tried. But there were other ways. He approached the stream again, tail awag, eyes glinting. As he neared it, he feinted, then darted to one side and caught up the hose six inches behind the nozzle.

Here the water could neither dowse nor strangle him. He was safe from it. He had seized upon the serpentine rubber thing which caused the mystifying spray. Having caught it, he set about demolishing it. His scissor-sharp teeth were half through the stout rubber before the Master called him off.

That was the way with humans: just as soon as a pup was having a really good time they always interfered!

But less and less often, nowadays, did these humans have need to interfere with Sandy. Imperceptibly, but steadily, he was learning the Law. In the depths of his queer pale eyes a quiet wisdom was beginning to dawn— a wisdom which was to last him for life and to make him an ideal pal and guard, and to reward a thousandfold the patience and time used up in teaching him the myriad things a puppy must learn if he would become a decent canine citizen.

Sunnybank Sandstorm was qualifying at last to take his future place in the roster of the loved house dogs of Sunnybank—Lad and Bruce and Wolf and Treve and Bobby and Gray Dawn. The promise of the pudgy two-month puppy was fulfilling itself in the gauntly huge year-old dog.

Sandy had "arrived."

XIV

* *

THE EXILE

* *

Thane Lovat whistled to his collie; then he started off
along the dusty road, toward the two-mile-distant railroad
station. As he came to the rise of the hill the man set
down his bulky handbag and looked back at the home he
was quitting.

Many thousands of men and boys have paused thus to
take a mental farewell to the place where they were born
and raised, and to photograph in their memories every
detail of it. But not many of those thousands have looked
back with the black hatred and smolder of wrath in their
hearts which encompassed Thane Lovat as he gazed his
last upon this home of his youth.

It was as though he were glaring into the face of a
mortal enemy in order to fix in mind the loathed visage,
for future revenge. Long and broodingly he scowled down
at the peaceful farmhouse set in its ill-kept land. If curses
could have prevailed, the house would have crumbled and
the rank fields would have turned to sandy desert, under
that blighting glower.

288

Then, the wrathful furrow between Thane's eyes softened and his hard mouth waxed less grimly tense. This because of a shoving pressure on his limp-lying hand. His collie, Gavin, had frisked gaily along in front of Lovat, glad, as ever, at the prospect of a morning walk with his loved master. Now, seeing Thane pause so long, staring back at the home they had just left, Gavin had paused, too, and trotted over to him and pushed a playfully remindful muzzle against the inert palm.

The man glanced down at the collie. Then with both hands he rumpled Gavin's classic head. The dog's plumed tail waved tumultuously at the caress.

"You're an old fool, Gavin!" growled Lovat, with reluctant affection. "If you weren't just a blundering, soulless dog, you'd have had sense enough to quit me, along with the rest of them. Why, even rats have enough wisdom to scamper free of a ship that is sinking. It's only a dog that hasn't the intelligence to see when a human ship is going down. You're a grand guard and you're a grand herder and you're grandest of all as a pal, Gavin. Any of a dozen folks would have been glad to take you—yes, and to pay me well for you."

Gavin wagged his tail anew at the repetition of his name.

"But what would have been the use? You never would have stayed with any of 'em. I know you well enough to know that. You'd have gone searching for me. They'd have caught you and lugged you back and whaled you with a horsewhip and kept you tied up, Gavin—you that's never been struck or kept tied. And you'd 'a' eaten out your silly heart, missing me. No, we're going to play this together, you and I. I don't know where we're going, after we get as far from this rotten hole as the train will take us. But we'll be together, anyhow, just like we've been all the four years of your life. . . . Come on, now. We've looked back at that dump long enough. Chase!"

Thane Lovat picked up his heavy handbag and started afresh on his tramp toward the station. But this was to be a morning of delays. A little topless runabout came chugging up the rise of ground from the direction in which he and the dog were traveling. As soon as it hove in sight around the bend, Lovat recognized its only occupant. Quickening his pace, and with his eyes on the ground, he sought to pass on without paying further heed to the vehicle.

But Gavin spoiled the fine effect of borishness by gamboling forward with a loud bark of welcome as he, too, recognized the chauffeur.

The car came to a halt. The girl in the driver's seat leaned far out to pat the collie as he reared his forefeet on the fender and grinned up at her. He and she were old friends. But today she gave the dog only an absent-minded pat. Her troubled gaze was on Gavin's master, who was striding past her with face turned ostentatiously away.

"Why, Thane!" she exclaimed. "Aren't you even going to speak to me? Dad said he heard you were leaving to-day, and I was going to stop and say good-by to you, on my way past your house. I ——"

"My house?" mocked the man, sourly. "*My* house? I haven't got any house. You ought to know that, if any-one does. It's your dad's house now. And all my land is his, too. There wasn't any sense in my waiting for the auction of the things in it. The cash for them will go into your dad's pocket, along with the rest of the loot he and my other dear neighbors have gouged me out of. I'm through with it and with the whole region and everyone in it. Gavin's the only one that's been dumb enough to stick to a down-and-outer. Best drive on, Molly. Some of the neighbors might catch you disgracing yourself by talking to a Dead One."

He made as though to go on. But Molly Brent would not have it so. The pityingly friendly smile which had accosted the man was wiped from her face as by magic, and that face's rounded softness took on a suddenly stern aspect.

"Thane Lovat!" she said, speaking hotly and fast, in an unwonted gush of indignation. "You need some one to spank you and then stand you in a corner. You're behaving like a sulky child that's smashed all his pretty toys and thrown his tin bank into the river; and then blames everyone but himself. You're making a martyr out of a shirker. You choose to think there has been a conspiracy against you here, among the kindly people who loved your father and your mother; and that they have robbed you and then driven you out of your home. Well, you're right, in part of it. There *has* been a conspiracy against you. A horrible conspiracy to ruin you and wreck you. And the one and only member of that conspiracy has been —yourself!"

"You gave me that same lecture the last time I came to see you," retorted Thane. "The time you forbade me to come there again. I won't bother you to waste any more breath on it. I'm in a hurry, now. And if I'm not fit to call on you at your house, I'm not fit to speak with you on the road. Good-by."

He took a step onward. Molly Brent slipped from the car and barred his way.

"If we hadn't been chums from the time we were little," she declared, "I wouldn't waste words on you as you are now. Yes, I would, too, if I could make you halfway sane again and as—as I used to think you were. You'll listen to me, whether you want to or not, Thane. I'm not going to let you go away from here thinking you're a suffering victim and that all the world is against you."

"I——"

"I'm not going to let you chew on the cud of self-pity, that way, till it sours your whole nature and makes you permanently worthless for anything in life. You're going to hear the truth. And, down in the bottom of your foolish heart, you are going to realize some day that it *is* the truth. That will pull you back to sanity and worthwhileness, if anything will."

Ostentatiously Thane Lovat looked at his watch and then at a timetable he took from his pocket. Molly did not take the hint. Her big dark eyes were aglow with excitement and her face was flushed. She confronted him there, in mid-road, again speaking with that hot rapidity so different from her wonted gentleness.

"I said you were like a cranky child," she went on. "And you are. A spoiled child, at that. From the time you were a boy, everything was made easy for you. Too easy. I'm not blaming your parents. It wasn't their fault, the dears! They just wanted you to have the best of everything. Then when they died and left you to fight the world, alone, you thought everything would keep on going smoothly for you. Well, it doesn't, with anyone. We have to fight, and fight hard, for any smoothness we get. And you wouldn't fight."

Again, with ponderous indifference, he looked at his watch and fidgeted. His whole manner seemed to ignore the emphatic girl who barred his way. Molly Brent continued:

"You had two bad years in succession with your crops. So did all of us, especially in the drought year. Then you used up all the money your parents left you, on those crazy irrigation schemes, before you had even taken the trouble to study irrigation or learn the first principles of it. Then you mortgaged your place and tried to branch out in all kinds of costly schemes that dad and everyone else told you were no use. When you went broke, you didn't try to fight your way back or to profit by your bungling. You got a second and then a third mortgage on the farm, and you took to drinking. That was why I told you to stop coming to see me till you could pull up and be a man; the time you came to our home dead drunk."

"I was not! I——"

"And now you're running away, instead of fighting back to what you might have been. Dad offered to give you all the reasonable time you needed, on the mortgages and on the two notes. But you flared up—you were drunk, that day, too, dad says—and you insulted him and insulted everyone around here; and you said we had all combined to ruin you and you never wanted to see this place or anyone in it again and that you were going away. . . . Well, go! But you're due to learn that nobody can change his luck or his nature by changing the place he lives in. When you have learned that, come home again, Thane," she ended, her voice and eyes softening. "You'll find this neighborhood just bristling with helping hands, to lift you back to where you belong. Mine—my hands—will be stretched out to you, clear in front of all the others. And ——"

The dark eyes misted. The clear young voice shook. Thane Lovat had to grit his teeth to force back the eager words that sprang to his lips at the sight. But a dumb devil still gripped his heart. Morbid hate still was scourging his brain. Without a word he struck out toward the town and for the railroad station, leaving the girl staring wistfully after him. Her indignant words were repeating themselves over and over in Thane's memory, searing deep into it; as did her heartbroken look and the sobbing catch in her breath.

Molly watched him out of sight. Then, fighting back her sobs, she climbed into the runabout and drove on.

Gavin, the collie, had stood between the two during the fierce colloquy, staring from one to the other in bewildered unhappiness. Something, he knew, was amiss. With a collie's queer sixth sense he felt the emotion and agitation that swept through these two people he loved. Now, following Thane, the dog thrust his nose once more consolingly into Lovat's palm. Crossly the man pulled his hand away from the appealing caress, and crossly he bade the collie run on ahead.

Obedient, as ever, the dog cantered onward in front of his master, but without his earlier buoyancy. Perhaps Gavin's preoccupation in Thane's unknown trouble robbed the collie of some of his usual road-caution. For he rounded the next bend at that same flowing canter, without thought of what might lie beyond.

Around the curve came a heavy racing-model motorcar, traveling at something more than fifty miles an hour. The machine skidded dangerously at the turn, but did not slacken speed. Its buffer smote Gavin crashingly on the head before the unaware dog could leap free. The car's momentum flung him perhaps fifteen feet, to the roadside. He crashed down among the dusty bushes, limp, and in a pitifully lifeless heap.

The car's driver either did not see or did not heed the smitten collie. For the racer tore onward, presently vanishing in a yellow upheaval of dust.

It was all over before the sourly brooding Lovat realized what had happened. He bent strickenly over his inert collie chum. Then he knelt beside Gavin, taking him in his arms. But there was no faintest sign of life. Thane had seen the car strike him, and he knew no such crashing blow on the skull could avoid being instantly fatal.

With unbidden tears running down his face, the man lifted the dog that was to have been his only comrade in the lonely life ahead of him—the dog whose death left him hideously and terrifiedly alone in a hostile world. Up the bank he carried the body, and laid it tenderly beneath a flowering apple tree that grew on the summit. There was neither time nor a spade for the digging of a grave. But there were thin flat stones piled up near by, which were to form the coping of a rough-cast wall in process of building, a few hundred feet away.

Thane carried several of these light slabs across to

where he had laid Gavin. Gently he covered the dog's body with them. Tearing off a branch laden with apple blossoms, he placed it atop the slabs. To himself he muttered, by way of epitaph, two lines from a poem he had had to recite in the days when he and Molly Brent used to go to school together; the verses Lord Byron carved above the grave of his own loved dog, Boatswain:

> To mark a friend's remains these stones arise.
> I never had but one. And here he lies!

Then, shamefacedly wiping the tears from his eyes, Thane Lovat hurried on to the train that was to bear him far from the region he hated.

Had Lovat been in a less foolishly desperate and more normal frame of mind, he would have explored Gavin's smitten skull for sign of fracture or of the supposedly inevitable bashing-in, before deciding the collie was dead. And he would have found no such sign. A collie's skull is not easy to break.

Moreover, Gavin had become aware of the onrushing car in time to check instinctively his canter and to leap backward. The car's buffer struck him at the very inception of the leap, but when he had just changed from a forward to a swift reverse motion. Thus the blow was robbed of much of its primal force. Gavin was tossed high and far. But he was stunned, not killed, by the partly averted impact.

It was perhaps twenty minutes later that the collie came slowly and groggily to his senses. His first feeble attempts to move were balked by a weight which held him down.

Presently, however, his full senses seeped back to him, and with them some of his wiry strength.

He found himself pinned to the earth by thin and loose slabs of stone which had been laid singly above him. The dog could not understand this odd situation. It vexed him. Gavin was not fond of liberties, except from his adored master; and assuredly it was a liberty to weight him in this way. Vexation lent him a fictitious strength. He struggled fiercely, writhing and twisting and straining.

As a result, one of the loosely laid flat stones slithered off its precarious balance; then another. A renewed struggle and he was able to crawl dizzily out from his impromptu covering.

He stood up, wavering a little. His body was bruised by landing so hard on the road bank. His head was in pain from the blow it had received from the car buffer. But he was alive and he was on his feet, and he was endowed with all an outdoor collie's glorious health and recuperative powers and physical fitness.

Not at all did he guess what had happened to him, nor why he was so bruised and shaken up. But he knew well where he was; on the familiar road. He was not half a mile from his own life-long home. Stopping only to drink thirstily from a bankside trickle of water, he started homeward. Then he remembered he and Thane Lovat had been out for a walk together.

Abandoning his home-going purpose, Gavin cast about in the road until he caught Thane's scent. Then, nose to ground, he loped onward toward the village. To a dog, trained as was he, the trail was as easy to follow as would be a painted line to humans. Down the hillside road

Gavin loped to the little town. There, without a check or a second's hesitation, he ran along the main street until he had reached the platform of the railroad station.

Here the trail of Lovat's steps was reekingly fresh. Gavin followed it along the platform, into the waiting-room and up to the ticket window, thence out again by the opposite door and to the very edge of the train platform.

There the scent vanished abruptly, where Lovat had boarded the train two minutes earlier. Cast about as he would, Gavin could not pick it up again. Always, when he crossed it, it led to the ticket window and out to the edge of the train platform. There, definitely, it stopped.

Puzzled, wholly at a loss, the collie did what most perplexed and lost collies try to do. He turned his steps homeward. Humans are not like dogs. Dogs know that. Humans have mysterious ways of locomotion, by car and otherwise, which make their trails disappear. Also, humans can open and shut doors, and can vanish in that way. But, almost invariably, soon or late, disappearing humans go to their own homes again. Dogs know that, too.

Homeward trotted Gavin, up the village street and then out into the country. Folk along the way paused to stare wonderingly at the dust-smeared collie with the cut on his head and the trickle of blood on his face and with his tongue hanging far out. One or two even prepared to bawl, "Mad dog!" But Gavin's elusively fast and choppy wolf-trot carried him speedily out of their ken.

Up the hill he trotted—the hill at whose summit bend he had been knocked over. As he breasted the top a car